# LEGEND OF A BADMAN

## RAY HOGAN

**SAGEBRUSH**
Large Print Westerns

First published in Great Britain by Thorndike
First published in the United States by Five Star

Published in Large Print 2012 by ISIS Publishing Ltd.,
7 Centremead, Osney Mead, Oxford OX2 0ES
by arrangement with
Golden West Literary Agency

**British Library Cataloguing in Publication Data**
Hogan, Ray, 1908–1998.
    Legend of a badman.
    1. Western stories.
    2. Large type books.
    I. Title
    813.5'4–dc23

ISBN 978–0–7531–9003–6 (pb)

Printed and bound in Great Britain by
T. J. International Ltd., Padstow, Cornwall

For my friend,
Marc Rupert,
in Houston, Texas

# TABLE OF CONTENTS

# Forword

In this Western I have combined my short novel about Robert Clay Allison with four short stories that I wrote some years ago at the behest of my German publisher. Of course, these stories at the time were translated prior to their publication in Germany but are included here for their first publication in the English language as I originally wrote them.

Many tales involving the feats and escapades of Clay Allison, outlaw, circulate around the southwest area where he lived and died. Conversely there are those who have knowledge of the New Mexico Cimarron country who maintain that he was no outlaw but one notch short of being an acclaimed and highly respected man. It is difficult to determine the truth, but, as the old saying goes, there is both good and bad in every man, only on occasions do circumstances compel one to overshadow the other, and it befalls subsequent generations to determine in their minds which was the most acceptable.

That Clay Allison was a man's man and many a woman's ideal is not to be denied. Much of this impression may have arisen from the multitude of yarns extolling his prowess, yet of a great number of these tales Allison himself had no knowledge. There are seven versions of the manner in which Clay Allison met a violent death. Similarly, all other events in the life of this turbulent Tennessean have through the decades become distorted, until anyone seeking the truth is confronted by a maze of legends, contradictions, and exaggerated half-truths.

Allison, unfortunately, had no biographer at his elbow during his hectic lifetime, as did some of the fabulous men of that day. No one bothered to note on paper the events, the explosive incidents that made up his life. We have only a few, perhaps prejudiced, newspaper accounts, the cold meager entries in court records, and many word-of-mouth reports from which to draw a picture. Thus, Clay Allison's story has been a matter of sifting through a multitude of second- and third-hand tales, a horde of legends, and dearth of facts. Version was matched against version, with date, time, and pure coincidence often being the yardstick for verification. From those comparisons came what appeared to be the true story.

To those whom I interviewed over almost twenty years on the subject of Clay Allison, and whose versions of certain incidents I did not use, I hereby apologize. Where I passed over these, I did so for but one reason: others appeared to stand better the test of truth. But the time they allotted me was not wasted, for it brought into sharper focus the man himself. Such errors are understandable. Allison was dead by mid-1887, and the memories of men approximating the century mark can easily stray far afield.

Was Clay Allison a badman?

Here again is a matter for dispute, if the criterion is to be the number of men he killed. Charlie Siringo, that rawhide-tough detective of free-range days, who claims to have known Allison well, says he slew eighteen or twenty men. But Siringo erred in his memoirs when at one point he placed Allison at a certain location when he was indisputably a thousand miles distant. He could be mistaken here, also.

Others say eight men fell before Allison's six-gun. And one individual claims for him a grisly total of thirty-two. Somewhere in between lies the truth, but on one thing they all agreed — and I myself invariably heard, when I talked with the old-timers around Cimarron town and other haunts of the famed Allison — that "he never killed a man who didn't need killing."

This is probably the key to the real Clay Allison. He was never a desperado in the sense of Billy the Kid nor was he a stanch defender of the law, wearing a star of authority and devoting his life to keeping the peace. He evolves, rather, as a man with a gun, a product of an era of violence, living and acting in accordance with his best judgment as to what was right and what was wrong.

I have heard him referred to by many as a sort of Robin Hood. Perhaps. If taking up for the underdog, for the weak and oppressed against the powerful, if living his life as he saw fit, in the manner he deemed wisest — which quite often meant the taking of the law

3

into his own quick hands — qualify him for that title, then this limping *caballero* deserves the appellation. This is not an absolutely factual account of the life of Robert Clay Allison, but one as nearly true as I could determine it to be. It is set forth in fictional form to heighten interest.

Ray Hogan,
Albuquerque, New Mexico

# Debt of Honor

He stood in the center of the cramped, heat-packed room, facing three men. He was not large but only of average build, yet there was an almost visible solidness to him, a quality that bespoke confidence, and a quiet undercurrent of determination that was as real and steady as the regular striking of his heart.

His clothing — dusty, travel-stained from the long ride down from Denver — was ordinary: flat-heeled Hyer boots, light-colored broadcloth trousers tucked within, thigh-length coat of the same color, a wide-brimmed Stetson hat. In spite of the day's wilting heat, he wore a buttoned vest, and a black string tie closed the collar of his white shirt.

"I am John Pole," he had said in a flat, declamatory way.

They had stared hard at him — McCreight, the banker, Tom Hale, who ran the Cattleman's Rest Hotel, and Joe LeForge, the owner of Dry Wells' largest general merchandise store. There was a sort of shocked dismay in their eyes.

"Good to see you, Marshal," McCreight said at last, hesitantly extending his hand. He introduced the others, and for long moments the silence held as each pursued his own thoughts. "You've changed some since I last saw you . . . in Las Vegas."

Pole nodded, feeling the continuous push of their gaze upon him. They were seeing the pure whiteness of his shoulder-length hair, the salt-and-pepper texture of his mustache, the gaunt leanness of his face. Time never waits for any man. And it makes its inevitable changes. He said: "That was a few years ago."

"Don't think about it," McCreight admitted bluntly. "Reckon you can handle this job?"

Before Pole could reply, Tom Hale said: "I don't know, Marshal. Job may need a younger man. No reflection on you, understand? But it's a tough, hard bunch that's moved in on us. We want them all run out . . . gamblers, rustlers, footpads, gunslingers . . . every mother's son of them."

John Pole was reading their minds, and their thoughts were not strange to him. Like considerations had been his constant, prodding companions since the day McCreight's letter had arrived, offering him the marshal's badge. The banker had remembered him from Las Vegas. The chore he had performed there and the power of his reputation had been such that it had touched the man and remained with him. But that had been several years ago. He had laid up his guns after that one, conscious of the relentless pressure upon his nerves. He had lived idly, proud of a legend, but no man can ever quit completely a way of life despite his determination. He was beginning to feel the demand when McCreight's letter came.

Now, at the moment of meeting, they were disturbed, disappointed, fearful they had erred, and their visible uncertainty increased his own doubts. He said: "Would I have rode six hundred miles if I hadn't figured I could handle it?"

"Well, let's hope we haven't made a mistake," LeForge said with a gusty, sliding sigh. "Things are bad. We got some of the worst in Dry Wells. People are leaving town. Wagon trains are avoiding us. Even the trail herds are taking a different road."

Pole looked out of the dust-streaked window of the office, fronting the jail. His eyes were an almost colorless gray, and the lines of his face deeply cut. His mouth was wide and firm. He let his gaze drift slowly along the street, down the rows of wood and brick buildings, and his thoughts moved back to other towns, other days. It was the same story: a raw village, growing and bursting at the seams, and seeking law and order. And the merchants — they were just the same, too. They wanted that law and order and were willing to buy it, to hire it done at no risk to themselves. But that was all right. That was to be expected. That was the way of it.

He swung back to the three men. "You hired me. I'll handle it. Now, be on your way, and let me get at it."

McCreight nodded and started for the door. Halfway there he paused. "I hope . . . ," he began and let the words die on his lips. Shrugging then, he moved on, followed by LeForge and Hale.

"Need me a room," Pole said to the hotelkeeper as he passed by. "You can put me up?"

Hale said: "All fixed for you, Marshal. Number Five. Key's at the desk."

For several moments Pole stood quiet, listening to their footsteps dwindle off. Alone then, his own doubts lifted anew and had their strong, undermining way with him. They turned him uneasy and chipped away relentlessly at his confidence. Time was against him. Time had slipped in stealthily, like a skulking Indian, doing things to him. It had laid a greater caution upon him and had colored his judgment, perhaps, but it had brought no fear with it. There was only a wavering uncertainty of his own abilities.

One thing was in his favor. Men's minds change but little, and the workings of a man's mind were as familiar to him as the fingers of his own hand. He knew what they thought, what they most likely would do under given circumstances, and that in itself was a powerful weapon, a strong ally. Youth had its advantages, but with age came experience, and maybe that counted most of all in this business of law enforcement.

He shrugged then, moving his thin shoulders with a slight impatience. He was weary of his own thoughts, tired of considering such things. He needed a bath, and he needed to lie down for a little while. It had been a long ride. He left the office and walked the short distance to the hotel. Getting his key, he made himself comfortable in his room, substituting a washdown from the tin bowl for a bath, and slept.

When he appeared later in the dining room, he had left off the coat and vest and had exchanged the broadcloth trousers for some of a darker, hard-finished cord material. The string tie was still at his throat, and he wore his shirt sleeves full-length, cuffed with gold bullet links. A gun, not visible before, hung in its holster on his right hip, its worn and polished handle lifting high out of the leather. He selected a table near the back of the room, ordered, and then sat idly, watching through the open door the steady flow of people in the street.

A few, coming into the dining room, attracted by the silver shine of light upon his hair, touched him curiously with their brief glances and passed on. Hale came over and spoke, commenting on the weather, and drifted on. The meal arrived, and he ate slowly, enjoying the food. Through, he arose, paid his check, and stepped out into the dusk, savoring those last few minutes of obscurity. He took up a position at the corner of the hotel, reached into his pocket, and withdrew the star McCreight had given him. He pinned it on his left breast, feeling at once the weight of its implication and obligations. From that instant on, he was a marked man, one set apart and away from the society of all others, good and bad, for in such times the end result was always questionable, and each faction feared the retaliation of the other should their cause fail.

He stood there, building himself a brown paper smoke, taking in the glances of men and women, moving up and down the dusty street. Like small ants, suddenly obstructed in their marching, they swerved out and around him in a wide arc, giving him short benefit of their interrupted attention. He was no longer a stranger in their midst, and while yet nameless to most he was the marshal, and that was identification enough.

Light faded and with it the day's driving heat. Shadows deepened, and, as he watched, window squares came to life, laying their yellow blocks out onto the loose dust of the street. A dog barked into the gathering darkness, and across the way a man spoke and a woman laughed. A piano broke into sound, the music high and tinkling above the muted hubbub, coming from Dry Wells' largest saloon and gambling hall, the Missouri. John Pole flipped the cigarette into the shadows and turned towards the bulky outline of the Missouri, a few doors distant.

He came into the saloon, feeling like a sudden blow the full blast of its noise and confusion, its boiling haze of smoke, mingled smells, and many lights. He stopped just inside, stepping slightly to the left, and let his eyes run swiftly over the broad room. He carefully took in the tables, the full-length bar with its long, flashing mirror and myriad of bottles and glasses that sparkled as they caught and flung back the lamp glow. It was a place just like a hundred others he had seen in his lifetime in El Paso, in Tucson, Albuquerque, Abilene, Cimarron, Boston City. They were all alike, and trouble would spring alive and violent from this one just as it had done from all the others. The piano's music died. The drone of voices lowered, ceased. A breathless expectancy suddenly enveloped the Missouri.

**10**

"Yes, sir?" the bartender asked, after a time had passed.

"You the owner here?"

The bartender shook his head. "Not me. He's out."

Pole considered the man's florid face for a moment. He said then: "This place closes at midnight. Start tonight."

A man coming through the swinging doors was caught up by the dead silence. He paused, then ducked quickly away, Pole's eyes flat and expressionless as they watched him. He turned back to the crowd, and every man jack felt the hard pressure of his search.

"Law also says no man wears a gun inside the town's limits. That goes back into effect at midnight, too. I catch any of you wearing one in the morning, I'll run you in. You don't like the law, then move on."

The stillness hung, and John Pole waited. Back in the depths of the crowd a girl tittered and a man's heavy voice said in a bantering tone: "Why, grandpa, you're a right hard *hombre!*"

Pole's face remained frozen, but within him he felt the quick rise of temper. He knew he should drag the man out and make an example of him. But that might be hard to do. There was no telling just who had said it. And then another voice spoke up, strained and hushed. "Shut up, Turk! Don't you recognize him? That's John Pole from Las Vegas."

"So?" the bantering tone came back. "Las Vegas was ten years ago. The John Pole then sure ain't the John Pole now."

There was a movement near the tables at the back of the room. A man detached himself and drifted forward. A young, thin man with sharp features and an underlying paleness beneath his tan. Pole started visibly.

"Why wait until mornin', Marshal?"

Bitter thoughts raced through Pole. The Mimbres Kid! Here he was again, insolent, surly, trouble, a bright thrusting scar lying across his face. Five years ago, after he had lain aside his star in Dodge City, he had faced him under different circumstances. The Mimbres Kid had been looking to build his reputation, and Pole had been elected to be a part of it. He had been a youngster then, scarcely turned eighteen, and he had humbled him, taken his guns from him, and told him to go home to his folks, refusing to draw a weapon on the boy for reasons best known to him. The Mimbres Kid, outraged and furious, had sworn his bitter vengeance.

Pole eyed him coolly, ignoring the blunt challenge. "Get rid of those guns," he said and, turning his back, walked through the batwings.

Outside he paused, listening to the suddenly unleashed clamor of voices. Shrugging, he moved off into the darkness. He made his tour of Dry Wells, stating his ultimatum in the four smaller saloons, noting as he did so the various alleyways and passages of the town and making himself generally familiar with the buildings. Satisfied finally, he returned to the Cattleman's Rest. As he entered, a thick-set, well-dressed man came up from a deep chair to greet him.

"Marshal," he said with no preliminaries, "I'm Jim Wyatt. Own the Missouri. My boys tell me you were by there tonight."

Pole nodded, remembering in that moment that Wyatt had not been one of those who welcomed him to Dry Wells earlier in the day.

"Pretty strong voice throwin', if you're planning to stay around long," Wyatt said then, keeping his voice normal. A thin smile was on his mouth.

"My job," Pole stated briefly. "And for the record, I mean what I said. Now, where do you stand?"

The saloonkeeper studied the question. Then: "Why, I stand for Jim Wyatt, Marshal," he said. "Reckon I always have and always will."

"Tells me nothing," Pole murmured. His eyes were reaching into the man, probing, searching. Wyatt stood to lose much by the elimination of those who now made the Missouri their headquarters, but it all would be regained once regular traffic again swung back through the town. Which did Wyatt prefer? The man's inscrutable poker face revealed nothing. "You can't ride and walk both, Wyatt," he said, turning away. "Better get your mind made up and do your choosin'."

Pole moved to a chair near the front of the lobby, next to a window. He had scarcely seated himself when Joe LeForge and the banker, McCreight, came pushing agitatedly through the doorway and halted before him.

"What's this we hear about the Mimbres Kid backing you down?" LeForge demanded in a high voice.

John Pole laid his cool, humorless glance upon the merchant, raking him from head to foot with complete contempt, and then turned back to the street, making no reply.

McCreight's voice said: "This is mighty serious, Marshal. Give that bunch the upper hand, and we'll never be able to handle them."

"Game's a long way from being played out," Pole observed dryly. "Fact is, it just started."

"But to back down in front of all that bunch . . . ," LeForge protested in his displeased, complaining way. "Sure looks like the wrong thing to be doing."

"Nobody backed down, mister," Pole snapped. "I've got my reasons for doing what I am. That satisfy you?"

LeForge shook his head. "Sure don't know about this. Looks bad to everybody."

"Guess maybe the marshal knows what he's doing," McCreight said after that. He turned for the door. "At least, we'll hope he does."

Pole watched them move out into the darkness and vanish into the shadows of the street. Without feeling he reflected upon the ways of men who hire another to do their dirty work and yet reserve the right to criticize the methods employed. But it was not a new thing. Shrugging, Pole settled deeper into the chair to wait out the hours. Somewhat after midnight he roused and went again into the street, making his check. The Missouri and the other saloons were closed. At least there was no trouble on that score.

Afterwards he lay on his bed, sleepless, thinking of the day's events. Time was when he would not have

14

countenanced either of the two incidents that had occurred at the Missouri, and his retaliation would have been swift and deadly. But now, here in Dry Wells, matters had assumed a different aspect. He knew it had been LeForge's and many others' hope that he would come into town and, with a gun in either hand, take over and carve out with gunsmoke the peace and orderliness they desired. And maybe, once long ago, he would have done it just that way.

But a man can do a lot of thinking in several years of inactivity and ask himself a lot of questions, such as how many times was bloodshed necessary? How many men were dead that might otherwise be alive, if he had not been so fast with his guns? He could never answer satisfactorily, but one thing had clarified itself in his mind: it would not happen in Dry Wells. He would proceed slowly, offer every man a chance to comply with the law or take his leave. Guns would be the final measure. And the Mimbres Kid? That was another matter entirely.

He rose long before daylight and, after dressing and checking his gun, ate his breakfast in the dining room as the pre-dawn gray of the morning gave slowly away to the full flare of sunrise. Moving out onto the porch, he watched as the street came grudgingly to life and full light crawled timidly into the narrow canons between Dry Wells' business buildings. This was the time of day John Pole liked best of all, the cool, quiet hour of muffled sounds when the world was yet awakening and the freshness of the night still lay upon the land like a bright, sparkling, dewy jewel. The burning sear of the sun was yet to come, and a man's thoughts could be gentle and kind, and he could forget all the old regrets.

People began to appear on the street. A wagon rumbled by, heading to LeForge's for supplies that would later be hauled back to some nearby ranch. Three 'punchers trotted in from the west and pulled up before Cardigan's stable. McCreight opened the doors of his bank, propping them back with a pair of chipped red bricks. The day had begun, bringing with it the hard-cored problem of trouble. Standing there on the porch, Pole had his moment of brief doubt that reached deeply again into his soul, questioned his abilities, and flung its challenge at the legend that had grown around him. It set him taut, and his nerves were suddenly tight as fiddle strings along which spun a shrill tension.

It had been a long time since he faced a man over that breathless span of space when violence finally came. And come that day it would, he knew. He expected it; he anticipated it; and, after those last lonely and bitter minutes prior to falling asleep the night before, he found himself almost welcoming it. In it he would find an answer.

He swung out into the street, feeling at once the lift of heat, and started walking toward the far end of town. People vanished from his line of vision, fading back out of possible harm's way. He was a deliberate, dark figure, and his eyes were sharp, roving probes, reaching into every corner, every door.

He made the long three blocks and came to a pause against the wall of Sandoval's barn, a fire-blackened relic still standing near the edge of town. Feeling the need for a cigarette, he drew out the makings and rolled one. He sucked on it lazily and, when it was finished, dropped the butt into the dust, ground it out with his heel, and began to retrace his steps. He had seen no one except a few fleeting faces, hurrying to get away, and no man had challenged him. Thus the play was squarely put to him. He accepted it and drifted towards the Missouri. From within it the beginning would spring.

No blast of music greeted him as he entered this time. Only a great and deep silence, loaded heavily with threat. The bartender met him with blank, empty eyes. The half dozen men, leaning against the bar, turned slowly and viewed him with a sullen stillness. He passed behind them, his gaze on their hips. They wore no guns.

"See anything, Marshal?"

Pole stopped, recognizing the insolent voice of the previous night. He pivoted about slowly.

"Shut up, Cud," the bartender said hurriedly. "No trouble in here, now."

Cud. Cud Rinson. Pole revolved the name around in his mind. He remembered it. He said: "Little far north for you, Rinson. Laredo get too hot?"

"No place ever gets too hot for me," the outlaw said. He shifted the ball of tobacco in his mouth and spat, sending a stream of tobacco juice to the floor between Pole's feet.

The marshal was a motionless shape. The thought — *a man like Rinson never changes* — rode wearily through his mind. It's always the same old tune, familiar, time-worn. Rinson, unarmed, knew he would take no action and, secure in such knowledge, pressed his advantage. Pole looked neither down nor away and after a moment moved on. He found no guns in sight. He turned, realizing suddenly the Mimbres Kid was not present in the saloon. He had a quick hope the young gunman had left, and he would see no more of him.

He threw his glance at the bartender. "Keep it this way, and we'll get along," he said and continued on towards the doors.

But things were wrong. The feel was there, and he could see it written across the men's faces as they watched him with a close, drilling interest. Alert, small flags of warning stabbing at him, he pushed back the doors and stepped out into the narrow street, meeting the full glare of the day straight on. The Mimbres Kid was waiting. He leaned against the hitching rail directly opposite the Missouri. He straightened slowly, sunlight glinting off the nickeled frame of the fancy gun on his hip.

"Looking for me?"

Pole's face went stiff as the mockery in the man's voice reached out to him. For a long minute he considered the words in the complete and dead silence. Then he slowly lifted his arms and deliberately crossed them upon his chest. He strode carefully towards the loose and easy figure of the Kid.

"Not necessarily," he replied softly.

The Mimbres Kid shifted uneasily, his face pulling into a worried frown. Pole noticed absently he was even younger than he had looked the previous night. He had a moment's pity for the boy, wondering, as he had done once before, what it had been that sent him off into the shadowy uncertainty of the side trails upon which a man eventually comes to a halt amid the smoke of gunpowder. His kind never lived long enough to outgrow the name affixed to them. He drifted closer to the Kid, arms still folded. He halted at the Kid's shoulder.

"Now . . . what the hell . . . ?" the Kid began, alarmed and suspicious of the marshal's actions. Crowded, he stepped angrily aside, and in that same moment Pole's hand snaked out and slapped the gun from its holster. It fell to the ground with a puff of dust belching from beneath it.

Pole said: "Don't move!" Leaning over, he picked up the pistol and thrust it into his own waist band. "This is your last chance, Kid," he said in a kindly voice that carried no farther than the pair. "Be out of town before sundown."

The Mimbres Kid stared at him, anger turning his eyes wild. And then a sort of sardonic humor moved in. "Nope, not me, Marshal. You're forgetting you and me have a little score to settle up. Don't be expectin' me to move until that's taken care of."

Pole shook his head. "Get out of town, Kid."

The Mimbres Kid smiled, his face becoming almost boyish. He turned away and swaggered to the Missouri. He entered without looking back.

Men came into the street, gathering in small groups. He heard Joe LeForge say, his voice heavy and

**19**

betrayed: "We've sure made a mistake." McCreight, standing next to him, made some unintelligible reply. Pole heard and cared little. He dropped back to the sidewalk and rolled a smoke, letting the tenseness drain out of his body. After a few minutes he started for his office at the far end of the town. He was conscious of questioning, wondering glances, of men looking at him directly and then lifting their eyes as if embarrassed. When he reached the jail, LeForge, Hale, and McCreight were already there, awaiting him.

"What kind of law enforcement you call that?" LeForge began, almost before he was inside. "What kind of a stunt was that?"

Pole laid the gun he had taken from the Kid on his battered desk and wheeled to face them. The accusation was plain in their eyes. They thought him afraid. He said: "Anybody can shoot a man down. My thought is to give a man every chance to pull out first."

LeForge's gaze was a relentless pressure. "Marshal, if you expect to live very long in this town, you'd better forget that!"

"That's your reason?" McCreight asked then.

Pole shrugged. Quite suddenly he was fed up with these three men. He said: "Let's get this straight. I never asked for this job. You asked me. Now, if you don't like the way I'm handling it and want your tin star back, say so!"

"Might be a good idea at that," LeForge said quickly.

McCreight cut in hurriedly. "No, wait now. Forget that. It's your job. We're having a hard time understanding you, Pole, but it's your job. Do it the way you want."

"Then," John Pole said in distinct, harsh words, "get the hell out of here and let me alone."

He caught the faintest of smiles on the face of Tom Hale. McCreight looked down, and LeForge, going slightly purple, turned and stamped from the office.

Pole made his check of Dry Wells shortly after the noon hour, finding even the Missouri almost deserted. He stopped at the hotel for lunch and after that returned to the jail where he dragged a chair to the outside. The slightest of breezes dulled the edge of the heat, and he placed the chair, tipped back, to where he could get its benefit. Ragged, cottony clouds drifted through the high blue overhead, and a little dust boiled up when a lone 'puncher rode by and pulled up before the Missouri. The town was quiet, but it was an uneasy peace.

Knowing the channels of men's minds, Pole knew the fight had just begun. His handling of the Mimbres Kid, while serving his own private reasons, would only whet the appetites and many ambitions of others like the gunman, and now, from many sources, he could expect trouble in plentiful quantities. And the affair was not over so far as the Kid was concerned. He thought about the boy. He wished he could make him understand, could get through to him. But he was having no luck on that score. Each move he made was a personal affront, according to the way the Kid looked at it.

The afternoon hours dragged by. Heat stiffened and died lower as evening approached. People began to move again in the dusty street, and Dry Wells slowly again came to life. A buckboard with two young girls on the seat clattered by, both waving gaily at him. The cowboy who had passed earlier, having satisfied his thirst for drink or company, returned, making his solemn-faced salute as he trotted back towards the short hills country. Shadows lengthened, and Pole, tired of the inactivity and knowing the time was near, dragged the chair into his office. He closed the door and headed off for the hotel. It was too early to eat, and he passed on to his room and had just laid his hand on the knob when two quick gunshots rolled down the street.

Spinning about, he traveled the long hallway in a half dozen strides. He came out into the lobby. A man burst through the door crying: "The Mimbres Kid just killed Cud Rinson! Killed him over a woman!"

Pole crowded past him and ran onto the porch. He flung a glance down the street. The Kid stood, spraddle-legged, over the form of Rinson, still writhing in the dust. Slipping off the end of the porch and gaining the alley, he ran the short distance to the back of the Missouri. Stopping there until his breath evened, he moved up along the separating passageway between the saloon and the adjacent building and stepped quickly into the street. The movement caught the Kid's eye, and he whirled.

He recognized Pole. A slow grin crossed his face. "You're right prompt, Marshal."

Pole said: "Drop the gun, Kid. You're under arrest for murder."

"Murder?" the Kid echoed.

"He's not wearing a gun," Pole replied evenly. "Now, raise your hands. Slow like."

"I reckon not," the Mimbres Kid drawled. "Not today. Not anytime."

"Don't push your luck," Pole said then in that cool, unhurried way of his. "It might run out quick. I've been trying to do you a favor, but you wouldn't listen. Now you've taken it out of my hands. Murder is one thing I can't let pass. Raise your hands and come along peaceable. I don't want to kill you, Kid."

"Marshal, I hear you talkin', but you aren't saying a thing. Looks like you'll just have to kill me. Or, at least make a try."

John Pole was a hard, rigid shape in the tight, breathless silence. This was not what he wanted. It was the very thing he had sought to avoid. But there was no dodging it now, regardless of his personal wishes and feelings.

"You're a fool, Kid," he said softly. "Better forget this and come along with me."

The faintest of breezes ruffled down the street, raising a light dust. The day's heat was now gone, and a freshness had moved in from the desert. A horse coughed, the sound hanging in the tense air, and Dry Wells was a suspended world.

The Mimbres Kid made his play. He buckled forward, hand sweeping down for the gun butt thrusting up from his hip. John Pole was moving, too.

His weapon came up sooner in that fraction of time. It laid two sharp blasts into the hush, shattering it completely, sending a covey of echoes rocking down the street. The Mimbres Kid pulled himself up to his full height as the bullets tore through him, and then he fell forward.

Pole, catching movement among the men, the Kid's friends who had gathered on the Missouri's porch, spun about, ready for more trouble. Wyatt's voice, coming from the batwings, broke the quiet: "Don't any of you go reachin' for a gun. I'm backin' this marshal's play." He waved the double-barreled shotgun in his hands for emphasis.

The saloon owner stood steady, a half smile on his face. There were the sounds of running feet behind Pole, and he turned to see Hale and LeForge, rushing up with a trail of other citizens behind them. He swung back to the men, silent under Wyatt's gun. "Get on your horses and ride out," he said. "This town's closed to you from this day on."

He watched as they moved to their mounts, swung to their saddles, and trotted off into the gathering darkness. Only then did he walk to where the Mimbres Kid lay. He was thinking: *The job is over. A dead outlaw in the street always cleans up a town. But why did it have to be the Kid? Why, of all the hundreds of gunslingers and outlaws did it have to be the Mimbres Kid?*

LeForge, standing at his elbow, cleared his throat noisily. "Guess we had you figured wrong, Marshal."

John Pole shook his head. He was remembering again that night long years ago when, crowded into a desperate corner by men such as Cud Rinson, with bullets fanning him closely from three sides, a man came unexpectedly from nowhere and said: "Friend, it appears you could use a little help." Together they had fought them off, and John Pole had been grateful. It had become a debt of honor.

He knelt down beside the young outlaw, his long hair a silver shine in the gloom. "I know this boy's daddy. Once he did me a mighty big favor, and I've been looking for years to pay him back. I tried to, but it didn't work out right."

Tom Hale said: "That's why you kept tryin to get him out of town with no shooting . . . You didn't want to kill him."

Pole nodded. "Have somebody take him to El Paso. Folks live there. Reckon that's the least I can do . . . Not much of a favor, however, sending a man the body of his son after you kill him."

"You tried, Marshal," LeForge said, his voice kindly. "Can't nobody say you didn't try to avoid it."

John Pole's eyes were on the bleak, boyish face, turned to the darkening sky. *Yeah, I tried,* he thought bitterly. *But, if I hadn't taken up my guns and been in this god damn town, he wouldn't be dead . . . and I wouldn't be sending sorrow home to a man I swore I'd never hurt.* Slowly he got to his feet. "Appreciate your taking care of everything," he said to Tom Hale and again fell silent, his gaze reaching out over the long distances. "And I reckon you better get yourself a new lawman . . . I'm through for good this time."

25

# Stranger in Black

We lived about a mile from town in those days, and, although Domino Wells was in the heart of the cattle-raising country, our place was not a ranch. I suppose you could call it a farm, but there were only a half dozen acres in all to it.

My mother said there had once been a ranch, a far-reaching spread miles from the settlement, where she and my father tried to make a go of the cattle business. They had failed and had wound up with only the six acres we had. I should remember something about the ranch for I was five years old when the trade was made, but I cannot. It seems to me we always lived on that hardscrabble slope in a sagging tarpaper and warped board shack, and I can't recall ever being referred to by the other kids in town as anything but a squatter. It never bothered me any, though, nor did it effect my brother, Lonnie. I guess we just figured terms like nester and sodbuster and squatter were on the same level as cowpuncher or wrangler or muleskinner.

I never really knew my father. He was gone most of the time, and, when I was little more than four, and Lonnie was yet to have his third birthday, he saddled up and rode off for good, leaving my mother to scratch out a living for herself and her two boys as best she could. She never spoke of him after that. She was that kind of woman. A bad hand had been dealt her, and she just took hold and played it out as best she could, without a whimper, asking no favors of anyone and giving none, either. It must have been a hard life for her, raising two sons with no man around the house to help, but I never heard her complain. While there were many times when I knew she was dead tired and ready to drop in her tracks, she just set her lips and kept on going.

Although I did not realize it at the time, she must have been a pretty, if not beautiful, woman. I remember her as dark and smooth-skinned, with a sort of heart-shaped face and deep green eyes. She was slender and tall, and her hair had a golden color, like the center of a summer sunset. Men were forever trying to make up to her, and, when we walked down Domino Wells' single street, they always turned around to have a second look as we passed. But she paid them no mind, just kept on going, her head high in a proud sort of fashion.

Domino Wells is what is commonly called a trail town. It was a sort of crossroads for cattle herds, coming up from New Mexico and Texas and even Mexico. In the summer and early fall there always could be found cowboys who had taken leave from the herds they were supposed to be driving, roaming about the street looking for refreshment and a decent meal or two. Sometimes they would be on their way back home, the trail drive over, their jobs finished. They were the wild ones, the noisy ones — and sometimes the bad ones. Their pockets would be full of money received in payment for their work, and quite often they would spend it all right there in town on drinks and dancing and other good times. Maybe they would lose it to one of the white-fingered gamblers who were always hanging around the saloons, shuffling a deck of cards in their soft hands.

Those times when the drovers were in town were the best for us. My mother would bake pies with the berries Lonnie and I picked from the thickly growing bushes along the creek and with apples from the two trees the previous owner of our place had fortunately planted. Then she would cut up and fry a half dozen chickens into crisp, brown portions and maybe turn out a few loaves of soft, white bread. On Saturdays we would load it all into a wheelbarrow that she lined with a clean muslin sheet, and the three of us would trundle it into town. She would sell the load to the restaurant where the cowboys ate, getting what I suppose was a fair price for her wares. Cowboys always seemed to like fresh pie and fried chicken, and I can't remember a single time when we did not return home with an empty barrow.

There were many times when we returned with something else, however. As I have said, my mother was most attractive, and men always seemed to think a young widow was fair game for masculine attention. When some persistent suitor did trail us home, my mother would send Lonnie and me out of hearing range. We would trot to one side and wait. It was never

28

very long, two or three minutes at the most. Then we would see the cowboy go stomping off across the hard pack, unsmiling, his face usually redder than normal and clearly angry.

Only once was I ever close enough to hear what was said on such occasions, and that time it was none of the itinerant drovers but Mr Dorcas who ran the store where we sometimes bought things we could not raise. We had stopped by his place for something or other, and Mr Dorcas followed us out into the dusty street. He was a short, thin man with not much hair left and had a way of rubbing at the end of his nose with his forefinger. Lonnie had trotted on ahead to look at the guns and knives and such like in the hardware store's window, but for some reason I had hung back.

I heard Mr Dorcas say. "Missus Starbuck . . . Laurinda, I could help you a lot more if you'd just be seeing things my way . . ."

I remember my mother going all stiff and straight, and her eyes sparked like a spinning grindstone when you lay an axe blade to it.

"I'll take none of your help, Mister Dorcas!" she said in that tone she used when she was mad. "I haven't asked for it nor have I given you any reason to think I would welcome it!"

Mr Dorcas hung his thumbs in the armholes of his vest and rocked on his heels. "Maybe so, but I'm thinking you need it. Ain't been a man around your house for six or seven years now . . . not since that husband of yours up and walked out on you. Ain't natural for a woman like you to live that way."

"Not natural for a man with a wife to speak out so to another woman, either," Mother shot back at him. "I'll thank you to keep such thoughts to yourself, Mister Dorcas. Good day!"

She whirled about, saw me standing there, listening to every word. Her face went a little paler, and her lips clamped down into a line. She grabbed me by the arm, and we marched off down the street, her skirts swishing noisily about her ankles. Needless to say we never again bought anything from Mr Dorcas.

That was the time she showed me how to use the rifle that hung on two pegs by our front door. I already knew how to shoot it. All boys in those days were sort of born with the knowledge, but I let on like it was all new to me. The gun was an old single-shot top loader that had been through the war. There were ten cartridges for it. After I had mastered the routine loading, cocking, aiming, and squeezing off the trigger, I was permitted to fire two of them at a target. The gun's smashing recoil shook me to my foundation both times, but I ignored the pain and went around for days afterward, walking ten feet off the ground, proud as a pigeon with six eggs in a nest.

Mother gave me to understand any more of the cartridges were strictly for emergencies — and the emergency was to be determined by her. If ever she told me to get the rifle and use it, I was to do so without question. The fact that the rifle was replaced on its pegs immediately daunted me a little. It was *my* rifle now. I was its custodian, and someday I might be called upon to use it.

I pictured myself in all sorts of heroic situations, standing off a whole crowd of drovers who were out to rob our house — of what, I didn't exactly know since we had no money and owned nothing of particular value; of fighting off a marauding band of Indians, lately rebelled and off their reservation; of facing down a desperate outlaw; of finishing off a hungry, prowling bear — although there had not been one in that part of the country for years. There was no end to the triumphs over danger I imagined myself accomplishing! The rifle was not touched for many years. And then I came near to killing a man with it.

Meanwhile the days rolled slowly by, one by one, made up of seconds and minutes and tedious or happy hours, whichever the case might be. It all totaled and built into a breathlessly hot life in summer or a brittle, painfully cold one in winter when we could never get a fire sufficiently hot or find clothing enough to turn aside the icy winds that swept in from the plains.

One year we lined the house with old newspapers my mother managed to get somewhere. We made buckets of paste and stuck the sheets to the uneven walls, always with the pictures and lettering right side up. The papers served fairly well as insulation from the cold, but I think they proved of greater value to Lonnie and me as textbooks.

Our education had been limited to what Mother could teach us. There was no law requiring us to attend school in town, and there was too much work for us around the place, anyway. Once or twice a week my mother would find time to gather us at the kitchen table after supper, and, under the single lamp we owned, she managed to teach us to read and write and cipher a sum. By the time we applied the newspapers, we were in a position to further enlarge and improve our knowledge by the simple method of reading the innumerable articles and news stories permanently affixed to the wall next to our bed and elsewhere in the house. I can remember my favorite reading matter was a ten-year-old account of President Lincoln's assassination. I read it so often that, after a time, it wasn't even necessary to look at the words. I knew them by heart.

My mother was a frugal woman and a very competent one. We finally were able to acquire a cow that kept us in fresh milk and butter. Later on came two hogs that were not long in producing a litter of eleven pigs. We had to keep a close watch on the old sow to see that she didn't eat her little ones, but, as it turned out, it wasn't necessary. She bypassed her cannibalistic tendencies, and soon we had a right smart number of the grunting, squealing animals rooting about in the pen Lonnie and I built for them.

We continually hoped to own a horse and a light spring wagon of some kind, but we never did. There were always more important things that came first — money it would take to buy even the most ancient and spavined bonesack and worn-out buckboard was always better spent for additional chickens or another cow or tarpaper for the roof which generally leaked during one of our infrequent rains.

As a result we continued to take our products to market in the wheelbarrow. It got to the point where I had a permanent set of calluses across the palms of my hands after I got large enough to manage it without my mother's help. To this day I shudder when I see one of the lopsided contraptions!

One thing I can say is that for all the discomforts and lack, we were never hungry. My mother always saw to it that there was plenty of food in one form or another, and I can't recall ever going to bed with an empty stomach. Cold and chilled, perhaps, or bone tired from the endless chores, sopping wet from the humid heat — but never hungry. Rabbits were plentiful, easily snared, and we ate them often, friend crisp and with a thick gravy and tasty bread made up in round, corrugated loaves. It was unthinkable that we should ever eat one of our chickens. They were strictly for the trade. But we did have eggs and fresh butter and milk and occasionally ham and bacon. Berries, of course, were always to be had, and now and then we would get lucky and find a bee tree filled with wild honey. We had a small garden where we grew cabbages and a little sweet corn and other vegetables, but my mother was never much for growing things. There was more money to be made in the finished product, and our six acres went mostly to natural food for the livestock.

As time went on, it never occurred to me to think much about my father until one day, when I was in town, two men stopped me and started talking. I had graduated to the exalted status of being allowed to make deliveries by myself on occasion, and this was one of those instances. Mother had been too busy to accompany me, and Lonnie, for some reason, had stayed home also.

After carefully counting the money Mr Gatlin, the café owner, had given me — and then going over it for a third time, since Mr Gatlin was not averse to cheating us if he got a chance, I tucked it deep inside my pocket and headed for my regular look in the hardware store window. I had just reached the display of glittering knives and blued pistols and rifles behind its dust-covered, wavy glass façade when the two men halted beside me. I didn't know their names, although I had seen them around town before and knew they were not drovers from one of the herds.

The tall one said: "Ain't you one of the Starbuck kids?"

I nodded, and the other one asked: "You the little one or the big one?"

There was a little more than a year's difference in Lonnie's age and mine, but I was almost a head taller. I said: "I'm the biggest. I'm Ashur."

"Ashur?" the tall man echoed. "Now where you reckon Ben got a name like that to hang on his kid?"

"Prob'ly that woman of his did it. She always was one for highfalutin' things."

I was about ten at the time, and it was all pretty much over my head, but I realized they were talking about my father. I stood there and listened, saying nothing.

"Kind of looks like Ben, don't he? Got them same little, yellow-colored eyes and that way of walking, like a cougar. You figure he'll grow up to be like Ben?"

The other man shrugged. "Why not? First colt always looks like the stud, I've heard tell," he said, and then they moved on.

When I got back to the house, I turned the money over to my mother. I went out and did my chores after that. I didn't want anything standing in the way when I asked my mother the question that was plaguing me.

Finally, I finished. I went into the kitchen. My mother was at the stove, stirring a big kettle of berries she intended to preserve for winter use. There were a dozen or more glass jars lined up on the table back of her. When she saw me coming nearer, she shook her head.

"Be careful and don't knock those jars over, Ashur."

I said: "Yes'm," and stopped. I waited a minute, getting a firm grip on my courage. Then: "Ma, who's Ben?"

She ceased her stirring for a brief moment. Without looking around she said, very quietly: "Get to your chores, Ashur."

Never before had I braved her as I was doing in those moments. Quaking but still determined, I pressed further along the forbidden subject. "They're all done, Ma. Was Ben my pa?"

The stirring halted again. She reached down, took up a corner of her apron in one hand and wiped at the beaded perspiration on her forehead. She removed the long wooden spoon from the kettle, tapped it methodically to dislodge the residue that clung to it, laid it aside. She picked up a pot holder, made of many folds of cloth stitched together, grasped the bail of the kettle, and moved it to the cool side of the range. After what seemed an eternity, she turned about and looked at me. I could see her face was taut, stiff, like it was when she was angry over something.

"He was," she said in a low voice. "Now, we'll not talk of it again, ever."

And that ended the matter between us.

But not for me, otherwise. I began to listen to conversations whenever I went to town, always hoping to hear a word or two dropped about Ben Starbuck, my missing parent. Nothing else ever came to my ears, and one day I summoned enough courage to approach Mr Kilosky, the blacksmith, who I knew was a sort of old-timer in Domino Wells, and openly broached the subject.

"Did you know my pa, Mister Kilosky?" I asked, trying to make it sound off-hand and casual.

The blacksmith was a huge, roaring man with a beet-red face and a bristling, black mustache. He was pumping the bellows to his forge at the moment, and he looked down at me from a towering height.

"Did I know Ben Starbuck?" he boomed out in his thickly accented voice. "And who did not? From Mexico to Montana, who does not know Ben Starbuck?"

I felt a sort of tingle lift suddenly within me and go racing up my spine. My father must be an important man to be so well known! I was a little vague on geography and couldn't remember exactly where Montana was in relation to Mexico, but Mr Kilosky made it sound like a long way.

I stood and watched, waited for him to say more, fascinated by the huge, corded muscles slipping back and forth beneath the dark skin of his thigh-sized arm as he pumped the wooden lever.

"Where is he now, Mister Kilosky?" I asked, convinced he was about to say no more.

"Who knows? Anywhere . . . everywhere! Find trouble and you will find Ben Starbuck!"

Again I waited for more that did not come. I said: "Why did he go away?"

"Why? Why does any man have a fiddlefoot? Why does any man want to see over the next hill? Some men are made to look. Some are not. He was one of those who would have his look." He stopped short. I looked up at him. He was no longer smiling, instead was glaring down at me with a fierce, dark impatience. "Such questions your mother it would be better to ask, boy. I say no more." And then, as if angry with himself for speaking what he had, he turned about and stalked deeper into his lean-to shop.

It was good advice I never followed. When my mother put her foot down on something, it was a thoroughly closed matter. Still I kept trying to find out from others in town, doing it on the sly, dropping what I considered innocent little questions here and there at strategic moments, all to no avail. Everyone, it appeared, was unwilling to talk of Ben Starbuck. I don't know if they feared my mother's wrath or some sort of swift and fatal retribution from my father, should he one day return, or if they simply didn't know anything. Anyway, the net result was that I continued to grow and live in ignorance of my absent male parent while time rolled slowly on.

Then one day something happened that changed everything. It was late summer. The sky had been dry and steel brilliant with heat for over a month. Dust from the herds five miles to the east hung above the horizon in a continuous, brown cloud, seemingly never to settle. The blistering days helped the town's business, of course. Everybody was dry, thirsty, and even our supply of fresh milk sold out. Mother and I were in town, making a second, extra delivery of pies and fried chicken. Lonnie wasn't with us. Someone had given him two goats, and he was engaged in building a pen which he hoped they could not batter down.

The street was ankle deep in powdery dust and was as near crowded as you could expect it to be. I was walking along ahead of my mother, perhaps ten feet or so, pushing the accursed wheelbarrow before me when I heard a man's voice speak out.

"Laurie!"

My mother's name was Laurinda, and I didn't realize for a moment that he was addressing her until I suddenly became aware that she was no longer following behind me. I stopped, sat the wheelbarrow down, and turned to wait, thinking it was another of the persistent cowboys still hoping to become friendly with her.

The man had his back to me, and I looked him over curiously. He was tall with wide shoulders and hips so narrow he almost had none at all. He was dressed fancy, entirely in black, wide-brimmed hat, shiny sateen shirt, and rich-looking corded pants. His boots were elaborately stitched with red and white butterflies and birds, and, although they were covered with a fine film of dust, they still gleamed from a high polish. What most caught my attention were the guns he wore. There were two of them, one at each thigh, worn low with their smooth bone handles tipped forward and slightly out in the way of a fast draw gunman. He carried them in soft, dark holsters that were decorated with silver and thonged tightly to his legs with narrow strips of rawhide.

"A long time, Laurie," I heard him say in a deep voice.

My mother did not answer. At least, I do not recall what she said, if she did answer. I was so engrossed in the guns and the fancy belt and holsters — and the man himself — that it could have failed to register on me.

"I know where you live. I'll drop by later tonight."

"No!"

My mother's reply was so sudden, so sharp, that I glanced up, startled. There was almost a fear in her tone, something I never before had recognized in her. When I saw the brightness in her eyes, the strained lines of her face, I realized she actually was afraid of the stranger in black. It surprised me. I didn't think anyone, or anything, could frighten my mother.

"You have no right . . . ," she said then, her words coming out haltingly. "You made your choice . . ."

The man laughed a low, rumbling sort of sound. "I have every right," he said in a silky, soft way, "every right. And I shall exercise it. I won't be late," he added, and then walked on down the street.

For a long time my mother just stood there, staring straight ahead. She wasn't seeing me or the other people nearby or the weather-beaten, faded buildings of the town at all. She was looking at something in her memory, something that disturbed her deeply and made her afraid. I saw this, and suddenly it began to worry me.

After a long while she recovered herself, and we started on home. She said nothing to me about the man in black, but I could tell it weighed heavily on her mind. I was at a loss to understand that. I had seen her handle a half a dozen or more cowboys who exhibited greater persistence than this one and not be the least upset. There was something else that made this one different.

Lonnie had given up on the pen for the goats when we arrived. He had now fastened ropes about their scrawny necks and tethered them to the cottonwood that grew about halfway between the chicken house and the ditch that carried water in from the creek. The ropes weren't going to be any answer, either. One of the animals had already chewed his into separate pieces. I would have to help Lonnie figure out something, but it would have to wait for a better time.

I guess you might say I grew up that day. At twelve years of age I abruptly was a man, going about my chores unsmilingly, worrying about my mother, and considering seriously what I must do to protect and look out for her.

We ate our supper, my mother moving about the house in an anxious, strained manner. I saw her glance nervously toward the road several times, and, when full dark came, and it was time for bed, she lost no time in getting us off to it. I lay there beside my brother and listened to her close up the place, pull down the windows despite the intense heat, and wedge them tightly with a length of wood we used for such purpose. She shut the front and rear doors and moved some piece of furniture up against them, a table or maybe it was the washstand. I could not tell which.

She went to bed soon after that, and I waited, wide awake, knowing what had to be done. My mother was upset, badly frightened by this strange man who promised, in a threatening sort of way, to see her. I could not let it happen. Why he was so unwelcome, I did not know, but my mother felt as she did and that was all the reason I needed. It was up to me, as the man of the house, to prevent it. I was almost glad it had come to pass. At least, here was something my mother could not cope with. I had not thought it possible, but it was. And . . . I had the answer to it.

Being careful not to awaken Lonnie, I slipped from the bed, wearing only my long nightgown. Somewhere in the hot and darkened house a cricket had been chirping busily. It hushed the instant my bare feet touched the floor. I crept to the front room, took the rifle down from its pegs. I obtained two of the precious cartridges from the box on the shelf, and paused. I listened for the faint snores that should be coming from my mother's room which would indicate that she slept.

There was a different sound this night — a muffled sort of sobbing. I heard it in amazed silence, not fully comprehending it. My mother was crying! It startled me again, shocked me. I had never heard her weep, not in all the twelve years of my life. It did something to me inside, as a book being suddenly closed. It was like discovering there was no Santa Claus, that something you fully believed in didn't actually exist at all.

I stood there in the center of the close, stifling room for several minutes, I guess, getting a grip on myself, renewing my flagging courage. Finally I went to the rear of the house where the kitchen was. Since we had no locks on either of our doors, I found how my mother had secured them by tipping a chair against the knob and then bracing the chair with another piece of furniture. There wasn't much real protection in such an arrangement. Anyone desiring to enter bad enough could have booted the whole works aside in a couple of tries.

Outside, the night was little cooler than in the house. The cricket, hearing me no more, had resumed his racket. Down by the creek the tree frogs were going at it strong, and somewhere in town a dog was barking in that lonely way of a dog when he just wants to hear his own voice. I loaded the rifle and slipped along the side of the shack to the small lilac bush that stood about halfway to the road. It was a thin bush, and it never did have many blossoms on it, probably because we didn't have time to give it any water or care. You can't eat or sell lilacs, so it had to get along the best it could on its own.

I crouched down behind the bush and watched the street, leading into town. I thought about my mother, about the fear, and the way the stranger had brought weeping to her. And suddenly I was angry, terribly angry at the man all dressed up so fancy in black who had brought it upon her.

Whoever he was, whatever he meant to her, had affected her greatly. She no longer was the calm, self-sufficient mother, so capable and fearless and independent I had always known. She was now just a woman afraid, weeping in the night, hiding behind a thin wall of warped boards and tarpaper. And this stranger had brought it to pass. What mysterious power did he possess that enabled him so completely to change my mother?

I huddled behind the lilac and wondered. The rifle grew heavy, and I propped it against my knees, remembering the way it was done by Indian scouts as pictured in one of the newspapers plastered on the wall of my bedroom. Minutes wore on, and I began to get sleepy but I fought manfully against such weakness. Noises from the town were distant but plain. Men laughed, shouted. Now and then I heard the higher pitched, shrill laughter of women. And once there was a gunshot, a sort of hollow pop as when you clapped the dry seed pod of a wildflower that grew in our field between the palms of your hands. Then, unexpectedly, there was a different sound, the soft *tunk-a-tunk* of a horse walking slowly in the street, its hoofs muted by the thick dust.

My heart began to pound, my temples to throb wildly. A great lump gathered somewhere in my chest as a torrent of fear washed through me. For the first time I had an idea of what I was actually doing — waiting alone out there in the night to shoot a man! Me, a twelve-year-old kid with a cumbersome old rifle that might not even fire, figuring to fight it out with a man who probably was a top gunslinger. I wouldn't have a chance!

But I thought of my mother, and somehow that steadied me. I took up the rifle and held it before me. The sound of the approaching horse grew stronger, nearer. I pulled back the huge hammer of the gun. It was loud in the darkness, so loud that I feared it would be heard and wished at once that I had cocked the weapon earlier. It apparently went unnoticed. The rider continued to draw closer.

He pulled up in front of our house, stopped. The night was pale, lighted only by starshine, but there was no mistaking the man. He was the one in black. The silver on his belt and holsters gleamed dully in the half light, and his face and hands and neck were soft tan in color. He sat in his saddle for a long time, it seemed to me, just looking at the house. He swung down.

Not thirty feet away I watched him drape the reins of his horse over a clump of brush, tug them into a slip knot. He started toward me, walking softly in a way that reminded me of the stray cat that came and lived with us for a spell until we caught him killing chickens. The man seemed to know exactly what he was about. He walked straight for the door. I raised the rifle, sighted down its round barrel at his chest. I pulled the trigger.

With the deafening blast I went over backwards. In my anxiety and nervousness, I had neglected to hold the gun snugly against my shoulder, had allowed it to recoil fully. Dazed, I scrambled to my feet. The man in black was sprawled out flat in the yard, his right hand clawing at his left shoulder, while a mixture of groans and curses spilled from his lips. Beyond him his horse, frightened by the rifle's fearful blast, reared and fought to tear loose from the clump where he was tethered.

Other horses were pounding down the road, and men were shouting questions. Apparently they had not been far away, had heard the shot, and now were coming to see what it was all about. But my mother was there beside me before they arrived. I heard a sort of gasp, looked around, and there she was. Her face was chalk white. Her eyes were spread into large, round pools. As I watched, an expression of horror covered her features when she saw who it was I had shot.

The three men rushed into the yard, leaped from their horses. They trotted to where the man lay and knelt down beside him.

"He dead?" one asked.

"Nope, not yet."

I heard a little sigh of relief slip through my mother's lips as though she were thankful I had not killed, but only wounded, the stranger.

"Bullet's smashed his shoulder. Done a powerful lot of damage."

"Know who he is?"

My mother sounded like her old self again when she spoke, getting out her words quick and hurried before anyone could answer the question that had been asked.

"That's not important now ... getting him to a doctor is. There is one at the far end of the street."

"Yes'm," one of the men said. "Give me a hand here, Herb. The lady's right. He could bleed to death while we're standing around yammering."

They got the man to his feet, walked him to his horse. They loaded him onto the saddle. Two of them rode off with him, one on each side, holding on to him to keep him from falling. The third man came back to where we stood. He pulled off his hat.

"Ma'am, just what happened here?"

I was beginning to recover a bit, the shock and excitement of those first moments finally wearing off. I started to reply. My mother's fingers pressed into my shoulder, warning me to silence.

"He was just a prowler," she said in a quiet voice. "My son shot him."

The man let out a low whistle. "He done just right! But I reckon he got himself more'n just a prowler. I've heard tell of that one ... he's a bad one. That button of yours has done what twenty men couldn't do ... shoot him down."

My mother said: "I hope he won't die ..."

"Likely he won't, ma'am, leastwise die the permanent way. But he's dead far as a gunfighter's concerned. That bullet messed up his arm so's he won't be fast drawing no gun ever again. I'd say the country owes that boy of yours a vote of thanks. Well, good night, ma'am."

We watched him wheel about and walk to his horse. He swung to the saddle, waved his hand, and his horse trotted off after his friends. When he was out of sight, my mother put one arm about my shoulders, her other around Lonnie who had come out with her, and we started toward the house. I was a little nervous, not knowing just how she was going to look at the matter. I wondered if I was going to catch it for taking down the rifle without her permission.

Halfway Lonnie asked: "Ma, who was it Ashur shot?"

I turned to look at her, wanting to be certain I heard her answer. She was not smiling, but her lips were very set in a relieved sort of way, and her face was once again calm and smooth.

"Only a prowler," she said. "We will forget all about him."

The answer satisfied Lonnie but never me. Not long after that night my mother sold our place, land, buildings and livestock, and we moved back to Missouri, to a small town near St. Louis called Montgomery City. During our years there I brought up the question several times, but the reply was always the same: a prowler.

Later, when I was grown, I paid a visit to Domino Wells — only it no longer existed. With the advent of the railroads the trail drives had ceased, and the reason for the town's presence had vanished. Now it was only a fading scar on an otherwise limitless landscape. Gone also were the persons who might have answered the question in my mind — who was the stranger in black I had felled that night in our yard?

I had my own ideas, but I never actually knew — not for sure.

# Mountain Man

Abner Galvan sat in Miguel Prieto's Taos Inn and sipped slowly at his cup of *aguardiente*. It fell just a bit short of hell's own brimstone in temperature, he reckoned, but it was good. It cut the dust, and it helped pass the time until Kit St. Vrain rode in with the wagon train from the east.

Ab had been down from the high country no more than three days — three days during which he had sold his winter's take of pelts to McTavish, bought himself a complete new outfit, renewed old acquaintances, and taken in a fandango at which he had gotten into a very satisfying scrap with another trapper. And now, somewhat bruised, money belt a bit lighter, he was whiling away time.

The cup went dry, and he glanced around the cool, low-ceilinged room, but he was momentarily alone, Miguel apparently having gone outside for one reason or another. *It could be a long wait for Kit*, he thought, and drew a knife from its belt sheath at his hip and began to rub absently at its handle. It had been made by his own hands, worked up from file steel and whetted to razor sharpness during the long winter nights. He tested it again as he had on a hundred previous occasions by wetting his thumb and running it lightly along the edge.

Moved by a sudden urge, he took the tip between thumb and forefinger and with a single, deft action flung it across the room where it plunged, quivering, in a pine roof support. Quickly, as if testing his own reflexes, he plucked another but smaller knife from inside his right boot and sent it flashing after the first one.

He grinned, thinking of the name his skill with knives had earned him among the Indians and Spaniards — Cuchilliero, the knife man. He thought, too, of all the endless hours he had spent, painstakingly learning to throw a blade so that it would strike properly and with deadly accuracy. But it had proven worthwhile.

Miguel came in, refilled the cup at Ab's call, and went out again. The mountain man retrieved his weapons and settled down once more in the low chair. Only then did he sense the presence of someone else in the room. He turned to see, and a woman's voice said: "You are the one known as Cuchilliero?"

She was an old woman, clothed entirely in black with the usual *rebozo* covering her head. She spoke in the stiff and stilted Spanish of the *ricos*.

"You are that one?" she pressed.

"*Estoy, señora,*" Ab replied in his own halting knowledge of the language.

"My mistress would have words with you," the *duenna* said. "Come with me."

Some of the imperiousness of the woman's tone and manner rubbed into Ab, irritating him. "Now, who the hell is your mistress?"

"That you will learn," the woman replied. "Come, we have little time."

Ab looked the woman over coolly, only the brightness of his eyes betraying the anger that had crawled into him. These *ricos* with all their fancy airs! They might be the top class and live in their big *haciendas* with the high walls, but they meant nothing to him. He owed them nothing — and he wanted nothing from them.

"Suppose you go tell your mistress that I'm not used to trotting around at everybody's beck and call. You just tell her, if she's looking for me, I'll be right here."

He settled back into the chair, but before he could pick up his cup, the old *duenna* was before him.

"But you will please to come this time. It is of so much importance. I implore you, *señor!*"

The note of urgency in the woman's voice got through, touching him and having its affect. He looked more closely at her and thought he could see fear in her eyes. Fear and anxiety and something else, perhaps a hopelessness. Silently he motioned for her to go and followed her outside.

She led him not across the plaza but by a devious route that took them behind squat adobe huts and rambling store buildings and along a narrow ditch that was heavily veiled in willows and scrubby outgrowth. They saw no one, and, when they finally entered a gate, Ab found them to be within a high-walled plaza. He paused a moment to gather his bearings and then at the woman's urgent — "Come!" — followed her across the hard-packed ground to the main house. This was a *rico* dwelling, sure enough, and he wondered at the strange invitation that would summon a usually forbidden *Americano* inside.

He followed the *duenna* into a large room, plush and elegant in its furnishings, and she signaled him to wait. He stood motionless, legs spread, hat still on his head, arms folded, and examined the dark oil portraits on the wall. Spanish cavaliers and one — the big one with the odd, sharp face — was probably the king.

The door reopened and the *señora* reentered, followed by a young girl dressed in voluminous, flowing white satin and lace. Her face was smooth as a cameo, and her black hair was piled high on her head, a white flower of some sort making its sharp contrast. Ab's breath caught, and his hand went to his hat, removing it.

"This is the one called Cuchilliero," the *duenna* said and moved back into one of the room's corners.

The man nodded in foolish affirmation, thinking that he had never seen a girl like this before. He had observed plenty of Spanish *señoritas*, but never one like this, no, not even in a carriage. They just didn't show themselves, but remained, pampered and guarded, in the *haciendas*. He was vaguely aware of the girl's voice, sharp and commanding, and that he was staring at her.

"You will remember your place!" she was saying.

Ab Galvan, possessing all the healthy and lusty feelings of a strong man, grinned but didn't take his eyes away. A thing of beauty, to him, was something to be looked at and appreciated, and he was doing just that.

"I am . . . ," the girl continued haltingly, and then stopped. She was confused and taken aback by his frank appraisal and didn't quite know how to cope with it. Furious, then, she returned his direct gaze and started once again.

"I am . . . but the name doesn't matter. I have need of a carriage and driver this evening. If you are willing to take the job, I will pay you a hundred dollars in gold."

Ab stirred. "Depends on the job."

"You will drive me to San Martinez."

San Martinez was thirty miles to the north, and there was nothing there but a convent. *She is running away from something*, Ab reckoned, but he said: "Sounds easy enough. What time do we start?"

"There is a possibility of danger. Great danger to yourself."

The mountain man shrugged. "There is always the possibility of that, *señorita*. You would like to start at dark?"

She nodded. "You will meet me at the side gate. I will be ready."

Ab turned to go, but she checked him at the door. "You will say nothing of this?" she cautioned.

He nodded and stepped outside. Pausing there momentarily to orient himself, he noticed that the carriage gate was to his left, some two hundred yards, and that a soldier stood at guard just inside. The high wall entirely surrounded the grounds. As far as he could tell, the only other exit was the small gate through which he and the *duenna* had entered earlier. Not liking it too well, he started to leave when he heard the *duenna* say: "He is a strong one and bold, too!"

"He will serve the purpose," the girl answered, but her tone carried more than just a simple statement of fact. There was a lift to it, a certain note of anticipation, and Ab, catching it, felt the swift roll of something through his body, something he couldn't identify but closely akin, perhaps, to hope. He left the *hacienda* grounds in a mood that firmly refused to heed the tiny pluckings of caution that tugged at his mind.

Later that afternoon he obtained a span of good horses and a light covered buggy from the livery stable and said he planned to head ostensibly for the river, some ten miles to the west.

"Who lives in the *hacienda* just beyond the turn in the road?" he asked casually of the hosteler.

"Captain Delgado . . . Felipe Delgado," the man said and added, "why?"

"The Captain has a sister?"

"No sister. A cousin, Margarita Vasquez. They are the last of the families."

The hosteler stopped short, as if struck suddenly by thought. He walked closer and peered up into Ab's face. "The *señor* does not have thoughts of visiting the *señorita*, does he? Have care there, friend! The captain is a violent and dangerous man."

"I'm headed for the river," Ab reminded him, and put the team into motion. He followed along the

54

well-beaten road that cut across the flat plains and dropped down into the canon and the riverbed that led, eventually, to Santa Fé, but he pursued its course only until the scattered buildings hid him from the hosteler and anyone else that might have been watching.

Cutting back to the north, he covered the uneven ground slowly. By the time he had reached the *hacienda*, it was full dark. Tethering the horses a short distance from the gate, he quietly let himself inside and waited. The girl was not there, and he slacked against the wall, enjoying the coolness the shadows had brought and listening to the sounds of the night, mingling in the soft air.

The minutes ran on, and still she did not come. A small worry set up inside of him, growing as the time ground by, until it had built itself into a definite thing that tensed him and made him wary. He waited another full ten minutes and then crossed the courtyard into the deep shadows. He pulled up short when the girl's voice, almost at hysterical pitch, came to him.

"I will leave this house!" she cried. "You cannot stop me. You can't make me become a party to your ambitions!"

"You will do as I say," a man's low voice returned. "My ambitions, as you choose to call them, have but one purpose and that is to maintain the prestige and standing of our family. This is our only means."

"I will not do it," the girl repeated.

Ab heard the solid smack as he struck her across the face and the quick gasp of pain when she recoiled.

55

Lifting the latch, he stepped quickly into the room, hand resting casually on his knife handle.

Margarita stood facing him, her eyes wide with a mixture of fear and astonishment. She was dressed for traveling, and near her on the floor lay a small bag filled, probably, with her belongings.

The man, too, looked at him in amazement, but it gave way to anger. "Who are you?" he demanded.

"Are you ready to leave, *señorita*?" Ab asked, ignoring him.

The girl nodded and picked up her bag. "I am ready."

She moved toward the door, and Delgado, suddenly aware of things, lunged at Ab. The mountain man sidestepped and drove a hard right hand into the man's face. The captain went down like an ox.

"You fools!" he gasped. "You won't reach the wall."

"We'll see," Ab said softly. "Now get up. You're going to walk there with us."

He dragged the man to his feet and pricked him gently in the back with his knife. "If you want to see morning, Captain, you'll walk quietly to the gate with us . . . and you won't call for your soldiers, either. I can drive this blade through your heart at thirty paces before you can take a step."

"He is Cuchilliero," Margarita said with false sweetness. "You have heard of him?"

Delgado muttered incoherently, and they started towards the door, the girl first, then Delgado with Ab walking closely behind him. To a casual observer they were but three people, sauntering towards the wall, and as such they crossed the patio and opened the gate. Ab saw Margarita pass through, and he kept the rigid figure of the captain moving steadily on.

Then sudden movement outside flung its warning at him, and he threw himself sideways. He caught a glimpse of soldiers and of the hosteler's grinning face. He shoved Delgado straight into them, seeing him lose his feet and fall flat, several soldiers piling over his thrashing figure. But there were more bearing down upon him. Margarita screamed his name, and then night crashed down upon him, and the last thing he was conscious of was that his knife had spun away from his fingers.

He came to, sick and throbbing all over. He was lying across a saddle, bound hand and foot, and at every jolting step of the trotting horse it seemed that his head would burst. Just as blackness was about to claim his reeling senses again, the horse stopped. Rough hands dragged him to the ground, and liquid fire raced through his body when they forced him to stand upright. Every tortured nerve in his being sang out, but no sound passed his clenched teeth.

Two soldiers grasped him by the arms, dragged him to a small building, kicked open the door, and slammed him to the floor.

"*Americano!*" one muttered and kicked him solidly in the ribs.

"Careful, Sergeant," Delgado's voice cut through the blackness. "We need this *gringo* for the morrow!"

Ab's senses were clearing rapidly now, and the stab of pain from the sharp-toed boot, searing through him, seemed to rouse his flagging brain more. But he lay motionless, eyes closed, listening to the movement about him. Someone produced a lantern, and then more men entered.

"Get him on his feet," Captain Delgado's voice ordered. "Cut the ropes on his legs so he can stand."

Ab was jerked upright where he swayed drunkenly. Through slitted lids he took in the assemblage — Delgado, a half dozen soldiers, and a new officer, resplendent in gold and braid that he had never seen before.

"The great Cuchilliero," the general echoed. He stepped closer, and Ab saw him to be fat and soft and with a repugnant coarseness about him that verified the stories he had heard around the territory. "Well, we shall see how great he is in the morning. Sergeant, you will have this man in the plaza at sunrise together with a firing squad."

"Yes, my general," the soldier said.

"Immediately after the wedding I shall bring the party there and, when we are all assembled, that will be your signal to carry out the execution."

Delgado turned to the man. "You mean to execute him in front of Margarita . . . before her very eyes?"

The captain's words drove into Ab's brain with solid force. Margarita was supposed to marry the general — that was why she had sought to escape to the convent. She was being driven into the contract by Delgado to save his rumbling political fortunes.

"Will it not be a masterly stroke," the general droned. "An object lesson for both my young bride and all *Americanos*."

The captain did not answer but stood silently, his eyes on the floor, and Ab read in his dejected figure the story of a man suddenly sick of his own bargain. Wordlessly the captain turned and walked from the small room. The general gave one more order to the sergeant, that a guard must be posted outside, and then he, too, left with the soldiers filing out behind him. Ab heard the bar drop across the door and then the muffled sound of hoofbeats, dwindling into the distance.

He remained as they had left him, standing in the center of the room, and he thought of the things they had said. He thought, too, of Margarita, the smoothness of her skin, her black hair, and the urgency of her, and how it had moved him. Slowly he began to pace back and forth, realizing suddenly that he could not permit this marriage even at the cost of his own life. And then he realized, suddenly and bitterly, that he was powerless to help, and that it was costing him his life.

He sat down on the hard floor, remembering all at once that his wrists were still bound. The belt knife was gone, lost in the scuffle at the *hacienda*, but his fingers found the other, safe in its scabbard inside his boot. He drew it out and, holding it backwards, cut through the rope.

For long minutes he remained there, considering his position, weighing and testing all possibilities in his mind. He got up then and moved to the door. Placing one ear hard upon it, he listened. He could hear nothing. Slipping the knife into his belt, he pounded on the thick timbers and shouted.

"Guard! Guard! I want water!"

No answer came. Either the man was gone, asleep, or could not hear through the thick walls. Satisfied that he could not get the soldier to enter on one pretext or another, and gambling that he could not hear, Ab crossed to the far corner. Dropping to his knees, he felt out the mortar lines between the adobe bricks and began to chip away at the brittle substance.

It was slow work, and he stopped periodically to listen at the door for the guard, but he could hear nothing and, therefore, concluded that the soldier could not hear him. The hours wore away, hot and breathless in the windowless room, and he thought of the coolness of his cabin, high in the mountains. It would be quiet there, too, but a different kind of silence with a light, magic wind drifting down from the peaks, moving the spruce trees gently and shaking the tall white aspens until they sighed and moaned. The dark, star-encrusted sky would be so low that you could almost touch it, and over everything would be that fresh, clean sharpness of wild and untamed country.

It never dawned on Ab that, should he effect an escape from his prison, the wise thing to do would be to forget the girl, flee into the hills, and remain there until the whole thing was forgotten. He was simply a man with a logical mind and an inherent sense of what was right and what was wrong. And this, to his manner of thinking, was all wrong.

He felt the first of the bricks loosen and paused to make one more check at the door. No sounds. He resumed the task, carefully working the adobe in, fearing that, if it fell out and away, it might create a noise that the guard would hear. It came finally, and for a long minute he sat before the opening, sucking in deep breaths of the meadow-sweetened air. The blocks came more easily after the first, and, when enough had been removed to permit his passing through, he made one last check at the door, heard nothing, and then crawled out into the night.

Lying there in the semi-darkness, he considered his best course of action. He guessed it to be a short two hours until sunrise. Realizing that it would be wise to get in touch with Margarita before the many people arrived at the *hacienda* for the wedding, he started to crawl the short distance from the jail to the brushy area bordering the ditch on the west. It was then that he caught the sudden drumming of horses, coming up the road from town. He flattened out instinctively, cursing his luck. The riders pulled up, and the guard brought a lantern to life. He waited until he heard the door creak open and then, coming to his feet, sprinted for the screening safety of the willows.

Instantly a yell went up behind him, and he knew he had been wrong. Only one of the soldiers had gone into the jail with the guard. The other had remained in the saddle and had seen him run. He heard the pound of the horse, and a gun blossomed in the darkness. He felt the wind of the bullet, speeding past him. But the willows were there before him, and he plunged into them, running low and fast.

The night became alive with shouting. The other soldier had caught up now, and they had separated.

Each was coming up the ditch, trying to work him in between them. Ab slid over the bank and dropped into the water, the coldness of it wrenching his breath momentarily, but he forced himself to remain motionless and clung closely to the bank, half submerged.

The horses galloped by, and he hung on for a full minute. Then, on all fours, he wormed out of the ditch and started for a thick grove of cottonwoods a hundred yards to the right. Before he had covered a half dozen paces, his ears caught the slow thud of a walking horse. Apparently one of the soldiers had decided to backtrack and was carefully searching the willow thickets again.

Ab went flat into the tall grass. The muted *tunk-a-tunk* of the horse's hoofs on the spongy humus drew closer, and the mountain man prepared himself for what he knew was his only chance. When he sprang, it was with all the deadly purpose and accuracy of a mountain lion upon an unsuspecting deer. He had a brief vision of the soldier's startled face as it swung toward him, and then it disappeared when Ab's locked hands smashed into the man and bowled him from the saddle. The horse reared, but Ab was half across the animal's neck, holding him down, and for a few moments there was nothing but the horse wheeling in tight circles as Ab fought to gain the saddle.

"Hey!" the soldier at the jail yelled, question riding his tone. "What's happening?"

An answering halloo came from up the ditch, anxious and querulous. Savagely Ab fought the horse into a semblance of calmness, gained the saddle, and wheeled for the grove. By now the guard was alive to the movement, and Ab heard the flat echo of a gun as the man fired, but the bullet was wide. He gained the cottonwoods in a headlong rush and pulled the animal up short.

Looking back, he could see the guard running across the open space, awkward and heavy, with the moonlight glinting off the gun he held half lifted in his hand. The other soldier was cutting diagonally to meet him, not coming fast, apparently fearing a trap.

Ab slid from the saddle and looped the reins about a sapling. Searching a moment, he located a stone. Moving to the near edge of the grove, he threw it with all his strength in the general direction of the approaching guard. It fell just inside the first outcropping of trees.

"Over here! Over here!" the man sang out, and the soldier broke into a dead gallop, swerving in his course.

Ab wasted no time to see what further effect the ruse would have, knowing in his own mind that it would be short-lived, but it had given him his opportunity. Returning to the saddle, he started north for Taos, threading in and out of the trees at a fast walk.

When he reached the end of the grove, he paused momentarily to listen, but the sounds were too far away and were lost to him. He reasoned at once that they could no longer hear him. Putting the horse to a full gallop, he circled the town and cut in sharply for Delgado's *hacienda*.

Tethering the horse in the willows opposite the gate, he paused again to listen and, hearing nothing, crossed over. The gate was closed, but not locked. Opening it, he let himself inside and waited until his eyes could adjust themselves to the deep shadows that still filled the patio. Above him the sky was streaking with the first morning rays, and he was impatient with his own caution, realizing, as he stood there, that minutes were sliding by rapidly, each claiming its own great value.

A few lamps burned in the *hacienda*, two near the rear of the building and one, much brighter, in the room where he had first talked with Margarita. In there, he judged, would be the general in the company of Delgado and possibly several others, celebrating the success of conquest and delighting with thoughts of the day to come.

Silently Ab moved to the back of the house and, pausing there only long enough to remove his boots, opened the door and entered. He found himself in a dimly lit hallway with doors turning off on either side. Losing no time, he lifted the latch on the first. The room was empty and dark, and he quickly moved on to the next.

He could hear the sounds of muffled laughter and the low drone of conversation coming from the far end of the hall where the large room was. The second door he tried also led to nothing. When he felt for the handle to the third and last on that side, tension was building up within him. Somewhere, off that hallway, was the girl, sitting out the long moments until sunrise, hope gone from her mind at this late hour.

Slowly he lifted the lock. A streak of faint light struck across his eyes, and he pushed in steadily, but making

**64**

no sound. Margarita was lying across the bed, face down. Warned suddenly by some inner voice, she whirled about. Her eyes opened wide with astonishment, and then fear took its charge, and she screamed. Almost too late Ab caught the warning and saw Delgado rushing across the room to meet him.

Lunging inside, he slammed the door and met the man's onrushing force. It carried him back, and his head thudded into the solid wood, momentarily stunning him, but he clung to the captain, pinning his arms to his sides as they wrestled about. Outside he could hear men pounding up the hallway, and with a burst of strength he flung Delgado from him, saw him strike the wall, and bounce away.

"Hurry!" he gasped, breath coming back to him in hard gulps. "The horse is outside the gate. I'll hold them off long as I can. Follow the road north. I'll catch up later."

There was no more time for words. Delgado was getting dazedly to his feet, and already the door was creaking under the weight of driving shoulders from the hallway. Ab seized the captain, spun him around, and drove a hard right into his jaw. Delgado crumpled.

"Stand here! When I open the door, they'll come falling in," he said to the girl. "When they do . . . run for it."

The girl shook her head, and in that fragment of a moment the mountain man had a better understanding of her courage.

"I'll wait," she said.

The door splintered. Ab grabbed up a heavy stool. He waited. When the panel burst wide, he sent the first soldier to the floor with a blow that broke the stool into pieces, leaving him with only a short leg as a weapon. The second man recoiled, but those behind him pushed him on. Ab dropped him with a wild swing.

A gun roared in the small room, and he heard the thud as the lead drove into the wall. The smoke crept into his eyes, smarting, but he flailed away with the stool leg, his huge shape outlined in the feeble light before the doorway. A man sagged into him. He heaved him back, and only then did he recognize it was the general. The way cleared momentarily, and he glanced back. Margarita stood as he had last seen her, a faint outline in the corner. Delgado was struggling to his feet again.

Ab flung a glance at the door where the two remaining soldiers and the general were preparing to rush him again. He swore grimly. He could no longer hold them back with the captain behind him and the two men on the floor coming into the fight. With a yell he flung the stool leg straight into the general's face and turned to Delgado, thinking to use him as a shield, but the captain threw up his hands to ward him off.

"Hold!" he cried. "In Holy Mary's name, hold!"

Ab backed away warily. For the first time his hand went to the knife, miraculously still in his belt. He flung a quick glance to the doorway where the two soldiers supported the sagging form of their general. Blood was streaming down his face, and his eyes rolled grotesquely.

**66**

"Put him on the bed," Delgado ordered, and the pair half dragged, half carried the man there.

"Now go," the captain said in a low, strained voice to Ab. "Take her with you while we're busy with the general." His eyes shifted to the girl, and his battered face softened a little. "We are lost," he added wearily, "but I had no real heart for the bargain."

The girl crossed over, and they moved down the hallway and out into the patio.

"Got to hurry," Ab said. "We'll ride double to the first ranch and then get a team and buggy."

"Where do we go?" she asked, tipping her face to him and looking into his own.

Her pale loveliness and the faint scent of her reached into the man, touched him, and had its strong, heady way with him.

"To anywhere," he said.

"To anywhere," she agreed.

Ab glanced at the sky, shot now with the full light of the morning. He thought of the cabin — *their* cabin now — sitting squarely, solidly, and comfortingly in the valley. Why not go there? The night would have just passed, and the air would be clear and sharp as flint. Probably sometime during the night a wolf had stood on the ridge and thrown his lonely howl into the pure silence just for the hell of it. And the magic wind would drift down from the peaks and over the valleys.

It will be wonderful, he thought, having her with him from this moment on, and then he grinned. He knew it was something that he could never make Kit St. Vrain understand.

# The Town Killer

He was christened William Thompson, but in later years they called him The Regulator — which is about as descriptive a name as you can give a hell-for-leather range detective. Little is known about his birth, his parents, or of the general background of this nemesis of frontier outlawry, but, from the first day he vaulted into blazing prominence in the mid-1880s until the melodramatic moment of his death, few who knew him ever forgot him.

He was a 19th-Century St. George who tried where entire posses feared to go, bearding the dragons of lawlessness wherever they might be, and it was his proud claim — no brag, just fact — that no prisoner ever escaped his sturdy fingers completely. There were two, with the help of an entire settlement, who tried — and regretted it, for in typical Regulator style he visited swift retribution upon the town and its inhabitants, not only wrecking the place but forcing its complete abandonment.

In the early 1880s, No Man's Land was that now peaceful Oklahoma Panhandle then known as the Strip. It contained nearly five thousand square miles of lush grassland, claimed by no state or territory, and as a consequence was ruled by those few first-come, first-served ranchers who possessed the derring-do to settle within its borders. This small dominion lay beyond the pale of federal jurisdiction and had its advantages; it existed in a tax-free ecstasy, was internally governed by its own residents, and had no outside problems other than the marketing of cattle which grew prime on the abundant forage. But, as is generally the case, this Eden soon found itself with a serpent — quite a few of them. Outlaws got wise to the fact that this Strip was beyond the reach of lawmen, settled in, and began living high on the hog off the ranchers' herds. The idea caught on and soon squatters, drifters, saddle tramps, one and all, having a yen for a thick steak or a succulent roast, simply looked around for the handiest prime steer, butchered it, and enjoyed their meal.

That the beef belonged to one of the various ranchers and bore his brand caused the filcher no lack of sleep. The rancher had plenty more — and what could he do about it? They were too busy looking for the rest of their herds to bother about singles and strays. And there was no lawman to yank them up by the collar on a rustling charge, so all lived well and luxuriously on good beef until one day the ranchers, tired finally of finding beef carcasses minus only the choicest cuts or discovering smaller than expected figures on the tally sheets at roundup time, got together and decided to do something about it. They combined their trouble, formed a pool to be known as the

Cattleman's Protective Association, and hired a certain man known to be long on nerve and fast with a gun to look out for their interests. That man was The Regulator.

At the time Thompson assumed this chore, he was said to be about forty years old. He was a stocky man, standing near five foot ten inches and weighing somewhat over two hundred pounds. He had glittering, jet black eyes, a full black mustache, and a marked weakness for cigars. Summer and winter his accouterments consisted of the usual heavy underclothes, boots, pants, wool shirt, hat, and vest. In the warm months the vest was worn open; in the winter, as a concession to the cold winds of the High Plains country, the vest was buttoned over his paunch. He was no two-gun man, but he was lightning fast on the draw and a deadly accurate expert with the one single action .45 he carried on his hip.

The Protective Association, when giving him carte blanche to clean the owlhoors and other undesirables out of the Strip, gave him also two deputies to aid him in the task. It is said he accepted them with reluctance, preferring to go it alone, but he eventually agreed, using them ever afterwards for the more mundane purposes such as driving the recovered cattle or horses back to their owners, standing guard, or searching for hidden camps. The Regulator, many say, trusted no one save himself and the heads of the Protective Association. He may have been right as the circumstances of his death would seem to indicate.

That he went to work with a will and with much success is attested by the innumerable tales of his exploits still bandied about in certain areas after nearly seventy years have passed and by the bald truth that he soon made No Man's Land a most unhealthy place for any man who swung a wide loop or carried a running iron in his saddlebags. One of the more famous of his encounters was one he had with two shady characters who maintained their financial solvency by the simple expediency of rustling stock in small bunches of five or six head at a time, driving them to the nearest market, or selling them to some trail herd *en route* to a railhead. The loss was small but annoying to the association's members, and they directed Thompson to put a halt to such nefarious operations.

The Regulator with his two shadows set out at once to do just that. In a few days they located the two rustlers in a small coulee. Sure enough, they had nine steers penned in a rope corral, all bearing the brands of an association member. Thompson called upon the two sidewalk ranchers to surrender, but they immediately showed a preference for flying lead to the usual rope trick customarily accorded rustlers, vaulted into their saddles, and fled. By some miracle they managed to escape with The Regulator and his deputies in close pursuit. They holed up eventually in a small rock house near the Cimarron River. There, well protected by the thick stone walls, they made their stand, confident they could hold out indefinitely.

They reckoned without The Regulator, always an impatient man in such times. When it became apparent to him they had reached a Mexican stand-off and that he and his men conceivably could stay there all summer, throwing lead at the unyielding walls of the hut, he decided such was not for him. He dispatched one of his men to the nearest ranch house for a few sticks of dynamite.

This accomplished, he called upon the outlaws to surrender. They refused, and Thompson, tucking a few sticks of the explosive in his hip pocket, crawled on his belly to the shack while bullets buzzed around his head and clipped dangerously close to the dynamite. He laid a charge against the wall, strung his fuse, and, when he had backtracked a safe distance, blew the works. There was a dust-filled minute of silence after the explosion, and then the outlaws, one badly injured, one thoroughly dazed, offered themselves up to their captors.

Another time three riders appeared in the Strip driving before them two hundred horses. It was near sundown, and Thompson, sighting the wranglers' camp, sent his deputies out to start the herd back for the nearest town while he talked things over with the men. Alone, he rode up to the hardcase trio who regarded his approach with half-raised rifles and surly suspicion.

Swinging off the saddle he was quoted as saying: "I'm mighty interested in these horses. They for sale?"

One of the men said yes, they were, that they were driving them to a Kansas market, but he reckoned they'd just as soon sell them right there on the spot.

That was fine with Bill Thompson. How about a look at the bills of sale?

Well, now, if he was one of those jaspers that had to have a bill of sale every time he made a trip to the outhouse, they'd just forget the whole blamed thing! They'd go ahead and make their drive to Kansas.

"Not today," said The Regulator, and, before the three horse thieves could act, he had drawn his pistol and was covering them.

Asked later how he was so certain the men had stolen the animals that he had already had his deputies driving them back, he merely shrugged his thick shoulders and said they looked like horse thieves. Later, the horses proved to be purloined and the men, well known in such circles active in that business, received punishment accordingly.

There was a squatter living near La Junta, Colorado, who had for himself a good thing going at the expense of one association member. He was suspected of helping himself to the rancher's beef, butchering it, and hauling the meat in to La Junta where he disposed of it at wholesale prices to waiting customers. The fellow was a clever operator. Everyone suspected him, but nobody had any proof.

A man named McKenzie, who headed up the Prairie Cattle Company, the unwilling supplier for the enterprising wholesaler, called for The Regulator.

"Bill, I want you to go out there and bring that man in. I want to see him."

"All right," said Thompson.

Two weeks later he was back in McKenzie's office. "I've got your man out here," he is reported to have said.

"Fine. Bring him in."

"Can't do that. Reckon you'll have to step outside to see him."

McKenzie followed Thompson to the street where a light buckboard stood.

"I don't see him," McKenzie said.

"That's him there, in the wagon. Rolled up in that sheet."

"Dead?" McKenzie exclaimed. "Hell! I said to bring him in so I could talk to him. Not kill him."

"You said bring him in," Thompson reminded. "He didn't take kindly to the invitation and drawed on me. Wasn't nothin' else I could do about it."

The wholesale meat venture ceased abruptly after that, but, whether it was because its principal operator was no longer able to function or for the reason that the fear of God and The Regulator had been instilled in those living in that area, it was never known.

Bill Thompson's fame had spread far and wide by the time of his clash with a tough Texan and his accumulating herd who chanced to cross the Strip. But the Texan apparently had never heard of him, or perhaps was one of those gentle souls of that particular time who never backed down from man or beast, dead or alive. It cost him his life.

It happened in mid-summer, so the story goes. The Texan was driving his considerable herd northward to market. Along the way he was collecting all the strays and small bunches of cattle he chanced to meet. Now that was, then, a more or less accepted practice among cattlegrowers as strays and quite often small jags, liking the company of herds, often forsake the brush and brakes where they have been hiding during roundup and join up with their kind. The honest trail herd boss, when he tallies out at the loading chute, keeps a record of the brands not his own and subsequently settles up with the proper owner.

But not so with old Tex. He conveniently carried along a few running irons, the type that simplified the changing of a brand to one more desirable and suitable for his own use. Every few days the added-on newcomers were cut out, their brands blotted, and one of Tex's own substituted. In Texas a man could claim several brands. Each county required a different mark, and, ranches being of the size they were, sometimes covering and reaching into several counties, it was not hard for an enterprising man like Tex to alter a brand to match one of his own.

But Tex ran squarely afoul of The Regulator. Several members of the association reported losing small bunches of cattle with the passing of northbound herds across or near their land. There were instances where twenty or thirty steers had been definitely known to be grazing one day, and then suddenly, after Tex's passage, they no longer were around. They all had their ideas of what had happened but to broach a customer like rough-and-ready Tex was a little out of their line. Anyway, they had Bill Thompson for just such a problem.

Thompson and his deputies set out that same day after Tex and the herd, reputed to be in the neighborhood of four thousand head. Estimates from the association members claimed that approximately five hundred were pickups from herds in the Strip. They caught up with the outfit late in the afternoon and rode boldly into the camp.

"Got all the trail hands I'm needin'," Tex greeted them.

Thompson, a cigar stuck in one corner of his mouth, didn't bat an eye. "I'm mighty good with a running iron. Hear you could use a man with the knack."

Even Tex was a little startled by that. He evidently figured he had been pretty slick about building up his herd. He looked the somewhat paunchy, moon-faced man and his two silent companions over carefully and decided he had nothing to fear. "Step down and we'll jaw about it a little."

Thompson and his deputies did as they were invited. The cook had coffee made, and they all had a cup while a dozen or so of Tex's trail hands stood around and listened.

Tex said to Thompson: "What makes you think I'm using a running iron?"

"What makes you think nobody knows you ain't?"

Tex shrugged. "Picked up a few mavericks, that's all. Of course, maybe a branded steer got in sometimes."

"About five hundred sometimes," Thompson said flatly. "I'm after them five hundred. You can cut them out of your herd right now, or we can do some more talking about it."

"A damn range detective!" Tex yelled and dragged at his gun.

With true Regulator efficiency, Thompson shot him squarely between the eyes before he could get his weapon out and then turned to the dumbfounded trail hands. "Reckon your boss forgot to tell you what to do. So I'll tell you for him. I want five hundred of the best steers in that herd cut out and headed back south where they belong. And I want it done before dark."

Two days later the members of the association who had reported missing stock had them back. The brands were a little confused, but they got a full count.

Probably the best known of The Regulator's exploits was his literal wiping out of a small town in Colorado. Boston by name, it was an unlikely collection of frame false fronts, tarpaper shacks, tents, and lean-tos about twenty-five miles north of the New Mexico border. It boasted some five hundred inhabitants, most of them unsavory characters with price tags on their heads that no one cared to claim. Principal among them was a gang of cutthroats, known as the Jennings bunch, who swaggered about in the best Billy the Kid fashion and generally made things miserable for everybody in that part of the country.

Boston was intended to serve, so they say, as a supply headquarters for the dry-land farmers who had moved in under the misconception that they could grow bountiful crops of corn and other grain without irrigation. They failed, of course, but the lack of water was no detriment to Boston. Who wanted water anyway, when every other building in the town housed a saloon with an inexhaustible inventory of red-eye? Not ninety-five per cent of the population of six hundred.

Boston had sprung up like a poisonous mushroom on the open range of the cattlegrowers which placed it in no small disfavor with them. It offered sanctuary for all manner of thieves, road agents, rustlers, and owlhoots, not to mention the painted-lady and whiskey temptations it placed before the working cowboys who, if they happened to be somewhere in the vicinity, always found a reason to swing by. But it was far outside the Strip, beyond the reach of Bill Thompson, the invincible cure-all who could exercise no authority within Boston's limits. But one day quite by accident, mind you, the detective with his deputies paused there with a pair of prisoners. They were delivering them up to the sheriff in Trinidad. The day was growing old, and it would soon be dark. Thompson reckoned they might spend the night right there in Boston and get an early start next morning. Was there a place in town where the prisoners might safely be locked up?

Boston, as could be expected, had no jail. A small store room was requisitioned, and the prisoners accordingly slapped inside. There was a hasp on the door, and a peg was shoved into the loop, making it secure. Thompson and his men then adjourned to the nearest bar where they had their meal and soon retired to a back room where they made pallets on the floor. Thompson knew he was no popular idol in the town, so all slept with rifles and pistols within easy reach. But they were not disturbed during the entire night.

Daylight found them on the street, walking to the storeroom to claim their prisoners. Unlocking the door, they entered to discover the prisoners gone. Someone, during the night, had liberated them and then carefully relocked the door with the hasp. That final act seemed to infuriate Bill Thompson. He decided the town must be taught a lesson concerning the courtesy usually extended a lawman and his prisoners. Or was that just an excuse?

Regardless, the six hundred residents of Boston next saw the most methodical and devastating job of town wrecking they ever dreamed of. Bullets were flying thick as bees converging on a hive, and, when it was all done with, Boston was a ghost town. There is no straight record of how many gunmen aspired to stand up to The Regulator, but it is known that a good many tasted the powdery dust of the town's single street that day, and those who declined the honor made haste to shake it from their boots and depart post haste. Nor did they ever return, except to claim what personal belongings they desired and haul off some of the lumber that was not bullet-splintered or fire-scorched.

Boston was no more after that. It had experienced a short, if a merry, life, and The Regulator had accomplished, quite by accident, something the cattlemen for miles around had hoped one day to happen. Now, you may be one of those analytical souls who wonders about certain aspects of the affair, such as why Thompson and his deputies did not stick closer to their prisoners if they were so important, or why they bedded down in the back of a saloon some distance away, knowing full well the town was peopled by owlhoots who would have naught but kindly feelings toward the prisoners. And why did it require The Regulator and his two deputies to take only a pair of prisoners to Trinidad? Ordinarily one deputy could have accomplished the mission.

You would not be alone in your wondering. Many are reported to have pondered over it. A few bolder men even voiced some questions, but never to The Regulator himself. As for the members of the Cattlemen's Protective Association, they just didn't care to speculate on the matter. Boston, a troublesome thorn in their sides, was no more. How Thompson went about bringing such a thing to pass was fortunate but of no deep concern to them.

The Strip country was a peaceable kingdom when Bill Thompson came to his death — dying with his boots on in the best tradition of his time. It was in the mid-Nineties, and it occurred in the back room of an old ranch house.

As could be expected, there is some cloudiness attending his demise, for so fabulous had been the man's life and activities that even the slightest incident was colored and charged, until it became difficult to separate fact from fiction. Some said the two men involved in the quarrel were only cowboys, virtually unknown to Thompson, and that he stepped in merely as arbitrator and was accidentally killed for his pains. Others say the two were his deputies, that a long, smoldering feud lay between them and was kept from erupting into violent gun play on previous occasions only by Thompson himself who stood for no nonsense where his own men were concerned. And there are a few who hint of pure murder, cool and simple by two men who, Thompson ignoring his own code, trusted.

There were two men quarreling. That much is fact. It grew quite bitter, bordering on gun play, and Thompson stepped in between them. He persuaded them to holster their pistols and sent one of the parties outside to cool off. The banished cowboy started to do as ordered, but, just as he reached the door, he had a change of mind. He whirled, drew his weapon, and fired, supposedly at his opponent. Thompson, who had turned to face the other cowboy, caught the bullet in the back of his head and died almost instantly.

Thus ended the life of The Regulator. I am not one of those who believes he, if he had a last fragmentary length of time in which to ponder, regretted his manner of dying. I believe he expected to die, as he did one day, with his boots on and from a bullet in the back. Maybe he was a little surprised at the perpetrator of the act, and again he may not have been. Only Bill Thompson, the invincible Regulator, could answer that. And likely he would not have done that for, as I have said, he was a close-mouthed man.

# Legend of a Badman

## I

Sixteen thousand dollars! That was how much was left after Dalton sold the herd and paid off the drovers. Sixteen thousand dollars. It was a lot of money. Clay Allison was thinking that as he strode into the bar of the Exchange Hotel in Santa Fé late that fall day in 1866. With him were his younger brother, John, and three more of the cowboys who had made the trip up from the Texas Brazos country.

Sixteen thousand dollars! The ring of those words in Allison's ears was like a siren call. Why should Dalton get all the gravy? That sixteen thousand could just as well be his, and John's, and their other brother, Monroe's, and Lew Coleman's. Even if it was cut four ways, it would be a hell of a lot better than drover's wages. He didn't begrudge Dalton his profit on the herd. That was why he was a cattleman — to make money. It was only that, if they were in business for themselves, the money would be theirs, not someone else's. And he was growing a bit weary of trail driving. Seems he had been in the saddle and on the move ever since they left Tennessee.

They bellied up to the bar, ordering their whiskey. The bartender passed some remark about the weather, and John Allison replied they likely would have a late winter and spring. Clay only half heard. Plans were formulating in his mind, building rapidly, growing, as possibilities presented themselves to him in quick succession.

They had their land along the Brazos, he and John and Monroe. And Lew Coleman, married to their sister, Mary, had his. They could forget the hardscrabble farming they had undertaken, unite their holdings, and concentrate on raising cattle. The market was good. Cattle were easy to come by. The brakes and badlands of Texas were full of strays that had reverted to a semi-wild stage during the war years when men were away. They had been left untended and allowed to drift far and wide. They needed only to be claimed and branded.

Clay downed his drink, setting the glass back on the bar slowly. Without turning, he said to John: "We're getting into this business on our own. You, Monroe, Lew, and me. We're going to start making that big money, not working our tails off for somebody else."

John, whose admiration for his older brother bordered on idolatry, nodded his head. "A partnership of us . . . sounds real good."

"With all of us handling the herds, we wouldn't have to hire many trail hands. We could save that way. We wouldn't have near the expense Dalton or Charlie Goodnight or some of the others have. It would be that much bigger cut for each of us."

Clay Allison talked of a new and richer life for himself and his brothers and sister. He was a ruggedly handsome man, standing over six feet, powerfully built, and with a wide breadth of shoulders. There was no fat on his one hundred and ninety pounds, only bone, lean muscle, and sinew hard as steel. Men from Tennessee to Colorado and points east had come to respect not only the dexterity with which he handled a six-gun, or a Bowie knife, but the power of his fists as well.

He wore his brown, curly hair long, scout fashion, and occasionally sported a closely cropped beard and mustache. But this was usually on a trail drive, when shaving was not convenient. He was a strong believer in cleanliness, almost to the point of being a fanatic on the subject, and in later years, when money was more plentiful for him, he was able to satisfy his need and desire for expensive clothing which he wore in excellent taste.

"Where's Lew now?" he wondered. "Let's get him, tell him what we've decided to do."

"He said he'd meet us here," John answered. "Said he and Lacy had some business to transact first."

Clay considered that. Ike Lacy was a small rancher of the Brazos country. He had strung along a few head of cattle with Dalton's, marketing them at the same time. Clay glanced around the bar. It was beginning to fill up, growing crowded. Several of the local citizens had come in along with more of the drovers. And there were more than a few blue-uniformed soldiers from nearby Fort Marcy and Fort Union to the north. Allison looked the latter over with disfavoring contempt. As far as he was concerned, the North had never won the war. In fact, hostilities yet existed, and usually after a few drinks he made that conviction apparent.

**84**

Outside the Exchange children played in the plaza around which Santa Fé drowsed. Their high, shrill voices carried plainly. San Francisco Street was far from busy at that hour. Only a few pedestrians and an occasional wagon stirred in the loose dust and heat.

A captain and a lieutenant entered the bar. They glanced along the counter, nodded to acquaintances, and took up places, more or less to themselves, at the near end. The lieutenant, studying the drovers for a moment, made a remark of some sort to the other officer, after which they both laughed.

Clay Allison stiffened. John quickly refilled his brother's glass from the bottle that stood before them. He glanced over his shoulder as the doors swung inward again. An expression of relief crossed his face.

"Here's Lew and Ike," he said. "Let's tell them about our going in together."

Clay's shoulders relaxed. He downed the drink John had poured him, turned to face Coleman and Lacy. They were smiling broadly, but their expressions turned serious when they saw Clay's face.

"What's wrong here?" Coleman asked quickly.

John shook his head. He motioned to the bartender for two more glasses. "Clay and I have a little deal we want to talk over with you, Lew. Let's get a table."

He gathered up the glasses and the half empty bottle of whiskey. The four men settled down in a corner of the room. Clay, his features still taut, chose a position that enabled him to watch the bar — and the two Yankee officers at its far end.

"Clay and me have been talking," John said, launching into the matter hurriedly. "We've decided we're tired of working for somebody else."

Coleman and Lacy exchanged glances. There was silence as John filled the glasses on the table. Then Lacy spoke.

"We got something we want to tell you two," he said. "Lew and me are partners now."

Clay Allison's attention swung from the blue-coated officers to the cattlemen. "Partners? Who?"

"Lew and me. We talked it all out, coming up here. We thought we'd throw in together as the Lacy and Coleman ranch and cash in on this big demand for beef. We already got ourselves a contract with Maxwell to take every head we can scrape up."

There was a long silence, broken only by the rumble of voices at the bar and elsewhere in the room. John Allison said: "Just the pair of you, that it?"

Lew Coleman nodded. "We want you two to work for us. Monroe's included in the offer, too, if he wants to get away from farming and work cattle. Clay, we figure to make you trail boss. You've been around this country quite a bit and know all the best trails. We'll stay on the ranch and get the herds together, and you drive them to market. Pick your own crew. What do you say?"

Allison refilled his glass. He twirled the tumbler between thumb and forefinger for a moment, stared at the gently sloshing liquid. He raised it to his lips, drained it without pause, and then placed the glass back on the table.

"It sounds great . . . for you two," he drawled in his Tennessee accent, "but count me out. I'm not interested."

"Not interested?" Lew Coleman echoed in surprise. "Why not? We figured you'd go for the deal. We're willing to make it worth your while as trail boss."

Clay again filled his glass. He stared moodily past Coleman's head to the bar and the line of soldiers standing before it. "Not interested," he repeated.

"You see," John broke in, directing his words to his brother-in-law, "Clay and me sort of had an idea that you, with Monroe and us, would form our own spread . . ."

"Forget it," Clay interrupted shortly. "We don't owe him or anybody else an explanation."

Ike Lacy stirred uncomfortably in his chair. "Now, wait a minute. I don't want to get smack in the middle of a family squabble. Maybe we ought to . . ."

"We've got a deal between us," Coleman said crisply. "If Clay doesn't like it, not much he or us can do about it. We get back to the Brazos, I'll tell Mary what's happened. Maybe she can make him use sense."

Clay regarded his in-law with cold contempt. "Don't lay any chips on it," he said. He swung his attention to John. "I don't know what you've got in mind to do, but I'm getting out of here. I don't like the company in this place. If you want to, go on back with them. I'm taking me a look at the Cimarron country."

He downed another drink of the raw liquor, sliding the empty glass to the center of the table. Fishing a gold coin from his shirt pocket, he laid it beside the glass.

"That ought to cover it, gentlemen. Now you can tell your grandchildren Clay Allison paid for the celebration that sealed your partnership."

He rose to his feet. He had drunk a considerable amount, but he was steady and in full control of his faculties. He had a vast capacity for liquor. One of his spurs caught upon the leg of his chair. He kicked free, sending the chair clattering against the wall behind him.

All eyes in the room turned to question the disturbance. Allison met the glances hostilely. He watched the two officers and saw them laugh again together at something that was said. The violent anger that characterized Allison's brief life roared through him.

"Lousy, stinking blue bellies," he said in a voice that carried distinctly through the crowded room.

John was on his feet beside him. "Let's head out of here," he said, taking his brother by the arm. "Got me an urge to see that Cimarron country, too."

Clay shrugged him off. "Later. There's a couple of Yankees I've got to teach manners to first."

Lew Coleman, their differences forgotten for the moment, rose to John Allison's side. He handed a glass to Clay. "How about another drink? Set down and let's talk this thing out." Aside to John he murmured, "Get Dalton. He's standing out front. I've got a hunch we're going to need him."

Clay took the proffered drink without removing his eyes from the Union officers. He brushed by Coleman and, with the glass still in his hand, slowly walked the length of the bar. He stopped beside the lieutenant. The bartender, seeing trouble in the air, moved up and began to rub the counter nervously.

"No fights in here, gentlemen. Please! It's bad for business. Why don't you go outside . . . ?"

"Outside is where these Yankee pigs belong," Allison said loudly. "Blue bellies aren't fit to drink with Southerners."

The lieutenant wheeled to face Allison. He got the Tennessean's glass of whiskey full in his face. He fell back a step, spluttering and rubbing his eyes.

The captain regarded Allison with no change of expression. "Bartender," he said in a level voice, "pour a drink for every soldier in the house. On me."

"You do and you serve it outside," Clay warned softly.

He reached out suddenly, grasping the officer by his coat front. He swung him toward the doorway. The captain's hand dropped to the pistol at his belt. Before his fingers could tighten about the butt, he was looking into the barrel of Allison's .44. A look of amusement spread across Clay's features. A low murmur swept through the room. No one, it seemed, had even seen Clay Allison draw, yet there was his gun in his hand, cocked, ready to fire.

"I'd suggest you try your fists, Yankee. Maybe you'll have better luck."

"You try that, cowboy," a voice from the depth of the saloon said, "then you've got every soldier in the place to take on."

Allison, gun still in hand, waved the lieutenant out of the corner where he stood to the side of the captain. He swung around slowly, facing the room. A half dozen soldiers had gathered in the center of the saloon, ready to back up their officers. Likely it was not because of any love existing for their superiors on the part of the enlisted men, but rather that this appeared to be a matter involving the reputation of the whole United States Army.

"I reckon that's all right," Allison said. "The odds are about even . . . eight Yankees to one Southerner. I consider that the proper proportions for an equal fight."

"Gentlemen," the bartender began, imploringly, "not in here. Go outside."

The doors swung in. John Allison, with Dalton at his heels, entered. They paused momentarily. The cattleman sized up the situation. He grinned at Clay.

"You want to hold up a minute. There's forty or fifty more soldiers standing out in front you can fight. You might as well make it a revolution."

For a moment there was silence. Then someone laughed. Tension broke as others joined in. Dalton winked at the Army captain, tactfully suggesting the door with a faint nod of his head. The officer considered, accepted, and, with the lieutenant at his side, moved through it. Almost immediately the tight little group of enlisted men followed.

**90**

Dalton eased up to Allison. "It's about time we were heading back for the Brazos, Clay. Are you ready to ride?"

Allison holstered his pistol. He swept the men yet in the Exchange with a still smoldering glance. "I'm ready to ride, but not back to the Brazos. I'm headed for the Cimarron. So long."

He turned abruptly, and with John Allison following, pushed through the doors into San Francisco Street.

## II

For supplies to cover the trip Clay and John Allison most likely stocked up at Seligman's General Store, which stood on the corner near the Exchange Hotel. Then they rode northward, following the ancient trail taken by the Spaniard, Oñate, when he journeyed through the land in the late 16th Century.

With the towering, snow-blanketed Sangre de Cristo Mountains on their right hand, they passed through small native villages and friendly Indian pueblos at a leisurely pace. They came finally to the settlement of Taos. Nights were cold in that seven-thousand-foot-high haunt of mountain men, and they did not tarry long there but pushed on, now on the well-beaten Santa Fé Trail cut-off which led them through numberless canons, around frowning escarpments, and beneath innumerable peaks lost to the clouds, until finally they broke out into the lower, lush country of the Cimarron and to the town that bore its name.

It was not Clay Allison's first visit. He had been through earlier that same year, 1866, with Charles Goodnight, trailing a herd of steers to a Colorado market.

"Finest cattle country I've ever seen, bar none," he had told John and his other brother, Monroe, upon his return to the Brazos. "Someday I'd like to own a spread there."

The land, at that time, was lorded over by a feudal giant, Lucien B. Maxwell, who possessed a grant estimated variously from one hundred thousand acres to just short of a million. No one, not even Maxwell himself, seemed to know how much of the fertile Cimarron country was contained in the Spanish land grant to which he held title. There existed a continuing case in the federal courts — it had been running for years and was destined to rock on for another score — in which some determination of the correct figure was sought.

One thing the United States government did recognize, despite the discrepancies between his claim and the acreage the various surveyors who plotted the land admitted, and that was the fact he did actually own a land grant. To Lucien B. Maxwell that was all that mattered. What difference is a few hundred thousand square acres, anyway? He could not productively use all the land he had, as it was. Nor was there anyone to dispute the acreage in question, other than government surveyors who usually got lost, were replaced, or else succumbed to the lure of the country and deserted the job long before it was finished. He was wealthy beyond the wildest dreams of man or king — and lived much as any royal monarch beyond the seas would live, with thousands upon thousands of cattle and sheep and horses, green gardens and broad orchards, all of which were tilled and cared for by feudal labor much in the pattern of the system prevalent in England and other far-off countries.

Maxwell had lucrative contracts with the Army installations in the territory as well as with various Indian agencies. While the rumors of gold to be found in several of the streams that crossed and recrossed his land were bringing scores of strange faces to his domain, he was not greatly disturbed by it. Squatters were something a man had to expect, particularly the sort who searched for the precious yellow metal the Indians occasionally found and traded for groceries and other items at the stores. Sooner or later they would tire and go away. That was the nature of their kind — dig a while, then move on in search of better opportunities.

Lucien Maxwell was not worried — at least, not at first. That was to come later and, when it did, it was to drive him into a frustrated sales maneuver, the result of which was a range war that drenched the land in blood and wrote the name of Clay Allison across the pages of Southwestern history in bold letters.

Late that fall of 1866, Clay and John Allison hung around the town of Cimarron for several days, enjoying the company, betting on horse races for which Clay had a fondness, and generally soaking up the feel of the country. Finally, with winter about to set in, they were compelled to come to a decision as to what they should do next.

"We can stay here and work for Maxwell," Clay said one morning as they sat in the bar of the hotel, "or we can ride on back to the Brazos."

John glanced quickly at his brother. It was the first time he had mentioned Texas since the incident in Santa Fé. "And work for Lew and Ike?" he wondered.

Clay shrugged. He pulled his long-bladed Bowie knife from its leather sheath, fondling its honed edge. "They aren't the only cattlemen in Texas. I reckon we could easy get a job with somebody else."

"Why not winter here? There's plenty of work around, like you said. It might even be a good idea to look into this gold business. I hear they're picking up nuggets out of every creek."

Clay shook his head. "No gold mining for me. I'm not of a turn to go grubbing in the dirt. And I'm sure not ready to settle down, regular like. I vote we go back to the Brazos."

John made no reply. He watched Clay take the blade point of the Bowie between thumb and forefinger and send it arcing through the gloomy room to strike, quivering, in a post thirty feet distant. His brother's skill with the knife had always fascinated him.

The bartender, the only other occupant in the saloon at the moment, wheeled at the dull thud of the knife, plunging into the ceiling support. He swung his attention to the Allisons.

"Here! I'll have none of that. If you want to practice with that thing, go outside. I won't stand for you destroying my property."

94

Clay got lazily to his feet. He crossed the room, retrieved the blade, smiling at the saloonman all the while.

"I apologize, friend. If you want me to, I'll go outside and cut down a fresh tree for you, so's you can replace that post I ruined. I didn't think I was about to bring down the roof."

The barkeep, mollified, returned the smile. "Forget it," he said. "I kind of have to watch things around here. If I didn't, cowboys would mighty soon tear the place apart."

Clay turned back to John. "Well, kid? What will it be?"

John said: "The Brazos, if you say so. Let's ride."

They started for the door. The bartender, hearing the last of John Allison's words, asked: "You leaving town?"

"Heading for Texas," Clay answered. "But we'll be back. Got our hearts set on a piece of ground right smack in the middle of Maxwell's grant. One of these days we'll be moving onto it."

The bartender shrugged, grunted. "Why not? Everybody else seems to be doing just that."

The Allison brothers rode eastward out of Cimarron until they struck the trail Clay had earlier followed with Goodnight on the Colorado drive. They then turned south, traveling easily, enjoying the country as they passed through.

When they reached Fort Sumner, they altered their course to the east, taking now another trail that eventually intercepted the Brazos River. Once there, they were in familiar country. In another couple of days they would be home.

## III

Home, for Robert Clay Allison, had once meant a small, starve-out farm in Wayne County, Tennessee, where, in 1841 he was born. There, he grew up with his brothers, John and Monroe, and their sister, Mary. His father, a part-time minister of the Gospel, sometime farmer, died when he was a small child, but his mother, whom he adored, held the little family together by dint of sheer faith and hard work and, at the same time, saw to it her brood received at least the average amount of schooling customary for the times.

That Clay was a restless boy soon became apparent. He was forever on the move, prowling the hills and valleys and along the creeks and rivers. He had little interest in the soil. His thoughts were elsewhere, far removed from the planting and growing of things. He dreamed and talked of the new country called Texas, where many other Tennesseans had gone, and to the wild and mysterious place referred to as New Mexico. He had been told by passing drifters, that Indians were to be fought in these places, as in the history books, and treasures to be found if a man knew where to look. It was an endless world of flat, open plains that ran up to halt at the foot of mountains so high the tips were buried in clouds. That was the sort of world he had dreamed of and had promised himself one day he would see. He never lost an opportunity to question the men who had made the long ride westward and returned with stirring tales of dangerous adventure.

Long before he had mastered his first reader, he knew the story of the Alamo, of Texas' independence as a nation all its own until it became a part of the Union. Before he had learned to write a legible hand, he was acquainted with age-old Santa Fé and its sun-flooded plaza and with Taos where mountain men gathered in the warm summer months. By the time he was twelve years of age, he was ready to pull up stakes and look upon those wonders with his own eyes. Only his love for his mother and strong sense of duty to her persuaded him the time was not yet at hand.

The years passed slowly for him, years in which a steadily mounting national tension went almost unnoticed in Wayne County. And then one day the air began to ring with strange voices that reached far and wide, touching even the most remote village. Powerful words of recrimination and threat. To a teenage boy it meant little, only that the elder men of government in faraway Washington were at odds over one problem or another. No matter what they said or did, it mattered little in Waynesboro. It was still necessary to work, to cut firewood in the summer for the cold winter months, to tend the livestock, to till the rocky fields — to live. Washington was a long way off. It held no interest for Robert Clay Allison, who still held tightly to his dream of the West.

As the teen years receded and a man began to emerge, the furor in Washington rose and fell, like a field of ripened grain, bowing in brisk winds. Clay began to hear new words, strange phrases — secession . . . state's rights . . . mobilization . . . conscription. And a new place — Fort Sumter. War came. Tennessee wrestled with herself over the problem of allegiance and conscience, eventually swinging with the states that would oppose the Union — to repel the blue-coated invaders from the North.

Clay Allison, just turned twenty-one, enlisted. He served as a scout under several commanders, principal among whom was Colonel Nathan B. Forrest. He participated in numerous engagements and was captured at Pittsburgh Landing — or Shiloh, as the Yankees called it. For a time he was confined with far too many other Confederate soldiers in an emergency camp, but finally was transferred to a larger prison compound on Johnson Island in Sandusky Bay, Lake Erie.

Soon the reckless daring the war had encouraged and brought to the surface in Clay Allison began to assert itself. He watched his chances, eventually escaping under the watchful eyes of Yankee guards. He swam the bay and in a few weeks was back in Tennessee.

He returned to the service almost immediately, only to be captured once again, this time in the uniform of a Union soldier and was, therefore, considered a spy. A court-martial was held, and he was sentenced to die by firing squad the following morning. The execution never took place. Sometime during the dark hours of the night Clay Allison killed the guard who stood over him and made his way to freedom. There seems to be no explanation of how he accomplished it.

One detail of the incident read: "Allison was shackled with chains. He hated the Yankees with such violence that it is not likely one of the guards felt sympathy for him and aided his escape." Other fellow prisoners could hardly have been of service to him. There was no way possible for contact. And even if there had been, there still was the matter of the padlocked shackles about his ankles and wrists. But, somehow, he did manage to get his hands on a knife, and that was all he needed.

He emerged, at the war's end, a lean, rangy, tough man, bearing a hatred for Yankees that he would carry to his grave. He made his way back to Wayne County. There, too, the old life had ended, just as it had come to a close elsewhere in the defeated South. Carpetbaggers were swarming, like greedy locusts, over the land, claiming all things of value, their activities sanctioned and enforced by the hated blue-belly soldiers. He was glad his mother had not lived to see it come to pass. She had died the year before. And Mary was now married to Lew Coleman, a man they all knew and liked. Thus, there were no ties left to keep him in Tennessee.

Late that summer of 1865 he called Monroe and John together at the shack where Mary and Lew lived.

"I'm pulling out. It's Texas for me. A lot of Tennessee people are moving there."

"What about the land . . . our farm here?" Monroe asked.

"Let the damyankees have it, if they want it. It's worked out, anyway. And there's no money here. If you had something to sell, you couldn't find anybody in the whole county to buy it."

Lew Coleman said: "I hear there's plenty money to be made in cattle. The government is needing beef for the Army posts and to feed the Indians. Is that what you have in mind?"

"It won't make any difference what we do when we get there," Clay replied impatiently. "If you want to farm, then farm. If you want to go into the cattle business, then it's the cattle business. No point in staying in Tennessee any longer." He stopped, and then moved restlessly about the small room. "And I won't stay. I'm leaving tomorrow. You talk it over among yourselves and decide what you want to do."

John Allison was nineteen at the time. And where Clay went, he went. Long years back he had made up his mind to that. Clay was everything he hoped to be — strong, handsome, reckless, expert with gun and knife and fists, and absolutely fearless. John said at once: "I ride with Clay."

"And me," added Monroe, who was of a more settled and serious nature. "I don't know what we'll find in Texas, but it can't be any worse than here."

That left it up to the Colemans to decide their own destiny. Lew took one look at his wife's face and knew at once her heart lay with her brothers. And Monroe was right. Texas could be no worse than downtrodden, ravaged Tennessee.

"We'll be ready to leave when you are," he said. "Farm or cattle, we'll decide that when we get there. Any idea whereabouts in Texas we ought to settle? It's a big place, I hear tell."

Now that it was decided, and in the way he had hoped, Clay, fired by the prospects of moving on, of at last realizing his lifelong dream, gave way to exuberance.

"It won't make any difference where," he said. "It's all fine country. But the people I've talked to who have been there or are heading out that way say the Brazos River country is the best. There's plenty of water, good ground, and the winters are never too cold."

"Where in Texas is the Brazos River country?" Lew wanted to know. "Like I said, Texas is a big place."

"More to the west side, I think. Almost below that strip they call the Panhandle. I reckon we can find it, once we start."

Lew Coleman nodded. "We'll find it, or starve. Right now we better get ready. Id like some help with this wagon of mine. Needs some work on it before we head out. And we'll need horses."

"I'll get the horses," Clay said. "John and I will do a bit of trading around."

They pulled out the next afternoon, Clay and John riding horseback, Mary, Lew, and Monroe with all their earthly possessions in the hastily overhauled wagon. They crossed the Mississippi at Memphis, angled south by west through Arkansas, and entered Texas at its northeastern corner. There they were fortunate enough to meet another party of immigrants bound for the same general destination, and, joining forces, they drove due west until, late one fall day, they were in sight of the Brazos River.

Twenty-four hours later they began to settle themselves for winter in a strange, new country that was a disturbing, unknown quantity. Lumber was scarce, and they set to work building a hut of sod and logs large enough to house them all. It would be the Allison place. Later, when time was not so pressing, Lew Coleman and Mary would choose a site for their own home farther along the river.

It was a precarious existence, with the possibility of raiding Indians and renegade whites always in the offing. They lived mostly on meat — quail and rabbit and stray beef that ran wild in the brakes. Monroe managed to get a small crop of greens out of the ground before it turned too cold and with that, and the meager stock of cornmeal, molasses, chicory coffee, dried fruit, and salt pork they had brought with them, they managed to get through to spring.

During the winter months Clay ranged far and wide along the Brazos, visiting the scattered ranches, the few settlements, and generally getting himself acquainted. He made friends easily, and, before the chill winds had ceased to blow, there were few who were not aware of Clay Allison's existence — or of his talents. He proved he could outride, outshoot, outdrink, and outfight any man on the Brazos. They learned he had a violent temper, that he was no man to underestimate in a serious disagreement, that a more polite or more

**102**

generous man never forked a saddle, that he was the champion of the underdog at all times.

He was a quiet man, almost shy, but beneath that thin veneer slumbered a mighty and turbulent force that, once aroused, was difficult to reckon with, as many who, mistaking gentleness for weakness, learned to their dismay. In the months after their arrival in Texas the handsome Allison became the reckless epitome of the drover all cattlemen needed when a herd was to be taken across the vast and lonely stretches of empty, unguarded land, plagued with marauding Indians and white raiders.

Charles Goodnight was the first cattlegrower to realize and take advantage of this fact. In the winter of 1865 he hired Clay as a drover and in the summer of 1866 rode north with him and several others with a mixed herd for the Colorado markets. That was when Clay Allison got his first glimpse of the New Mexico Cimarron country.

## IV

It was Goodnight's praise and prompting which decided Clay Allison that the life of a drover was what he desired. In the spring of 1867 a new market for cattle opened up to the east — Abilene, Kansas. Beef prices soared high, and there followed a mighty rush of cattlemen to get their herds together on the trail.

There were others, not necessarily in the business, who took profit in the forthcoming drives — the Indians and bushwhacking whites who immediately moved in to haunt the seven hundred empty miles of country that lay between the Brazos and Abilene. Goodnight, and others, realized it would take a special sort of man to get a herd through, a man unafraid, ingenious, and with the physical ability to keep his drovers on the job when they were tempted to desert.

Clay Allison answered all the requirements. He might be wild at times, but, when he was on the trail, taking a herd to market, he was strictly business. He kept the beef moving. He held his riders in line and on the job with an iron hand.

Thus Abilene, surging under its new prosperity, came to know him well. So did Newton, Ellsworth, Wichita, and a host of other cities. In no time at all he became the prototype of the hell-raising Texan, spending his money freely on whiskey, women, gambling, and a good time. He fought at the wink of an eye for any reason whatsoever, be it money, marbles, or the smile of a dance-hall queen. Peace officers soon learned to be busy elsewhere when Clay Allison and his cowboys were in town, celebrating the end of a drive.

His fame as a quick-draw, amazingly accurate pistol artist spread far and wide, a reputation that also served to dissuade any of the current and present gunmen from matching skills with him. They much preferred to join in with the tall Tennessean in his fun rather than flaunt fate by crossing him. They, like many peace officers, learned the curious and amazing fact that Clay Allison, drunk, was as deadly and dangerous with knife or gun as was Clay Allison, sober. Liquor seemed wasted on him except that it brightened his spirits, although now and then it persuaded him to engage in an old boyhood prank in which he enacted the role of an Indian chief doing a war dance and which always called for a minimum of clothing on his muscular body.

He was the idol of the men who rode for him and the bane of lawmen and saloonkeepers in every town they visited on the return route to the Brazos. His behavior varied according to his whim. Men liked to see him in action, particularly when soldiers were involved. He went out of his way to pick a fight with a blue-uniformed man, never lessening that special sort of hatred he held for Yankees.

It was on a return trip from Abilene or some similar market that he had differences with Zach Colbert, a man he termed a carpetbagger and who operated a ferry on the Red River in Texas. No one seems to know exactly what precipitated the brawl, other than the fact that Colbert was a Northerner and that he made a disparaging remark relative to the quality of Confederate courage. The fight was one of magnificent proportions. It lasted the better part of a half day and ended when Allison tossed Colbert into the roily waters of the Red. Later they shook hands, and, while it is not probable they ever became good friends, it would have been typical of Allison always to respect Colbert for his courage.

Thousands upon thousands of beeves were driven to market by cattlemen that year, although not always to eastern pens. Many herds went north into New Mexico, Colorado, and points beyond that.

Clay, soon restless, began to tire of the long, monotonous drives. He dreamed of a ranch on the Cimarron where he would raise his own cattle and make big money. The lengthy drives seemed foolish to him, anyway. They walked pounds of good fat off the beeves which thus brought lower prices at the markets.

Why not raise them close to the sale pens? In that way a drive could be eliminated, along with its attendant loss of poundage and the assorted trail dangers of stampedes, Indians, and raiders. It made sense to him, the more he thought about it, and the ideal location for such a ranch would be in the Cimarron country. There he could raise beef and sell it to Lucien Maxwell. There would be no long, hazardous trek to a faraway market, no loss sustained from Indians or other marauders. And the beef would be top prime.

He would need a starter herd, a nucleus from which to build. That was the drawback. He had no cattle of his own or the money with which to buy some. What wages he had made as a drover or trail boss were gone, spent in the wild towns, gambled away on cards or horse racing — or turned over to Monroe and John to aid in the building of their place along the Brazos. Thing to do, he decided one day, was to start now, accumulate a herd of his own. When he had what seemed to be a sufficient amount for a beginning, head them up and move to the Cimarron.

He was considering the further possibilities of such a procedure as he cut across his range one morning, headed for their still poor holdings. He topped out a low rise, pulling to an abrupt halt. A movement to his right at a water hole caught his attention.

He recognized the man working the shovel as Tom Johnson, a neighbor with whom he had exchanged harsh words several times before. The matter of the water hole's ownership stood in dispute between them, and Clay, concluding the time was at hand to settle the matter once and for all, rode down the slope to where Johnson waited, now aware of his presence.

Allison came directly to the point. "I've warned you before, Johnson. You're trespassing here."

"Not the way I see it," the rancher replied. "This is my land. You're the one who trespasses."

Allison climbed down from his saddle. "That's a bald-faced lie! And you're a liar when you say it."

Johnson took the insult with a half smile. He looked Clay over carefully. "If you figure to provoke me into drawing against you, then think again. I'm smart enough to know I wouldn't stand a chance."

"Maybe you've got a better idea how we can handle this," Allison said in a hard voice. "The question of who owns this water hole is going to be answered today."

"My sentiments, too," Johnson replied. His eyes dropped to the blade in Allison's belt. "You fancy a knife?"

"I've used one before."

"I've heard tell. Are you agreeable to fighting it out with the blade, winner take all?"

"And buries the loser," Clay added. "I'll agree to that."

Johnson said: "Good. It'd be only fair to warn you, however, I'm no greenhorn when it comes to a Bowie. I've been told I'm mighty good."

"Obliged for the information," Clay replied, removing his gun belt and hanging it on the saddle horn. "I've had some experience myself. I'll take my chances. Let's get at it."

They stripped to the waist and, with Johnson's shovel, hollowed out a grave of the usual proportions. That finished, they paused to recover their breath.

"I reckon we ought to make this easy as possible," Johnson suggested. "We'll fight it out in the grave. Then all the winner need do is throw in the dirt. That suit you?"

"Suits me fine," Clay said, and dropped into the pit.

Johnson followed, took up a position at the opposite end. Knives in hand, they faced each other.

"Winner take all?" Johnson repeated their agreement.

Allison nodded, and Johnson struck out instantly. His long-bladed knife sliced downward in a glittering arc. Clay blocked the blow with a forearm and slashed with his right. Johnson yelled and leaped back, a thin line of blood streaking across his belly as the needle-sharp point in Allison's Bowie split the skin.

The rancher swore, lashing out again. Allison, grimly intent, parried the thrust, driving his blade straight for Johnson's breast. The rancher jerked aside, and the point missed. He struck back, arm moving like an attacking snake. Clay felt pain and saw blood flow from his own shoulder in a quickly welling spring.

**108**

Johnson certainly was no stranger to a Bowie. Clay realized that he must be on guard every instant if he expected to survive this fight. He kept his own blade whipping back and forth horizontally before him, setting up a wicked guard through which Johnson would have to break if he would reach him. The rancher tried, taking a deep slash in the forearm for his effort. He recoiled, curses again streaming from his lips. He lay back then, beginning to play a cautious waiting game, watching for the moment when he could drive his blade deep in a death thrust.

He thought he saw his opportunity several minutes later. Allison seemed to lower his guard, allowing himself a brief time of carelessness. Johnson lunged, his knife extended rigidly before him. Clay threw himself to one side of the pit. He struck hard and fast. Johnson gasped. His head snapped back, his arms flung wide. He sagged against the wall of the grave, caught himself by the elbows momentarily, and then crumpled to the bottom.

Clay leaned back upon the cool wall of the pit, sucking for breath. Both arms were streaked with blood, and there was a vivid scratch tracing across his chest. He glanced down at his own torso. He had come out of the fight lucky. He had only one deep cut in his shoulder, along with several minor scratches. He picked up Johnson's bandanna, emptied into it the contents of the man's pockets, and climbed from the pit.

He completed the burial and then cleaned up as best he could at the water hole. Afterward, he mounted up and, with Johnson's horse on a lead rope, rode to where the rancher lived. Two men came from the sod house when he entered the yard. He knew neither of them. He halted before the pair and swung down.

"What are you doing with Tom's horse?" the older of the two asked suspiciously. "Who are you, mister?"

"The name is Allison. Tom and I settled our argument over that south water hole. I buried him."

"Allison . . . Clay Allison, the gunfighter?" the younger man asked. "That who you are?"

"I'm Clay Allison, sure enough. But I'm not a gunfighter."

"You say you buried Tom? How'd it happen?"

"The way he wanted it. With knives." He handed the lead rope to Johnson's horse to the older man, the bandanna containing the rancher's belongings to the other. "The agreement was winner take all, but I don't want anything except an understanding that the water hole is mine, which it was in the first place."

The older man shook his head slowly. "Tom was my brother, and I know him right well. He was mighty good with a knife. It's a little hard for me to believe you could have got the best of him in a fair fight."

Allison stiffened as anger rushed through him. "It was a fair fight, old man," he snarled. "If you got any doubts about it, go dig him up. Take a look and see if there's any holes in his back, knife or bullet."

"Maybe we just ought to do that," the younger man said, his voice trembling somewhat.

"Help yourself," Clay said, and moved back to his horse. "You got my permission. But once that's done, get off and stay off. I find either of you on my property

**110**

again, I won't bother to bury you." He swung onto the saddle and wheeled about. He threw a still-faced glance at the pair. "Don't get any ideas when you see my back. You'd never make it," he said, and rode out of the yard.

When he reached the road, he looked over his shoulder. The two men stood where he had left them. It was plain they had no desire to argue the matter any further.

# V

August of that same year, 1867, saw Clay Allison once again on a drive, this time pointed northwest for the Cimarron country. He had fully intended to settle down on the Brazos with his brothers, start building the herd with which he would begin the spread he dreamed of in New Mexico. But when he heard that Tom Dawson and several other ranchers were pulling stakes and heading for the Cimarron, he could not resist the opportunity to have another look at the country. He signed on immediately as a drover.

There were several herds making up the whole, and not all were to stop on the Cimarron. Many of Dawson's neighbors decided to settle in New Mexico's Pecos Valley area. Too much trouble was brewing on the Cimarron, they said. A man couldn't hire help, nor could he protect his holdings. Best he find a more peaceable place where there was no dispute in progress, no gold seekers to contend with.

None of such talk altered Clay Allison's opinion of the Cimarron. It was his country — the long plains and valleys, deep in sweet grass, flowing with clear water, the short hills, the high, towering mountains to the west, where lay Taos, and farther down Santa Fé. That was the place for him. Someday he would settle there and own his ranch. And, if there was trouble to be met, he damned well would meet it. The Cimarron was worth fighting for.

The party moved slowly for Allison, anxious to see New Mexico again. There was little he could do about it. The herd consisted not only of beef cattle but of horses and oxen and of the rancher's families and household possessions. There were innumerable delays and shutdowns for one reason or another. Before many hours had passed, Clay Allison promised himself he would never again sign on where a wholesale move, such as this one, was being made. Had he not given Dawson his word, he would pull out now on his own and leave the slowly creeping train behind. But he had promised, and Clay Allison had never broken his word to any man.

The morning of the seventeenth day out of the Brazos found them camped near low-lying hills, still many miles from the border of New Mexico. Allison was asleep, having just turned in from nighthawking Dawson's herd, when a scatter of gunshots and a sudden rush of horses brought him to his feet. They were being attacked by Indians.

The camp was in utter confusion. Men, half dressed and heavy-eyed, were running about, shouting questions. Women and children filled the air with frightened screams and wails. Breech-clouted Comanches were

**112**

everywhere. Allison pulled on his boots, strapped his gun around his waist, and legged it for the remuda where his horse was picketed. Several other experienced drovers, who had weathered similar situations previously, were doing likewise.

The picket rope had been slashed, and the horses were loose. Half a dozen Indians were trying to drive the milling animals toward the hills, where more braves had already stampeded a fair-size number of cattle. Clay opened up on the Comanches who were after the horses. He knocked two of them off their mounts. Other cowboys began to shoot. The remaining Indians instantly abandoned their purpose and wheeled to follow their brothers.

Clay caught up a horse, getting a bridle and saddle on him. By then the other riders were mounted. Dawson, along with several ranchers, came onto the scene. The Comanches were out of sight in the brushy, rolling hills, but they rode at once in pursuit.

The trail was not difficult to follow. The Indians had split up almost immediately after getting a few miles from the camp. There were now a dozen or more parties, each with a small jag of the stolen stock, which included not only beef cattle but a number of milk cows, oxen, and horses as well.

"We'd better separate," Clay said to Dawson when they paused. "You take half the men and follow that bunch to your left. I'll go after this other party."

They rode off, each pursuing what appeared to be the two largest fragments of the scattering marauders.

Their mounts were not too fresh, but soon they began to overtake the Comanches.

The Indians, knowing the rugged country well, had managed to stay ahead for a time, but the stock they were driving slowed them down. When it became apparent they could not hold their lead, they began to slaughter the animals, shooting them down as they ran.

"Looks like, if they can't keep them cows, they ain't going to let us get them back either," one of the men with Allison observed when they came upon half a dozen dead steers.

Rifle shots sounded from where Dawson and his party had gone, indicating that the rancher was encountering the same problem. Allison called the chase to a halt. They could not recover any of the stock, no matter how far they pursued the Comanches, and it could be dangerous to get so far from camp. The Indians might, conceivably, attack it again.

Dawson came to a similar conclusion. A few minutes later he appeared with his men and signaled Clay to abandon the chase. Dawson's group had failed as completely as Allison's. There was no point in continuing.

Back in camp Dawson dispatched a wagon and men to the nearest slain beef with the thought of salvaging part of the meat for food. He then set himself to calculating losses. Not counting the milk cows, the oxen, and horses, he estimated that a total of two hundred steers had been taken by the raiders. Their loss, however, did not disturb him nearly as much as did that of the horses and oxen.

It all registered deeply on Clay Allison's mind, and it altered his plans somewhat for the Cimarron. A man would work a long time to accumulate two hundred steers — and he could lose them in a matter of minutes.

The fallacy of his previous thought to raise a herd in Texas, drive it to the Cimarron, was apparent to him as he rode on with the train that morning and relived again the Comanche raid. In his mind's eye he saw once more the slaughtered stock along the trail, underwent for a second time that feeling of helplessness when he realized there was no recovery possible despite the fact that he had personally slain at least six of the Comanches. On the ranch he planned one day to own, to suffer the loss of two hundred head of stock would mean the difference between success and failure.

The idea of a drive was out. Even with the best drovers he could hire, they could not adequately protect a herd in such country. Better to accumulate his starter herd on home ground, on the Cimarron itself. Then he could avoid the possibility of trail losses. It might take longer to follow such a method, but it would be more certain. When he reached the Cimarron, he would look into it further. One thing was sure. He would need cash with which to buy his first steers — and cash did not come easy.

He would have to see about that, too, when he reached New Mexico.

115

## VI

There was no quick and royal road to riches. Clay Allison discovered that in the following two years, during which he trail-bossed drives for half a dozen different outfits, bucked the tiger in many a wild town, and tried his hand at horse racing, which generally proved to be the most profitable venture of the three.

He did well for a time in southeastern New Mexico, where later the ground was to run red with blood from the Lincoln County War and a semi-illiterate delinquent called Billy the Kid. Then he drifted back to the Brazos country, where his brothers and sister, Mary Coleman, still lived.

Time had softened some of the ill feeling he had conjured for Lew Coleman and his partner, Ike Lacy. Under the influence of Mary, he began to work for them again. By that time he was a familiar figure in trail towns from the territory of Arizona to Abilene, from Matamoros to Cheyenne, and his fast gun and rock-hard fists, not to mention his uncanny skill with a Bowie knife, went unquestioned and seldom challenged.

Although he reputedly killed three men during this period in gun duels, he resented being termed a gunman and, unlike most other desperadoes who sought fame along such lines, continually played down his talents. He was more interested in being known as an excellent trail boss and drover — and a gentleman owner of a string of race horses with which he won consistently. There were still the wild and violent hours, but they usually came at the end of a particularly tough, hard drive and, to the merchants who benefited from the money he spent, were generally harmless enough.

Early in 1869 he delivered a herd for the Coleman and Lacy outfit to a rancher named Wilburn near the town of Raton in northern New Mexico. Wilburn accepted the herd and told Clay he would pay off the next day at the Clifton House, a hostelry built several miles south of the town by a Texan, Tom Stockman. Cattlemen often gathered there to talk over mutual problems and bet on horse races held at a small track just below.

Allison took Wilburn at his word and, paying off his drovers from personal funds, he returned to Stockton's to await the rancher. Wilburn failed to show up. Thinking about it, Clay decided something had arisen that prevented the rancher from keeping his promise. A man's word was something you could depend on, and there were no doubts in his mind as to Wilburn's sincerity. But, after several days had passed, he discovered that Wilburn had been at the Clifton House, usually while Allison was down at the track, betting on the horses. Wilburn, he concluded, was deliberately dodging him and did not intend to make payment for the herd. It was time to bring matters to a head. He rode to Wilburn's place, his anger rising with each passing mile, and asked for the rancher. He was informed that Wilburn was away for the day on business and was not expected to return soon.

Allison, holding onto his temper, nodded understandingly. "Well, you tell him I couldn't wait any longer. Had to go on back to Texas. I'll pick up my money next trip."

He departed immediately, heading southeast as if to reach the Brazos. As soon as he was beyond view of the ranch, he swung back to the Clifton House. He was waiting in the bar when Wilburn entered, an hour later.

"I'll take my money now, Wilburn!"

The rancher was startled and completely frightened. The reputation of Clay Allison was not unfamiliar to him, and he knew that in his present mood he was no man to cross. But he clung to his nerve.

"All right, Mister Allison. But I don't carry that kind of money on me. I'll have to go get it. Take my word as truth, I'll be back quick as I can."

Clay studied the trembling man for a moment. "Your word's not worth much to me, Wilburn, but killing you won't bring me my money. I'll give you until four o'clock to pay off. If you haven't by then, I'm coming for you and the herd both."

Wilburn left immediately. Four o'clock came, and he had not returned. Allison rode to his ranch. The place was deserted. Only the stock, now scattered on the range south of the buildings, was left. Clay went back to the Clifton House, scouted out what riders he still had around, and next morning rounded up the stock. He sold them to another rancher the same day, collecting this time on delivery and getting as good a price for the steers as he had expected.

But he had lost time — an entire week, at least — waiting on Wilburn and that irked him. He was a restless man in a hurry to accumulate money enough to strike out on his own. He should, by this time, be well on his way back to the Brazos, where another trail job awaited him.

With five of his riders he started back at once. Before the day was over, he had altered his plans. Word came to him that the huge dust cloud lying along the road south of Raton Pass was a herd of mules *en route* to various Army posts in the territory. This, at first, interested Clay Allison only mildly. When he learned a few minutes later that the herd belonged to a Yankee general by the name of Granger, it was an altogether different matter.

Here was a chance to recover some of the money he had lost by waiting for Wilburn. With his cowboys he rode parallel to the herd until darkness fell and the muleteers had called a halt for the night. When the camp settled down, Allison struck. They scattered the saddle horses so that pursuit would be impossible, overturned the chuck wagon, and then drove the mules eastward into Texas, where Clay made a quick deal for their purchase.

He spent a part of the proceeds on the drovers at the next town, giving them a time they would not soon forget. The balance he added to the stake he was building. The fact that it had been an effective bit of mule rustling bothered him not at all. Yankees, particularly Army officers, had no rights to his way of thinking.

Back on the Brazos once again, he took on several more small jobs that added steadily, if not in any large quantity, to his fund of cash. It was mounting far too slowly to suit his impatient desire, but he hung on, reluctant to begin under a handicap. Each time he saw the Cimarron, however, the clamor to stay, to begin, grew more powerful.

And then luck swung his way. When he returned to the Brazos ranch from a job, early in the spring of 1870, surprising news awaited him. Lacy and Coleman had bought land from Lucien Maxwell. They had decided to move to New Mexico — and the Cimarron. And to get their three thousand head of stock transferred, they were willing to pay him well. One steer to him for every ten he delivered.

The move got under way shortly after that, and Clay, drawing on all his experience of trail driving, managed to get the herd through with few losses. They reached the Cimarron country which, in his mind, meant practically the entire New Mexico county of Colfax, and there they split, settling in different localities. Clay, with John and Monroe, claimed the three hundred or so cattle due them and chose a site in the Ponil Creek area for their ranch, not far from the town of Cimarron. The Lacys and Colemans went farther north and east.

For Clay it was the fulfillment of an old dream, and with his two brothers he geared himself to the hard and steady work of building up a ranch and herd that soon would amount to something. In the beginning everything went into the care and management of the cattle. The men got along with bare necessities, built only the simplest dugout for living quarters, subsisted on what they could grow. A fine house of stone and timber, with all the fancy trimmings, would come later, when they could afford it.

They worked long and hard those first months. No time was lost erecting pens, building corrals, enlarging the water holes. Clay's string of horses, the majority of which he had accumulated for racing purposes, were pressed into service, only the proved runners being reserved for track use. John and Monroe, lovers of the soil who had never fully rid themselves of the need to till and plant, got a small crop into the ground that supplied a good portion of their food needs.

Everything was to Clay's liking. He finally was ranching in the Cimarron country. The old restlessness disappeared, and he looked forward to being settled, to becoming a man of substance. To realize that boyhood dream had taken twenty-five years, the last nine of which had taught him well the trade of violence he must know if he was to hold his own in this soon to be turbulent land he had chosen.

Shaping up like a monstrous, threatening cloud of trouble, however, were the problems of Lucien B. Maxwell. Although his wealth had piled up with astounding rapidity, the steady rape of his holdings by settlers, squatters, small-time ranchers, and gold seekers was a persistent thorn in his side. The government readily assured him his claim to the vast grant was valid and just as steadily refused to do anything about keeping off the trespassers. That was a problem entirely his own, they said, and, while there was a fair-size garrison of soldiers at nearby Fort Union to the south, they were forbidden to give him any aid in controlling the persistent depredations.

Small towns, mining camps of varying sizes, had sprung up here and there over which he could exercise no control. Principal among these was Elizabethtown. It lay to the northwest of Cimarron, a genuine, twenty-four-carat hellbender of a community, if ever one existed. Any given Saturday night appeared to be a contest in which violence was the sole measure of the winners.

Maxwell decided he had taken enough of it. He had ample money, and, if he sold out his interests to the Dutch and English syndicate that was pressing him for a favorable decision along such lines, he could retire as the wealthiest man in the territory. Why continue to worry and sweat over a possession he could not hope to hold for much longer? Why not accept the offer that was being dangled in front of his nose and get out while he had the opportunity?

The Dutch-English company signed the papers and assumed Lucien Maxwell's vast spread on April 20, 1870. The price was a million and a quarter dollars. It was immediately renamed the Maxwell Land & Railway Company, and plans to colonize it were put into effect at once. The Maxwell Land Grant War was born.

Clay Allison was to become its stellar attraction.

## VII

Clay with a neighbor, Pete McQueen, rode into Cimarron late in the afternoon. It was Saturday, and the sharp promise of the cold months ahead hung in the autumn air.

"Going to be a hard winter," McQueen said. "The Indians are saying so."

Allison, riding his favorite horse, a gelding black as a raven's wing, shook his head. "Doesn't bother me half as much as this vigilante talk that's going around."

McQueen, a thick-shouldered, husky cattleman, glanced at Clay. "Well, that's coming, too, sure as hell. When Maxwell sold out to the syndicate, he made a real smart move . . . for himself. Knew he'd never be able to clear the grant of the squatters and jacklegs that had drifted in. Syndicate's finding that out now."

Allison did not reply immediately. He sat straight in the saddle, his lean body rolling gently with the motion of the gelding. His eyes, blue as the steel-colored sky overhead, stared out over the swells and shallows of the country, the Cimarron. He found what he had long sought in this lovely, lonely land. And now trouble was coming to it. He could feel it draw nearer with each passing day, almost see it, in fact.

"The syndicate people have their rights, there's little doubt of that," he said finally. "But so have the people who settled here. They've filed their claims and built their homes and ranches and put a lot of work into the land."

123

"Sure," McQueen said, "and I guess there won't be many siding with the big money, right or wrong."

"I blame the government for a lot of this," Clay said. "They should have clarified these titles, not let them just hang in the wind like they have."

"Well, one thing's sure. When the lid blows off, a man's going to have to take a hand. There'll be no middle ground. Where do you figure to be, Clay? With the ranchers and settlers, or with the syndicate?"

Allison shrugged. "That time comes, I'll make up my mind."

They turned into Cimarron's main street, hearing at once the sounds of laughter and loud voices coming from Henri Lambert's saloon. A dozen horses were tied to the hitch rail along its front and, farther down the dusty way, spotted here and there, were more.

"It looks like some of the boys got in early," Pete McQueen observed.

"Bunch of Texas trail hands. They delivered a herd up north, near Trinidad, couple of days ago. Henri'll be lucky if they don't take his place apart, bit by bit."

"Henri won't mind, long as they've got the money to pay for their drinks and the damage," McQueen said. "I'm dry. What d'you say we have a couple of snorts ourselves?"

"One thing I never say no to," Allison murmured, and headed the black into the rail fronting the hotel.

They dismounted, looped their horses to the log, and started for Lambert's. Cimarron's streets were deserted. Saturday, from midday on, was no time for the timid to be abroad. Farther along, a derby-hatted man moved into the doorway of the sheriff's office, threw his glance at Allison and McQueen. He lifted a hand in recognition.

"It appears Rinehart's on the job," McQueen said. "I wonder how many extra deputies he's got lined up for tonight?"

Allison laughed. "Not enough, you can bet on it. Cimarron and Elizabethtown sure aren't healthy for a lone lawman on a Saturday night."

They entered the saloon, making their way to the crowded bar. Lambert, with one assisting bartender, handled the trade. He saw the ranchers come in and nodded to them. Without waiting for them to order, he reached under the counter and produced two bottles, one bearing Allison's name, the other, McQueen's. He slid a pair of thick-bottomed shot glasses toward them. A clamor at the far end of the bar drew him away before he could open a conversation.

Allison poured a round of drinks from his bottle. He picked up the glass and held it before him.

"Here's to the hell I hope won't ever come," he said. "I've had my time with trouble. I sort of like this peaceful way things have been."

Pete McQueen clinked his glass against that of Allison. "*Salud.* But I think it's a little like a dog barking at the moon, that wish."

Clay set his empty glass on the counter. "Could be, but a man can sure hope."

McQueen stood the second round of whiskey. At his shoulder a dark-faced cowboy with reddish hair began to pound on the bar. Lambert glided up to him.

"All right, mister, what is it?"

"Whiskey," the redhead said, "and don't give me any of that skunk juice you've been pouring. Give me some of that good stuff you got saved away for the regular customers, like you give these two jaspers."

"Their own private bottles," Lambert said coldly. "You want to buy special whiskey, lay the money on the counter, and I'll produce it."

"I'll sure do that," the cowboy said, and dug into his pockets. He went through them all and came up finally with a few coins.

Lambert glanced scornfully at the money. "Friend, you ain't even got enough there to buy yourself one drink, much less a bottle!"

A man farther down the bar laughed. The redhead spun, facing him, his eyes sparking. "You braying jackass! What you laughing about?" He thrust aside the men standing between himself and the offender and squared himself. His right hand was poised above the worn gun, slung low on his hip.

To Clay Allison it was as if he were again living the hundred and more nights when he rode the trails and haunted the towns along their way. Smoke curling about the ceiling, the smells of whiskey and beer, or sweaty men and burning coal-oil lamps. It was all behind him now, but the thrill of such moments still touched him, reaching deep.

He saw the inevitable lines shape up. The five or six men who would back the man who had snickered now were easing off to one side out of the line of fire, but they would wait and be ready. A dozen more would be the neutrals. They would side neither man. Clay Allison knew their kind well — the sort who like to watch, who are ever quickest to egg on a fight and pound trouble to satisfy an odd desire on their part to see a man die. They were always plentiful.

The redhead stood alone. If he was aware of it, he gave it no consideration. Allison, measuring the odds mentally, poured a drink from his bottle into the cowboy's glass. In the tense hush the sound was loud.

"Here, Red," he said, "have a shot out of my bottle. You'll probably find it no different than what Henri's been serving you."

The breathless quiet broke with his words. The man who had laughed allowed his shoulders to sag in relief. He grinned weakly at the redhead.

"Hell, friend, I didn't mean no harm."

The cowboy relaxed, turning slowly back to the bar. Others crowded in, refilling the line. Lambert brushed at the beads of sweat congregated on his forehead. The redhead picked up his glass, studied it for a moment, and then carefully tasted the liquor. His eyes still glowed with a hard anger, and color was slow in returning to his broad face.

"Good stuff," he said after the first swallow. "A man always gets rooked in these trail towns."

"I know what you mean," Allison said.

The redhead took another swallow. "You done a turn at trail driving?"

"Enough," Clay replied. "A long five years of it."

"I reckon you sure do know what I mean! I want to thank you for the drink, Mister . . . ?"

"Allison. Clay Allison. My friend here is Pete McQueen. We're ranching this part of the country."

The cowboy shook their hands. "The name's Davy Crockett," he said. "This is my first time through here."

McQueen filled the glasses from his bottle. "You say Davy Crockett? I thought you got killed by the Mexicans down in Texas somewheres . . . a place called the Alamo."

Crockett wagged his head in disgust. "Lousy joke. And I'm always hearing it. You'd think people would figure there could be more than one Davy Crockett. Hell, they's plenty of John Smiths and Charlie Browns running around. That Crockett was from Tennessee. I'm from Arkansas."

Allison smiled. "I thought I caught a bit of razorback drawl in your voice."

"It sounds like you might be from that neck of the woods yourself."

"Tennessee," Allison said. "Wayne County."

The screen door to Lambert's slammed, and Sheriff Isaac Rinehart's bulk darkened the entrance. As the lawman swept the room with his hard glance, talk ceased momentarily and then gradually resumed.

Rinehart said: "I want you boys to know you're welcome to stick around here tonight, long as you behave yourselves. Otherwise, you better ride out come dark."

There was silence for a moment, and then a voice from the depths of the saloon said: "Why, sheriff, you ain't being hospitable at all!"

"Mind what I said," the lawman snapped. "I got a jail big enough to hold all of you . . ."

"Maybe," another voice said in a promising sort of way. "Just maybe it's big enough but ain't strong enough."

Rinehart made no answer but moved in a step farther, his eyes searching for the speaker. Crockett, his face pulled into a deep frown, stared at his half empty glass, seemingly unaware of the conversation taking place.

"Allison . . . Allison," he muttered. "Seems I recollect that name from somewhere. I heard a few things up and down the line. Wasn't you the one who was always tangling with Yankee soldiers and giving the badge-toters fits? Ain't you the jasper that used to shoot the heels off their boots, right out from under them?"

Allison shrugged. "Long time ago, that."

"Then you're the same man that got the marshal of Hall City down on the floor of a saloon and poured him full of whiskey until he was rolling drunk! He'd tried to stop you from doing that Indian dance of yours."

McQueen looked at Allison in surprise. "Just because you were doing a war dance? It must have been a mighty stiff-necked marshal."

"I reckon it wasn't the dance the marshal was complaining about," Crockett said, "but the fact that Allison here was wearing only his gun belt and boots at the time."

"I was the big chief of all the redmen" — Clay laughed — "and it was a warm night."

Rinehart moved in beside McQueen. He placed his attention on Allison. "You staying in town tonight, Clay?"

Allison motioned to Lambert for a clean glass. He poured the lawman a generous drink. "I don't know for certain, Isaac. It could be."

Rinehart downed the whiskey, smacking his thick lips in audible appreciation. "Thanks. I thought maybe you and Pete might give me some help, if things get out of hand. It ain't enough I got to look after this bunch of wild trail hands, too. All I need now is for a couple of miners loaded with dust to blow in."

"The best thing you can do is go home and go to bed early, like everybody else around here does on a Saturday night," McQueen said. "Then you won't know what's going on."

Rinehart grunted. "I wish to hell I could do just that. But you people pay me to keep things right around here, so I got a job to do. See you later."

The sheriff turned, leaving the bar. He was a good lawman, and Clay liked him. But being a lawman for Cimarron and the surrounding towns was a mighty frustrating job.

Crockett, well warmed by the liquor he had drunk, had drifted off into the crowd when Rinehart came up. Now he was busily relating some of the incidents he had heard of Allison's time of trail driving and his fame as a fast gun and expert with a knife.

McQueen listened for a few minutes, then slapped Clay on the shoulder. "It sounds like you're bound to be a hero around here before this night's over."

**130**

Allison grinned. "A man never gets away from his past, I reckon. But they'll forget it quick now. Here comes some of Henri's girls."

"There's nothing like a woman's bare hide to catch a man's attention," McQueen admitted. "About ready to eat?"

"Ready," Allison said, and corked his bottle. He shoved it toward Lambert. "See you later, Henri."

With McQueen he waited while the four girls who worked for the saloonkeeper as entertainers moved by, smiled their recognition, and began to mingle with the trail drovers. Then the two men walked to the doorway, pushing out into the street. A group of soldiers from Fort Union, all Negroes, had ridden in, their uniforms gray with dust from the ride. They had tethered their mounts in front of Sternberg's Clothing Store and were now heading for Lambert's to quench their thirst.

Allison felt a vague anger rise within him, as it always did when he saw the uniform of the Army, but he said nothing and continued on.

"Clay! Hey, Clay!" The voice of Davy Crockett reached out from the depths of the saloon, halting him. "Hold up a minute."

Allison and McQueen turned to wait for the redhead. They saw him gain the door at the same moment as the soldiers, colliding solidly with them. Crockett ripped out a curse. The soldiers fell back a step. Then came the sudden, rapid blast of gunfire.

Allison and McQueen wheeled, rushing toward Lambert's. Behind them came the pound of bootheels

**131**

on the hard-baked dirt of the street as Isaac Rinehart hurried to investigate.

Three soldiers were dead, a fourth slightly wounded. Crockett had a bleeding furrow across his left arm. The sheriff and his men stepped over the prone bodies and examined them briefly. The lawman pushed his hat to the back of his head and swung his scowling attention to Crockett.

"How did this happen?"

The cowboy, his stocky frame tense, shrugged. "Me and Gus Heffron was coming out the front door, following Allison and McQueen. The soldiers were all coming in. They tried to shove me out of the way. Hell, Sheriff, I don't shove easy."

"So I see," Rinehart said dryly. "And it looks like you shoot real easy, too." He glanced to Lambert. "You see this, Henri? Is that the way it happened?"

The saloonkeeper nodded. "It's the way I saw it, Ike."

A man standing at the bar said: "Self-defense. That's what it was. Them soldiers was looking for trouble."

Rinehart grunted skeptically. "Self-defense maybe. It's a little hard to figure how he could shoot four of them before they could wing him once."

He shifted his attention to the remaining soldiers, poised and waiting. The threat of violence still hung heavily about the doorway of Lambert's saloon.

"You men put your guns away. And pick up your friends here and lug them over to Doc Jackson's place. He'll look after the bodies and fix up that wounded man. I'll ride down to the fort tomorrow and make a report to your commanding officer."

They complied reluctantly. Crockett, observing their activities with narrowed eyes, said: "The Army's got no business putting uniforms on slaves. They don't . . ."

"Enough of that!" Rinehart snapped angrily. "Start marching toward the jail, cowboy! I'm holding you until I talk to the colonel at Fort Union. Maybe he'll want to ask you some questions."

"Questions?" the cowboy echoed. "Questions about what? You heard everybody say it was self-defense."

"I heard. Every time a man gets killed hereabouts, I'm told by somebody it's self-defense. Well, maybe it is, but I'm locking you up for a few days, anyway."

There was a murmur of disapproval among the trail hands gathered in the saloon. Allison threw them a speculative glance, stepping forward.

"No need for that, Sheriff. Crockett is going to work for me. I'll stand good for him."

Rinehart stared at Allison in surprise. "Since when is he going to work for you?"

"Since right now. Is that good enough?"

Rinehart hesitated a moment. "All right, Clay. I reckon you know what you're doing, but people are going to talk, you standing up for a killer like him. If I want him, I'll ride out to your place for him."

He moved back through the doorway into the street. The men from Fort Union had picked up their fallen comrades and were carrying them toward the office of Dr. Jackson, who doubled as undertaker. Crockett swaggered up to Allison.

"Much obliged, Clay. But I reckon you didn't need to have done it. That tin star would have never got me inside his jail without a fight."

"That's just what I figured," Allison replied. "And I meant what I told him, Davy. You're working for me."

Crockett studied Allison for a time. "Are you taking up for them Yankees?"

Allison's jaw snapped shut. "You know better than that! There's enough trouble around here without starting more. Rinehart's the one man who's been able to keep things halfway under control. I don't want you or that bunch of trail hands shooting him and shooting up the town."

Crockett still found it hard to understand. "I always heard you didn't cotton much to lawmen. How come you're backing this one?"

"Like I said, I don't want to see trouble coming into this country."

McQueen picked up the explanation. "This isn't just any saloon brawl we're thinking about, cowboy. There's a range war brewing here on the Cimarron that could turn out to be a second rebellion. We're trying to head it off, if we can."

"So that's how the wind's blowing!" Crockett exclaimed with a broad grin. "Well, man, I'll be real happy to stick around and lend a hand. Range wars are right up my alley."

"There won't be one if it can be helped," Allison said, and turned away. "Let's go eat."

But if Clay Allison was able to circumvent that incident, there were others more serious over which he could exercise no control. Land disputes and claims arguments erupted throughout the Cimarron country suddenly, and blood flowed. Twenty-six men died violently within a thirty-day period, and it became a macabre sort of joke around the settlement to ask: "Who got killed at Lambert's last night? Anybody I know?" The gulf, on the one hand, between the merchants and the native Spanish and Mexican residents and, on the other hand, the cattlemen and cowboys steadily widened. And to increase the tension, the syndicate, dissatisfied with its progress to civilize and colonize its vast holdings, redoubled its efforts to drive off the squatters and ranchers, believing that a more tractable element would replace them.

Other influences, in the form of politicians in the distant capital of Santa Fé, began to make themselves felt. The suddenly ore-rich county of Colfax became a ripe plum, needing only to be plucked. A group of greedy men, who became known as the Santa Fé Ring, began to move in and exercise their power. Claims were unexpectedly voided. Records were altered or else disappeared entirely. Out-and-out cheating by officials where ranchers were concerned became too common to be accidental.

The cattlemen reacted violently. They banded together and held a meeting to discuss what appeared to be discrimination on the part of the "Yankees who held county and state offices," and what should be done about it. It was probably such a meeting that was taking place in Pearson's Saloon in Elizabethtown late in September when Dulcy Kennedy, the wife of an innkeeper who maintained a lodging house on the road to Mora, staggered into the room. She was smeared with blood, badly beaten, and her clothes were in shreds. She was almost frozen from the bitter mountain temperature.

"Charlie . . ." she gasped. "He's killed another man."

Allison and Crockett helped the distraught woman to a chair near the stove. One of the other ranchers brought her a stiff drink.

Allison knew Charlie Kennedy. He was a one-time mountain man and trapper who had married Dulcy Maldonado, daughter of a native family in the small town of Arroyo Seco. After the marriage he settled down to a life of running the inn, wife-beating, and hard drinking. There had been rumors of missing travelers having last been heard of around Kennedy's place, but there was never anything definite about it.

"What do you mean . . . another man?" Crockett asked when the woman had recovered herself somewhat.

"There are many, many others," she replied in rapid Spanish. "They stop for the night. Charlie kills and robs them."

"What about their bodies? What does he do with them?"

"They're buried in the cellar."

There was a long minute of silence. Allison finally asked: "How many, Dulcy? How many men are buried in the cellar of the inn?"

"Six, maybe seven. And he killed my baby!" The woman trembled violently. "He will kill me, too, if he knows I've told you."

"He won't have a chance to hurt you," Allison replied. He turned to Crockett. "Davy, go get the deputy. We'll bring in Kennedy."

They placed Dulcy Kennedy in the care of a local family and rode to the inn. They found Kennedy behind the house. Coals still glowed in a pit where he had been burning something.

The deputy stepped up to him and disarmed him quickly. Unsteady from heavy drinking, Kennedy watched as Clay and the others poked around the smoking ashes.

"Bones," Crockett said, kicking some of the remainder to one side. "And this sure looks like cloth of some sort."

"He must've realized his wife had gone to tell on him," one of the ranchers said, "so he tried to burn the evidence."

"She said something about him burying them in the cellar," the deputy recalled. "Maybe we ought to have a look there, too. A couple of you go inside and see what you can find."

Crockett and another man went into the house. They returned after several minutes.

"There's been some digging going on in there, sure enough," Crockett reported. "It looks to me like the woman knew what she was talking about."

The deputy nodded. "I'll take Kennedy in and lock him up for the judge. Get a sack and bring along what bones you can find. And those bits of cloth. We'll need it all for evidence."

Davy Crockett crossed his arms over his chest and cocked his head to one side. "Now, why go to all that bother, deputy? We know he's guilty. It would be better just to hang him right here and now."

The lawman stiffened. "Now, just a minute. Maybe I agree he's guilty, but he'll still have to go to trial. I'm not heading up any lynching party."

"Then why don't you just ride on back to town, and let us bring him in?" Crockett suggested slyly.

The deputy wagged his head stubbornly. "Nope, that wouldn't work out, either. Something is sure to happen on the way. We'll all ride in together, and I'm looking to you men to help me see he gets to my jailhouse."

Allison, inclined to agree with Crockett and his views, asked: "When will the judge be around to hold court?"

"He's here now. The hearing can probably get started tomorrow morning, if we push him hard enough."

"Then let's get going," Allison said. "If word gets out what Kennedy's done up here, we'll have a lynch mob nobody will be able to stop."

It was waiting for them when they rode into Elizabethtown. Dulcy Kennedy's words, overheard by bystanders in Pearson's Saloon, had passed quickly through the settlement. When Allison saw the gathering before the jail, he knew they were in for trouble.

He drew his gun, riding out ahead of the others a few paces. Davy Crockett spurred to side him.

"I'm Clay Allison," he said, drawing the crowd's attention. "Most of you know me. I feel the same as you about this man, Kennedy, but the law says he's entitled to a trial, guilty or not. If I guarantee you justice will be done, will you break this up and give the deputy no trouble?"

There was a shout of agreement from those who knew Allison, a mutter of dissent from those who did not and who took no stock in the proposal. Another man spoke up. Clay recognized him as the judge, Ben Houck.

"All of you people," he called, "do what Allison says, and I'll start the trial right away. Quick as we can find a place to hold it."

One of the town's better-known merchants stepped up beside the judge. "It sounds fair to me. What about it? Let's break this up and meet at Salton's Dance Hall one o'clock. The judge can hold the trial there."

The crowd reluctantly agreed and began to melt away. Allison and the men with him saw the deputy and his prisoner to jail, after which they returned to Pearson's to await the trial. There was no doubt in their minds as to Kennedy's guilt. It was a matter for the court to state officially, and they were willing to go along with the due process of law.

At one o'clock the court convened. Judge Houck heard the witnesses and saw the evidence that had been gathered. During the morning hours a number of Kennedy's friends had got busy and hired a lawyer, who now began to present the innkeeper's side of the story.

Allison, sitting in the large audience with Davy Crockett, wondered where Dulcy Kennedy was, and why she wasn't present to repeat her story to Houck.

A man beside him leaned over and supplied the answer. "Kennedy's lawyer fixed that. She don't have to appear unless she wants to, and they've scared her out of it."

Allison wished then he had listened to Crockett's earlier proposal. Kennedy's lawyer produced several doctors and defied them to say definitely that the bones exhibited as evidence were human. All declined. Judge Houck, suddenly caught in a maze of legal technicalities, was beyond his depth. He ordered Kennedy returned to jail to await the regular term of district court at which time expert opinions could be introduced.

"This is only a hearing," he explained to the suddenly angry, muttering crowd that faced him. "And since there is no clear-cut evidence, there's nothing I can do but hold the prisoner for regular court session."

The deputy, aided by Kennedy's friends, slipped the prisoner out a side door and back into the safety of a jail cell before many knew he was gone. This served to heighten the tension, and many looked to Allison now to make good his promise.

"Kennedy's lawyer is a slick one. He'll get him off sure."

"Charlie will never hang . . . not with the help he'll get."

Charlie Kennedy did hang — and that very night. A large crowd of outraged citizens, including Clay Allison, Crockett, and the ranchers who had been in on the innkeeper's arrest from the beginning, took him from the jail and meted out the justice they feared he would escape.

No one particularly regretted the incident. All were convinced of the man's guilt. His brutal treatment of Dulcy alone was sufficient to incur the death sentence in the minds of the men. But the forces opposed to Allison and the settlers on the grant made the most of it, and thus more fuel was added to the smoldering fire that was soon to burst into flames along the Cimarron. From Raton to Santa Fé, from Las Vegas to Albuquerque, and across the territory, word was passed with the speed of light. A report was carried in newspapers:

**Clay Allison, leading a lawless band of wild cowboys, has defied the law again. He has broken an accused man out of a jail cell, a man awaiting trial for his life, and strung him up. Isn't it about time the law called in the Army to help bring this criminal to justice? How much longer must Colfax County endure the ruthless activities of this gunfighting desperado?**

Clay heard the vicious words and brushed them aside. People who knew him would not believe the incident had occurred in the lurid manner set forth in the report. That he had participated in the hanging of a killer, yes — that he had violently flaunted the law with a gang of wild cowboys, no. They would not believe it true.

141

But what Clay Allison and the others in the Cimarron country overlooked was the most important factor of all: for the first time the opposing forces had singled out Clay Allison as the leader of the resistive faction. The battle lines had become more sharply defined.

## VIII

Winter came early and stayed late. Snow swept in upon the Cimarron from the towering mountains to the north and west, and the bitter winds from the plains of Texas and the Indian Nations blew ceaselessly. Ranchers, squatters, and town residents alike were hard put to keep their interests intact during the rigorous season. Activities of the syndicate and the Santa Fé Ring, likewise, were fortunately brought to a halt. Even the vigor of Saturday nights at Lambert's saloon toned down considerably and were livened chiefly with demonstrations of shooting skill by Clay Allison, at the behest of Crockett and other cowboys familiar with his proficiency.

Spring finally did come in 1872, and Allison, following his usual custom, rode north in the early summer for the Clifton House. Other ranchers would be making the same pilgrimage to get together, talk over the winter's problems and summer's prospects, and participate in the horse racing that customarily took place. This year Davy Crockett was with Clay, and both men looked forward to making some good money on a little sorrel mare that was an excellent runner on a quarter-mile track.

They traveled the relatively short distance to Stockton's place from Cimarron at a leisurely pace and arrived there in the mid-morning. Pete McQueen and a number of other ranchers were there ahead of them, and Allison spent the first hours in the bar, renewing acquaintances and rehashing the tribulations of the hard winter. He was sitting at a back table with Crockett, McQueen, and rancher Sam Harris when two men, both strangers to him, walked up.

One was a short, thin man in a dusty blue suit, the other a husky, broad-faced cowboy, wearing a gun low on his hip. The latter was fairly drunk, and, as he pulled to a stop, facing Clay, he brushed his hat to the back of his head and grinned.

"So you're the great Allison, eh? Well, you don't look such big shakes to me! More like a four-flushing dude, was anybody to ask me."

The bar instantly hushed. Allison stared at the man, obviously a gunslinger looking for trouble. Crockett swore under his breath.

From the far side of the room, Stockton's brother, Matt, spoke up. "Don't start a fight in here, Chunk."

"Fight?" the gunman echoed. "Who's looking for a fight? I've just been hearing a lot about this Clay Allison and wanted to have me a look at him. From what I've been told, he's a real ring-tailed cat."

"You can lay money on it," McQueen said. "Now, how about moving on?"

"Sure, sure. But I got to say I'm some disappointed. Like I mentioned, he don't look so much to me."

Anger began to move through Allison. "The kind of opinions you have could get you a place on boot hill," he said coldly.

Chunk laughed. "There've been a few other yahoos before you got that idea. Seven of them, to be exact. But they're the ones planted on boot hill, not me."

"And you're looking for number eight, is that it?" asked Crockett.

Chunk let his glance shift to Davy Crockett, sitting tense and ready at Allison's shoulder. He shrugged. "No, sir, no such a thing. Me and my friend, Cooper, here are just around to make a little money on the horses. I hear you got a sorrel you figure is mighty fast. Well, it so happens I got me a bay, a genuine Thoroughbred from Kentucky. I've got a hunch he can run off and leave your sorrel like she was standing still."

"You got the hunch," Allison said quietly, "but have you got the money to back it?"

Chunk raised his left hand slowly, carefully. He dug his fingers into the breast pocket of his shirt and produced a wad of bills.

"Here's twenty-five dollars that says so."

"You got a bet. We'll meet you one hour at the track."

Chunk nodded, and with Cooper trailing along behind, left the saloon.

Crockett watched the two men depart in silence. Then he spoke. "This is some sort of trick, Clay. He's not interested in any horse race. All he's looking for is a chance to gun you down."

Allison murmured, "It would seem so. Who is he, anyway?"

Sam Harris supplied the answer. "His name is Chunk Tolbert. He rode in about a week ago from Trinidad. He got himself quite a reputation as a gun slick. He's supposed to have killed seven men, and I think he heard of you, and, knowing you'd be here, he's decided he wants to add your name to his list. There's been quite a bit of talking going the rounds about how good you are. I reckon he figures, if he can get you, it will be quite a feather in his hat."

"And Cooper?"

"Sidekick of his. He runs with him all the time. The law in Trinidad would like to have Tolbert for something he did up there. The sheriff followed him down, but he got a little too careless the other night and shot the wrong man in the dark. He didn't wait to explain or make another try for Chunk, but just turned around and lit out for Trinidad."

There was silence for a time after that. Crockett finally asked: "Are you going to go ahead with that race?"

"Sure, why not?" Allison replied. "I'll put that sorrel of mine up against anybody's horse in a quarter mile."

Crockett shrugged. "Well, if that's the way you want it. I'll keep my eye on that jasper, just the same, in case he gets any ideas about getting around in back of you."

"You watch Cooper," Clay said. "I'll look after Tolbert."

Two Englishmen, reportedly in the country to look over the syndicate's holdings in Colfax County, were chosen to be judges of the race when it got under way at the specified time. A large crowd had gathered, and considerable betting was done.

Chunk Tolbert had a fine horse. Allison saw that when the gunman led him out onto the track. The long-legged bay looked like a good runner — and proved the fact when he came in, nose to nose, with the sorrel mare. The crowd shifted over to the judges and awaited the decision. It was several minutes in coming.

"The bay, only by inches," one of them declared.

Chunk Tolbert was jubilant as he collected his winnings from Allison. "I knew I had the best horse," he crowed. "But to show you I'm a good sport, I'll stake you to a dinner."

"That's one way to get some of my money back," Clay said, still not trusting the gunman any. "Where will it be?"

"The Gonzales place," Tolbert said, naming a small café at the side of the Clifton House.

"Does that invitation include my friends, too?"

Tolbert said: "Nope, just the two of us. It'll be a good chance for us to get better acquainted."

Crockett was against the proposal immediately when told of it. "He's got some trick up his sleeve," he said. "I don't trust him."

"Neither do I," Allison replied, "but I'm not going to walk around the rest of my life, wondering if he's somewhere behind me, just waiting for a chance to add a new notch to his gun. He's determined to have a fight. I'll give him one."

"I'll be hanging around the outside," Crockett said. "If you need help, sing out."

Clay met Tolbert in the bar shortly after noon. They had a drink together and then went next door to the Gonzales place. It was empty when they entered, except for the native woman who operated it — and Tolbert's friend, Cooper. He sat in a chair against a far wall, his hat slanted down over his eyes.

"I thought this was to be just the two of us," Clay said, glancing at Cooper.

Tolbert laughed. "Oh, you mean Coop there? He don't count. Here, set yourself down," he added, pointing to a table in the center of the small room.

Allison shook his head, ignoring the invitation. He moved to the side and settled down in one of the booths that lined the wall. In that position, his back and right side were protected. Cooper was at an angle where he could be watched.

Tolbert, abruptly angry, took a place opposite Clay. He did not like the change and showed it, but Allison was satisfied and gave no indication of being willing to move. Señora Gonzales came in, bringing the food. The two men began to eat, Allison wary and thoughtful, Tolbert again trying to be offhand and make light conversation.

Halfway finished with the meal, the gunman paused, squirmed. "This here pistol of mine," he said, "sure makes me uncomfortable. If you don't mind, I'm going to lay it on the seat."

Danger warnings flashed through Clay Allison's mind, but he said: "Sure, go ahead. I think I'll do the same."

Through half-shut eyes, he saw Tolbert's arm drop to his side — and come up fast. There was a sharp crack as the barrel of the weapon accidentally struck the edge of the table and a deafening blast as Tolbert pressed the trigger. Clay's own weapon echoed the explosion. Tolbert jolted as the bullet smashed into him, driving the life from his body.

Allison whirled to face Cooper. The man was on his feet, his hand resting on the butt of his gun.

"Draw it and you're as dead as your friend here!" Allison snarled.

Cooper hesitated a moment. He shook his head, allowing his hand to fall away from the weapon. At that moment the door flung open. Crockett, McQueen, Stockton, and several others rushed in. They glanced at Tolbert, at Cooper, and then at Allison.

"What happened?" Crockett asked.

"Chunk tried a sneak draw on me, under the table. I guess his gun barrel hit the edge and caused him to miss. I didn't." He got to his feet and walked to Cooper. "Let's go," he said coldly. "Get your horse. I'm going to personally escort you down the road a piece. And, if I ever see you around here again, I'll kill you just like I did Tolbert."

Cooper hurried toward the doorway, moving out into the open.

Clay was only a step behind him. To Crockett and the others he said: "I'll be back shortly. Hold the funeral until then."

He waited while Cooper saddled his horse, collected his few belongings, and stuffed them into saddlebags. Then, swinging up onto the black gelding, Allison rode northward with Cooper for Raton Pass and the Colorado line, some distance beyond.

## IX

It was late in the afternoon. Allison had returned from voluntarily escorting Cooper from the vicinity. Several more horse races were behind him in which the sorrel had justified his faith in her abilities. He was in the saloon at the Clifton House, feeling good.

Two soldiers entered, taking places at the bar. Clay and Crockett looked them over while Stockton poured each a drink.

"Are you up from Fort Union?"

One of the soldiers, a sergeant, shook his head. "No, just passing through. We've got a herd of mules we're delivering."

Allison's interest arose. "Some of General Granger's?"

The sergeant said: "Yeah, some of the general's. Last time he sent a herd through here with some civilians in charge and lost the whole kit and caboodle. He ain't taking any chances this time. He's got this bunch under military command."

"Good idea," Allison said, and winked at Davy Crockett. "Where are they now?"

"They're corralled for the night on a ranch south of here, at a place called Crow Creek."

"I know it," Allison said. "The old Lear ranch, it was. Well, good luck with the general's mules, Sergeant."

The non-com ducked his head. "Thanks, but I don't figure we'll be needing it. There won't be any mule rustling this time."

Allison, in high good spirits and recalling the first time he had come upon one of the Yankee officer's herds, motioned for Crockett to follow him into the yard.

"Round up some of our boys," he said. "Tell them to meet me here at dark. We're going to give that damyankee general something to cuss about again."

Crockett departed at once, and Clay spent the balance of the day in the Clifton House, talking and playing poker with some of the ranchers who yet remained. The soldiers soon left, and exactly at dark Davy Crockett reported in.

"I could only find three of the boys," he said. "They're outside now. What's up?"

Allison threw down his cards, getting to his feet. "You'll see," he said. He followed Crockett to where his riders waited and came immediately to the point. "There's a herd of mules belonging to a Yankee general bedding down for the night at the old Lear place," he said, his eyes bright with excitement. "We're going to do the mules a favor and turn them out."

The cowboys were instantly agreeable. "Just like before, Clay, that it?" said one of those who had been in on the previous raid.

"Just like before," Allison repeated, "only this time it might not be so easy. The general sent soldiers along

**150**

with the herd. I guess he figured he'd better not take any chances going through here."

"Blue-belly soldiers won't change things any," another of the cowboys observed. "When do we get started on this shindig?"

"Right now," Allison said. "Mount up."

They rode south from the Clifton House for a short distance and then, keeping to a deep arroyo, angled toward the west. They soon came in sight of the camp's night fires and halted. Leaving the men behind, Allison and Crockett rode in closer for a better look at the situation. It was made to order for what they had in mind. The mules were all in a pole corral, a lone sentry pacing a beat at its gate.

Most of the soldiers had already rolled into their blankets, Clay judged, for there were only a handful sitting around the fires. And one by one they, too, were moving off into the darkness and turning in. Another hour and all would be quiet.

At his shoulder Clay heard Crockett ask: "What's this all about? You ain't got no use for mules."

"Let's just say I haven't any use for Yankees," Allison replied, and turned back to where the other men waited.

Quickly he outlined his plan for action. They would slip in under the cover of night. One man would take care of the sentry by knocking him out quietly and getting him out of the way. Allison and Crockett would handle the corral gate while the others got the mules moving. It would be done fast, silently, so as not to arouse the sleeping soldiers.

All went as scheduled. The sentry was drawn off to one side where a sharp blow to the head greeted him before he could sound an alarm. Allison and Davy Crockett rode in, opening the gate. Like all such gates, it had been hung at an off angle which caused it to swing shut automatically when pulled back. Allison, astride his black horse, took up a position before it to prevent its closing. Crockett and the remaining cowboys eased into the enclosure and began to haze the mules through the opening.

A shout lifted from the camp. A gun blasted, setting up a chain of echoes. Someone had been awakened by what was taking place at the corral. The mules, stubborn and sleepy, began to mill about, clogging the gate.

"Get out of there!" Allison shouted to his riders. "Soldiers coming!"

More gunshots broke through the night as the Army got under way. Crockett and the cowboys were having a hard time of it, bulling a route through the lethargic mules. Clay fought to keep the gate open, but the gelding, nervous and frightened from being crowded and thumped by the sluggish mules, was hard to handle.

Clay heard the whine of bullets overhead and realized the sentries had spotted him. He threw a glance at his cowboys. All but one were out of the corral, in the clear. He reached for his pistol, intending to unload it at the feet of the oncoming Yankees, now rushing for the enclosure. It might slow them down a bit and give him and his men a few more seconds in which to withdraw. His fingers closed about the weapon. He drew back the hammer with his thumb.

152

The black reared suddenly, falling against the gate as a huge mule let go at him with both heels. The revolver in Allison's hand fired as the impact of the unyielding gate slapped it hard against his leg. Pain flared through his foot and raced up his body.

"Let's get out of here!" Crockett yelled, surging in close.

The black swung in behind Crockett, the other riders following them rather than obeying any direction on Allison's part. They rode hard for a quarter of an hour before they pulled up to listen. There were no sounds of pursuit, and they concluded they had shaken the Yankees, if, indeed, the soldiers had given chase at all. Most likely they were too busily engaged in rounding up the general's scattered mules to do anything else.

Allison dismounted and sat down to examine his wound. Crockett and the others crowded up, aware for the first time of the accident. The bullet had entered Clay's right foot on the top, passed through, and was lodged in the instep. It was bleeding profusely, and Allison was in considerable pain.

"It's a hell of a note, when a man wings himself," he said in utter disgust.

"It's a bad looking wound," Crockett said, not smiling. "You able to ride to Cimarron?"

Allison shook his head. "It'd be better if you fetched the doctor here. Get Longwell this time. I don't trust that Jackson. We'll wait at the old Santiago place."

Crockett agreed. The Santiago place was a deserted shack only a couple of miles distant. Cimarron would be a long trip for a man injured as badly as Allison.

**153**

"Maybe Longwell won't want to come," Crockett said. "Would it be all right for me to bring him anyway?"

"Bring him anyway," Allison replied.

The physician returned with Crockett after a considerable delay, during which Allison suffered badly, from both pain and the loss of blood. Longwell, his jaw set and showing plainly his displeasure at the forced summons, examined Clay's foot.

"How did this happen?" he asked.

"Never mind how it happened!" Allison snapped. "It's been done. Now get busy and do something about it. You sure as hell took long enough getting here!"

The doctor reached for his leather satchel. "If I had known who it was, I wouldn't have answered the door," he said coolly. "I'm getting a bit tired of patching up you and that wild bunch of jackasses that run with you."

"You always get paid," Allison said.

"I admit that, but sometimes I wonder if I wouldn't be doing the country a favor by refusing to make a call such as this one."

"Any time I send for you, Doc," Allison stated in a low voice, "you'd better come. I mean it."

Longwell, working steadily at his task, paused and looked up. "Is that a threat?"

"Take it any way you like, but I mean it."

The physician resumed his treatment. "I suppose I ought to be scared, having the great Clay Allison talk to me in that manner. Only I'm not . . . not one bit."

Allison's tone relented. "I don't expect you to be, Doc. I guess waiting for you, with that foot hurting like all get out, sort of sharpened my nerves. How much longer is this going to take?"

"It's about finished now."

"Good. It's time I was riding. I've got to get back to the Clifton House."

Longwell paused again, looking at Clay. "You're not going anywhere except to my place. You're lucky you aren't losing that foot . . . and you may yet. I'm taking you to my house where I can keep an eye on it for a few days."

Allison started a protest, then suddenly changed his mind. "Is it that bad, Doc?"

Longwell nodded. "Every bit that bad. It's going to require constant attention for a spell." He turned to Crockett. "Help him into my buggy. You can look after his horse and do whatever he wants done at Stockton's."

Clay went along with the physician, offering no more objections. The thought of losing the foot was no pleasant prospect. He rode back to Cimarron in silence and settled himself in a bed at the doctor's combination office and residence with no argument.

"How long will I have to stay here?" was his only question.

Longwell, finishing with his follow-up treatment of the injury, said: "A week, at least."

Allison groaned. "A week!"

Longwell shrugged. "Why? Are you in a hurry to go somewhere? I expect your brothers can look after the ranch without you. I hear they've been doing it most of the time as it is, with you out rousting around, day and night."

Allison eyed the medical man closely. "You've been taking pot shots at me all night, Doc. What's on your mind?"

"Nothing's on my mind except a little sleep. I don't give a hoot and a damn what you do, only it seems to me you'd do better to settle down and get lined up with the right sort of people. There's lots of talk going around about you, Clay."

"Talk? What kind of talk?"

"About the sort of people you run with . . . killers like this Crockett . . . and the trouble you're always getting yourself into. Shooting scrapes and so on. Your reputation is going to catch up with you someday."

"Reputation is something that never leaves a man, Doc," Allison said quietly. "And as far as talk around here is concerned, I expect it all depends on which side of the fence you're standing as to how you feel."

"Well, I know how the right people feel about you. You would do a lot better if you lined up with them."

"A man's got to do things the way he thinks is best," Allison said, shaking his head slowly. "The way I look at it, in this lifetime it's just once around the track, and then you're done. I've got to do it the way I see it."

"You could just as well be doing some good as bringing trouble down on other people," Longwell said stubbornly.

"I guess that depends on who you think is in the wrong, and who's right."

"I'd say the choice you've made is a bit stupid."

Clay stared at the medical man. "Meaning what by that?"

"Meaning that the Maxwell Land and Railway Company isn't going to put up with you and your kind much longer. They want this country to tame down, to start amounting to something, so they can settle it with decent people. The way they see it, there's nothing but riffraff around here now, and they've got you tagged as the leader of that element."

"The way I see it," Allison replied, his tone faintly mocking, "is that this riffraff are all good, hard-working people the syndicate is trying to drive off their own property. There are two sides to the story, Doc."

Longwell said: "Maybe, but your position in this isn't very popular in Santa Fé, either. They've got you pegged as a troublemaker. Sooner or later you'll be hearing from them, too."

Allison laughed. "That Santa Fé bunch doesn't worry me, no more than does the syndicate. If they want to start something, I figure I can finish it."

"It's up to you," Longwell said. "I just thought I'd give you an idea of how things were shaping up." He rose and walked to the door.

"One thing, Doc," Clay called, halting him. "Just where do you stand in all this?"

"Right smack in the middle," Longwell replied. "I'm doing all I can not to line up with anybody . . . on either side. My place is to patch up holes for both, once the war gets started."

Allison nodded. "Good. That's the way to stay nice and safe. I'm obliged to you for all the advice, even if I can't take it."

"I didn't really figure you would," Longwell said in a weary voice, and left the room.

## X

After the second day at Longwell's, Clay began to rest, even to enjoy his convalescence a little. The constant prod of restlessness tapered off and the long-forgotten recollections of Tennessee, of his home there, his life with his mother and family before the war, came back to him. He began to remember the easy, tensionless way of things before the clash between the states brought it all to an end and made a different person of him.

Mrs Longwell cared for him as though he were her own son. He dined on expertly prepared food and reveled in the innumerable little attentions that only a woman can show a man. This pointed up sharply all the multitude of fine things he was missing by pursuing the semi-solitary path he had chosen in life. He thought a great deal about what had gone before and what might lie ahead. Considering the latter, it seemed to him there was little room in the scheme for a home and a wife.

Plenty of men were abroad who would like to take his life, not only because of personal grudges and ill will — for no man could live as Clay Allison lived without making enemies — but there was also the siren clamor of reputation. His fame as a fast gun, as an expert with a knife and fists, was a magnet attracting would-be desperadoes who felt the addition of his name to their list would raise their own stature. For years he had been a target for any gunman on the make along the frontier. It would not end soon, and it could only end with his death. Thus he had never thought much about taking a wife. Then, too, he was a reckless man who dared any and all things, but for some reason was never at ease around a young woman. In fact, he was decidedly shy in most instances, although his exceptional masculine good looks and inbred politeness invariably drew women to him.

Only twice in his lifetime had he become interested in a girl. Both times the parents of the young ladies involved put an end to it. They stated, in no uncertain terms, that their daughters were not going to waste their lives on a hell-raiser, a man feared because of his gun — successful cattleman or not. They respected Clay Allison for what he was, but he was unacceptable to them as a husband and a son-in-law.

With John Allison, his younger brother, it was a different matter. He was steady, dependable, and never in any trouble. He spent his time working the ranch. At the moment he was keeping company with a girl named McCullough, who lived with the A. J. Young family up in the Vermejo River country. Nobody would object to John Allison, or Monroe, either. They might have a wild, irresponsible brother, but they could hardly be blamed for that.

Clay had just had a visit from John, near the end of his week of convalescence, when Dr. Longwell ushered in two more visitors. One was the Reverend Thomas Harwood, the circuit-riding Methodist minister. The other was a tall, dark-haired girl with soft, doe-like eyes.

"We were calling on the sick when we heard you had suffered an accident," the minister said. "Thought we might drop by and cheer you up a bit."

"I appreciate that, Parson," Allison said. He thought the girl with Harwood was the most attractive woman he had ever seen, and he wondered when the minister was going to get around to introducing her.

It was Mrs Longwell who handled it. "Miss McCullough," she said, "I would like for you to meet Clay Allison."

Allison saw the girl's eyes widen and knew at once his reputation had preceded the actual introduction. But, if she was repelled, she managed to conceal it. She smiled, extending her hand. He took it, feeling awkward and not a little embarrassed at being in a nightshirt and in bed. Longwell had told him he must stay off the injured foot and that, even so, he would likely always have a noticeable limp. At least he would not lose the foot, as he had feared at first.

"Miss McCullough," he repeated, suddenly aware the name was familiar. He frowned. "McCullough . . . ? Are you acquainted with my brother, John?"

The girl smiled. "Very well. I see him quite often."

This, then, was John's girl. He felt a tremor of envy. John had made a good choice, and he deserved her. He was a good, hard-working man.

The Reverend Harwood said: "Don't let the things you hear about Clay Allison frighten you, Dora. I happen to know many things about him, all good. He is one who is always ready to help the church when a donation is needed. And I know of several families who

**160**

would have had a mighty bad time of it if it hadn't been for his generosity."

Dora smiled. "I've heard such reports, too. Perhaps the good by far outweighs the bad."

"Well, maybe balances it, anyway," Dr. Longwell said with a slow grin, as he entered the room.

Allison laughed with the others. This was the sort of woman he would marry, if ever he found one who would have him, who could accept him for what he was. But he would fool no one but himself about his past and probable future. Considering that, he doubted if he would ever find a woman who would take him on such terms. He said: "I hope I haven't caused my brother any embarrassment with you and the Youngs. You mustn't blame him for what I do."

Dora McCullough's full brows arched. "Well, I won't say your name hasn't come up many times . . . where my sister and John are concerned. But . . ."

"Your sister?" Clay broke in, half rising from his bed. "Aren't you John's girl?"

"No, I'm not John's girl. She's my younger sister."

It was Clay's turn to smile broadly, to settle back. Relief spread across his features. "I'm sure glad of that," he said. He glanced at the Longwells, at the Methodist minister, wishing they all would take their leave. They showed no signs of moving. He said: "Once I'm up and out of this bed and in the saddle again, do you think it would be all right to pay a call on you?"

Dora said: "I'm sure it would be, Mister Allison."

"Then please expect me . . ."

"You'll have to mend your ways, young man," Dr. Longwell cut in, "if you expect Mister Young to allow you on his place. He's likely to take a horsewhip to you."

Everyone laughed again, Allison a bit ruefully. But Dora McCullough gave him reason to hope. "Don't worry. Come some evening with John. That will make it easier to get started."

They left the room soon after that, the medical man with them. Mrs Longwell came to Clay's side and sat down on the edge of the bed. She looked down at him for a long minute before she spoke.

"I think you were attracted to Dora," she said. "She is a wonderful girl. She would make you a fine wife, Clay."

He nodded soberly. "I realize that. The question that's in my mind is what kind of a husband I would make her, or any woman?"

"That's something only you can decide," the physician's wife said. "It would be up to you whether you loved and cherished her, as the Good Book says, or broke her heart. It lies entirely with you."

Clay thought much about that all the rest of the week and was still pondering it when Davy Crockett dropped by to see him. It was the day Longwell said he could rise and try out his healed foot. He was in the parlor, testing his weight on it, when Crockett entered and sat down in one of the heavy leather chairs.

Crockett watched Clay limp slowly about the room for a time, then asked: "Clay, you know a man named Wilson? Jim Wilson, I think it is?"

Allison halted and thought for a bit. "No, I can't say that I do. Is he from around here?"

"I don't recollect ever seeing him before, myself. He's a real hardcase, tough looker."

Clay resumed his walking. "He's a stranger to me, far as I know. Why?"

"I heard him talking over at Lambert's. He said he rode all the way down here to have it out with you. Only now he couldn't, because he won't draw on a cripple."

"Cripple!" Allison flared, instantly angered. "What's my foot got to do with my gun hand? Where's this Wilson now?"

"I just saw him going into the county clerk's office a few minutes ago. You want me to go fetch him?"

Clay shook his head. "No, you ride on back to the ranch. Get me a horse. I'm ready to leave here tonight."

"What about Wilson?"

"Forget him. I'll look him up later."

Crockett departed on his errand, and Clay continued to exercise his foot. But within him anger was steadily rising as he thought about Wilson, and what had been said. After an hour he could stand it no longer. He buckled on his belt with gun and knife and quietly let himself out of Longwell's side door into the street. He stood for a moment, searching along the buildings. At that hour of the day Cimarron appeared almost deserted. He turned then, still a bit weak and unsteady from the days in bed, and made his way to the office of the county clerk, recently moved there from Elizabethtown.

A man, sitting at a desk, glanced up as he entered. He looked at Allison briefly, deliberately ignored him, and resumed the writing he was engaged in.

"There a Jim Wilson around here?" Allison asked.

The man at the desk continued at his task of scribbling in a thick book.

Allison repeated his question. "I understand he came in here."

The clerk, in the surly manner of many public officials, turned around slowly. He pushed his green eyeshade higher onto his bald head. "Mister, if you think I keep track of every sodbuster or cow tramp that comes in here, then you . . ."

He got no further. Allison took one step nearer, seizing the man by the shirt front. He jerked him to his feet, whirled him about, and slammed him against the wall. Anger flared in his pale eyes. "I don't think anything about you, rooster!" he barked. "All I want is a civil answer to what I asked. Where's Wilson?"

The impact of the clerk's body crashing into the wall brought a second man from the back room.

"What's the trouble out here, Lee?"

Before he could reply, Clay said: "My name's Allison. I'm looking for a man called Jim Wilson. I was told he was in here."

"He's not," the newcomer said flatly. "Now, let go of Lee and get out before you find yourself in trouble. I've heard of you, Allison, but you don't scare me one bit."

"And who are you?" Clay demanded, releasing his grasp on the clerk's shirt front.

"My name is Mills. Melvin Mills. I'm a lawyer."

"Have you seen this Wilson I'm looking for?"

Mills shook his head. "And what's more, knowing your reputation, I wouldn't tell you if I had. Are you getting out of here, or do I use this rifle?"

The attorney half turned, reaching upward for a gun hanging on the wall. Allison's hand moved swiftly. His Bowie knife glittered, slicing through the air. It struck with a dull thud, pinning Mills's coat sleeve to the wooden paneling. Angrily Mills jerked loose. He spun to face Allison.

"You'll regret this," he said in a low voice. "It's a good thing I'm not armed."

"You won't have to go far to get a gun," Clay replied coolly. "I'll wait right here for you."

The door slammed. Dr. Longwell, his face flushed from running, entered, accompanied by Lee. He pulled up in the center of the office, glancing about.

"What's going on here?" he demanded.

Melvin Mills did not turn to him. "If you have a pistol on you, Doctor, I'd like to borrow it."

Longwell gasped in astonishment. "Are you crazy, Melvin? You want to try to outdraw Clay Allison?"

Mills nodded. "I mean to kill him."

Longwell wagged his head in disbelief. "You've got less sense than I gave you credit for. Allison would shoot you full of holes before you could even touch your weapon. I don't know what started this, but take my advice . . . forget it. Get on out of here. I don't want to be mopping up your blood, if I can help it." Without waiting for the lawyer to reply, he turned to Clay. "And you'd better get back to the house. My wife is looking for you. She said you left without her knowing about it. You've got some explaining to do."

Allison, his anger cooled, nodded and walked back into the street. As he started for Longwell's house, a thought occurred to him in that moment. The story of what had taken place in the clerk's office would make the rounds quickly, and he would have someone to explain the matter to Dora McCullough.

Dr. Longwell had judged correctly the reaction of the A. J. Youngs to the attention shown their niece by Clay Allison. They recoiled immediately, and the fabulous Allison, afraid of no man that walked, bowed his head and meekly accepted their displeasure. But he did not give up.

That night, a week after his first meeting with Dora, as he and John rode homeward from the Young ranch, he let his feelings be known to his younger brother.

"If I thought she felt about me the same way as I feel about her, I wouldn't care what the Youngs said. I'd ask her to marry me, anyway."

John said: "Could be she does. You might try asking her."

"Me?" Clay exclaimed. "Hell, man, I couldn't do that!"

John, amused, glanced at his brother. "For a man who never backed down from anything in his life, you're mighty scary about asking a girl a simple little question."

"Different thing altogether," Clay said.

They rode on in thoughtful silence for a mile or so. Then John said: "You really want to marry Dora? You're dead sure she's the woman you want?"

"Dead sure," Clay replied. "I've met a lot of women in my life, usually the wrong kind. There's been a couple or three nice ones I had a notion I'd like to marry. But none of them come up to Dora, or the way

I feel about her. It's the real thing this time. I know it now. She's got me where I can't think of anything else but her."

"Dora's a nice girl," John said. "She and her sister are the best. We're thinking about getting married, too. I might step in and ask Dora for you, if you're sure." John Allison paused. "The only thing is, Clay, you got to be dead sure. I won't let Dora get hurt."

"Hurt?" Clay echoed. "That's one thing you don't have to be afraid of. I'm a one-woman sort of man. If she will be my wife, she'll never have cause to regret it. Oh, I don't say I'll change much . . . not overnight, anyway. But there's one thing certain . . . she'll be the only woman I'll ever look at, long as I live. That's already a fact, John."

The younger brother nodded. "I believe you, Clay. And I don't think Dora would expect to change you, as long as she was the only one that counted. She's that sort of girl."

"Talk to her for me, then, will you? It's not my way to ask favors of anybody, John, not even of you. But I'm asking this one. Maybe we could make it a double wedding."

John said: "That's a good idea. I'll mention it."

That next day and evening were long ones for Clay Allison, and he waited impatiently for the return of his brother. He met him at the corral, his question plain, although unspoken.

John dismounted with exaggerated deliberation. "She said to tell you," he began, keeping his expression solemn, "that she felt the same as you . . . but that you would have to ask her to marry you yourself. She refuses to be proposed to by proxy."

Allison let out a yell that echoed down the valley. "I'll ride over now . . ."

"Now?" John said. "Do you realize it's going on to midnight?"

"Well, first thing in the morning, then."

"She said she would meet you an hour after dark, tomorrow evening. In the cottonwood grove below the Youngs' place."

"Fine, fine. How about the double wedding idea? I'd feel a lot easier if we went at this thing together."

"They thought it was a good idea. We can get Reverend Harwood to perform the ceremony."

"The sooner the better," Clay said. "But we can't bring them here," he added soberly. "We'll have to build a decent house for them to live in." He paused, his thoughts racing on ahead. "I know a good piece of ground east of here I can get my hands on. It would be the perfect place for a home. I'll go over tomorrow and buy it up. Then we can start building a house."

John, usually stolid and easy-going, was caught up by his brother's enthusiasm. The next day he accompanied Clay to the land and agreed with him it would be a fine place for their new home. They procured the property at once and began construction.

The wedding, performed by Harwood, went off as planned, after which the four of them went to tell the Youngs. The Youngs were shocked at first. Elopement was not the proper way for a girl to give herself, but the fact that the Methodist minister had spoken the vows

**168**

over them, and not some justice of the peace, softened the blow. They gave their blessing and the girls, with their belongings — some from the old family home in Sedalia, Missouri — moved to the new house east of Cimarron town.

That was in 1873. It was the next year Clay met Mace Bowman, the only man he ever faced who could outdraw him.

## XI

The meeting with Bowman, a gunfighter who was soon to be made a deputy sheriff, came about by accident at Lambert's. Davy Crockett, as usual, was regaling several newcomers with tales of Allison's proselytes, topping off his remarks with the claim that his friend unquestionably was the fastest man alive with a six-gun, faster even than the famed Wild Bill Hickok.

Bowman, a quiet, soft-spoken man who had said nothing all evening, shook his head. "I doubt that, my friend," he drawled in a distinct Southern accent. "I'm not bragging when I say I can outdraw Hickok. I simply mean I know how fast he really is, and I don't think your Allison can match him . . . or me."

Clay overheard the observation. He moved to the bar where Mace Bowman stood.

"I'm Allison. You sound like you might be from the South."

Bowman said: "Right. Served my time in the Confederate army, if that means anything to you."

"It does. I was with Forrest."

The two men shook hands.

Allison said: "I heard what you said about Hickok. I've never matched speed with him, so I don't know. Davy there has seen him in action and thinks I could beat him if ever we come together. But about yourself . . . you care to make a little bet on how good you are?"

"That I'm faster than you?" Bowman asked. "Sure. I'll lay you a gallon of good whiskey that I'm the best man."

"You're on," Allison said. He reached for his pistol, unloaded it, waited for Bowman to do the same. When the Southerner had finished, they walked to the center of the room and faced each other.

"You give the word, bartender," Bowman said to Lambert.

The room was quiet. The two men were tense. Henry Lambert suddenly said: "Now!"

Allison's hand flashed down — and up. He was looking into the barrel of Bowman's gun before his own weapon was in firing position. He stared at the Southerner in amazement, unable to believe what had happened. Perhaps it was an accident.

"Again," he said.

Once more Mace Bowman demonstrated his startling speed. Allison conceded his defeat, paid Lambert for the gallon of whiskey, and stood drinks for the house. Then, with the jug under his arm, he started for the door with Bowman.

"We're going some place where we can be alone," he said. "I'm going to learn how you do that."

**170**

When they were where he could study Bowman's movements, Allison quickly saw that it was a matter of snapping the wrist upward in the final motion that made the difference. He and the gunman practiced continually the balance of that night and off and on in the days that followed. Soon Clay had mastered the system and had it down to perfection. Unquestionably, at that time, he was one of the peers of the frontier quick-draw artists — a select group, comprising not more than five or six other men.

The chance meeting with Mace Bowman had made close friends of them. With Davy Crockett they rode the range, visited Las Vegas, Raton, old Santa Fé, and all the other settlements in the area, sometimes for business purposes, other times in search of diversion. But Bowman, always a drifter and never long for one place, soon turned restless. When winter set in that year, he decided he would go into Texas, perhaps even Mexico or California. He didn't like cold weather. Late on the afternoon of December 24th he and Allison met to have a farewell drink together. They ate a meal at the St. James in Cimarron and then began a round of the bars.

Sometime near midnight Clay remembered that it was Christmas Eve. Being a man of strong religious principles and, therefore, having a profound respect for the holiday, he sobered quickly. Most of the town's establishments, in deference to the occasion, had closed. One bar, however, a place generally known as the Brick House, was going full blast. Cowboys, miners, painted ladies, and townspeople alike were whooping it up in genuine frontier fashion when Allison and Bowman walked through the doorway.

Allison strode directly to the bar. He drew his pistol, firing once into the ceiling to draw attention. Quiet settled over the crowded room immediately when he was recognized.

"Ladies and gentlemen," he said, gun still in hand, "this is Christmas Eve. What you're doing is no fit way to celebrate the birth of Christ. I suggest that those of you who have families, go home to them. The rest of you will stay, and we'll have proper services here."

He paused, waiting as a half a dozen or so men left the building. He turned to the piano player.

"A hymn, please. One of the Christmas kind."

The man at the piano removed his derby hat, hanging it on a chair post. He began to play *Silent Night*. A few voices took up the carol, a weak response at first but strengthening gradually as the rest of those in the room joined.

When it was finished, Clay glanced about. "Is there someone here who can lead us in prayer?"

After a moment a young man, dressed in the clothes of a prospector, stepped forward. "I can, sir. I started out to be a preacher once."

Allison said: "That's fine. From here on, this meeting is in your charge. My friend and I," he added, pointing to Bowman, "will see to it that order is kept in the congregation."

Thus Christmas came to the Brick House in the Cimarron country, perhaps forcibly, but with complete reverence. When daylight came, and the services ended,

Mace Bowman rode out, striking southward. It was the last time Clay was ever to see him. Bowman ended up finally in Trinidad, Colorado, where he died in 1893.

## XII

There was a new settler along Crow Creek that year, and Clay Allison found the man strangely interesting. His name was Oscar McMains, and there was nothing about him physically to draw Allison's attention. He was short, of nondescript appearance, and continually had trouble with his teeth. He was a preacher by avocation, which possibly was the key factor in his appeal, since Clay perhaps saw reflections of his own father in the seedy little man.

The Cimarron was moving steadily ahead under the constant push of the Maxwell Land & Railway syndicate, and settlers were at last heeding the call to colonization. The town itself began gradually to grow as cattle raising and mining progressed, and the interest of the third point of the triangle, the Santa Fé Ring, began to increase as Colfax County developed in wealth.

A new editor replaced Sullivan at the head of Cimarron's *News & Press*, this one a man named Dawson who dedicated himself to a finish fight against the political forces in Santa Fé. It was rumored that the ring planned to divide the county into quarters, which could be more easily controlled by themselves. McMains went to work for Dawson, filling in now and then in the pulpit of the local church. He was a speaker of no mean ability, and soon Oscar McMains found

**173**

himself the spokesman for the settlers who had been there before the syndicate and, in turn, who were feeling the wrath of the mighty land barons.

A tenseness settled more noticeably over the Cimarron, and men began to walk and talk carefully. Nights became hours of alarm with mysterious riders galloping over the plains and through the valleys, leaving behind flaming barns and houses and not a few dead and wounded men who had sought to prevent their depredations.

Allison, visited often by McMains, was increasingly aware of the violence that was steadily becoming a part of the way of life on the Cimarron. Responding to McMains's constant reporting of ruthless activities and cruelty on the part of the syndicate, he assumed a sympathetic attitude toward the nearly defenseless settlers, and his own dislike for the syndicate grew. To incense him and the other ranchers further, cattle rustling flourished with no help forthcoming from the law. It seemed to Allison, and those who automatically gravitated to him, that the politicians were deliberately hoping to discourage and ruin them financially by refusing aid. They began to take the law into their own hands and soon were meting out justice to transgressors in the time-honored way of the West.

Slowly, but surely, the Cimarron became a mighty, smoldering time bomb composed of three distinct but interlocking factions, awaiting only a spark to set off the explosion. That spark, in the shape of a gentle, completely honest and likable man, F. J. Tolby, rode in from Indiana one summer day. Unlike Oscar McMains,

Tolby was a minister by profession. He had heard of the booming Cimarron country through the circuit riders and persuaded the Methodist Church leaders to permit him to claim the area as his own particular field for salvation. He had the blessing of the syndicate, which recognized the need for an organized religious movement, and it provided him with a house in which to live while his own home was under construction.

Clay Allison, impressed with the Reverend Tolby, threw his considerable support and influence behind the man who very quickly drew himself up to a place of prominence and authority in the burgeoning community. There was no middle ground with Parson Tolby. And this Allison admired. A thing was either black or white, with no intershading grays, and, when the first evidences of the Santa Fé Ring's activities reached Tolby in absolute and indisputable force, he denounced them publicly from the pulpit in no uncertain terms.

McMains immediately leaped to the Indiana minister's side, even to the point of delivering confirming denunciations of fiery eloquence from Tolby's pulpit at various times. The two men's causes became enmeshed. Tolby's battle was against the greedy politicians who would enslave Colfax County for their own pecuniary benefit. McMains cried forth for the little man, the downtrodden squatter and settler, the miner, and small cattleman whose lands the syndicate would tear from his grasp, reclaim as its own, and sell to newcomers at a profit.

At times the issues became confused. Tolby would champion a settler, allegedly a victim of some crime laid at the syndicate's door, and McMains would find himself at war with a petty politician, controlled by the powers in far-off Santa Fé. But the Reverend Tolby's fight was primarily with the ring, and he veered seldom from that purpose. He became more vehement in his accusations, bringing forth figures to prove his point, citing the names of men high up in government positions who, he claimed, were bleeding the country dry. And on September 14, 1875, he was dead.

Two cowboys, hazing strays from the brush, came upon the parson's body, lying a short distance off the road to Elizabethtown. They loaded him up and took him into Cimarron at once.

News of the murder spread fast. Oscar McMains saw in it the fine, ruthless hand of the syndicate, but others were not so sure. It was the Santa Fé Ring, they said. Tolby had known too much, had been striking too near the truth for the comfort and safety of the politicians in Santa Fé. McMains believed that to be only a cover-up to hide the real killers, throwing the taint of murder onto the most apparent suspects. It was the syndicate, he declared from every step and pulpit he could command, and he would devote his life to catching the hired killers and avenging the death of the gentle Reverend Tolby.

Cimarron was in turmoil. Men lined up according to conviction or in response to outside pressures directly related to their own interests. The time of distrust and suspicion, like a terrible, enveloping plague, was at hand. A man's friends could be his enemies. Men, who had walked in peace and quiet, buckled on their guns, and Cimarron became an armed camp. Accusations were plentiful, and half a dozen men suspected of Tolby's murder were taken, questioned, and eventually turned free.

Oscar McMains, clawing for the topmost point of leadership in the county, despaired of reaching it unaided and, recognizing his own limitations, knew he alone could not bring the syndicate to its knees. He could raise the indignation of his followers to a certain level, but there it wavered, lacking the decisive leadership that it demanded. A man of greater stature, of unquestioned strength and honesty — a man feared and respected — was needed. Clay Allison.

There were well over a dozen men in the party. Led by Oscar McMains, they rode into Allison's yard shortly after noon on a fall day and pulled to a halt. Dora greeted them from the doorway.

"Missus Allison," McMains said, "we'd like to speak with your husband. Is he around?"

Clay, hearing the riders, came from the rear of the house at that moment. The men dismounted, and all shook hands with him. John, also drawn by the sounds, came out into the yard.

"We've come to ask your help, Clay," McMains said. "Murder has been done here on the Cimarron . . . the first of what will probably be several. We feel we must move at once to prevent more bloodshed."

Allison nodded. "Has the sheriff found Parson Tolby's killer?"

"No, and it doesn't look like he intends to. We represent the citizens of town and the surrounding areas and believe it is time we acted."

"What about Rinehart? He's a good man."

"There's nothing he can do. Between the syndicate and the politicians, his hands are tied. They don't want him to find Tolby's murderer."

The old craving for excitement began to rise within Clay Allison. He had kept himself steadily at work since the day he and Dora were married, with only an occasional truancy, usually a harmless one. He was lonely for action. Davy Crockett was gone, killed by a lawman in another territory. Mace Bowman was off in Texas or Mexico, or some other distant place. The trail was a thing of the past — and he was little more than a day-to-day plodder. The restless blood within him began to stir.

"Tolby was a friend of mine," he said, as if defending to himself his freshly aroused desire to ride and fight again. "I want to see his killer brought in as bad as any man. What do you want of me?"

McMains was blunt and to the point. "We want you to head up the vigilantes. You're the one man on the Cimarron who can bring them together and lead them."

Allison did not take long to consider. He said: "All right, I'm agreeable to the job. We'll meet tomorrow morning in back of the church and decide what's to be done. Pass the word around for every man who wants to see something done about things around here to be on hand."

Oscar McMains smiled his satisfaction. He had expected it to be much harder to enroll Allison in the cause; instead, Clay had almost jumped at the chance. Now the time of reckoning was at hand. A small army of hard-riding, hard-fighting men led by the feared and prominent Allison would make the syndicate sit up and take notice. He would show them Oscar McMains was no man to be trifled with.

The next morning there was considerable activity on the streets of Cimarron when Clay rode in. He pulled up at Lambert's. McMains came running to him at once.

"Rinehart's made one arrest," he said. "Could be he really has caught Tolby's killer."

Allison stared at him. "I thought you said the sheriff wasn't doing anything about it!"

"Well, as you knew, he has done some questioning. This seems a bit more likely than the others."

"Who is it?"

"Cruz Vega."

"Vega . . . the mail carrier?" Allison exclaimed. "Why would he want to kill the parson?"

"That's what we've got to find out," McMains replied. "He was probably paid to do it. We've got to learn who did the hiring."

Allison frowned, considering that for a time. "Where's Vega now?"

"Rinehart's got him locked up. I was just going over there when I saw you ride in."

Vega, a native, had been the mail carrier for some time. He worked for Florencio Donohue who held the government contract for service in the area. When

Allison and McMains entered the jail, Vega was being questioned about Tolby by Sheriff Rinehart and Melvin Mills, the lawyer Clay had met previously in the county clerk's office.

Vega admitted to seeing the Reverend Tolby on the Elizabethtown road. He had watched him pull off the road and stop near Willow Creek. He guessed the parson had halted to water his horse, since it was a very warm day. A little later on he saw him again, this time two or three miles farther along. He was riding slowly. Then he rounded a turn, and Vega never saw him again.

Rinehart and Mills were inclined to believe Vega had nothing to do with the murder. So was his employer, Donohue, along with many others, including Clay Allison. But Oscar McMains saw it all as a piece of the massive plot he felt was engulfing the Cimarron. He insisted there was more to it than Cruz Vega was telling, that he was shielding others, and that he should be made to talk.

In the end McMains had his way. Derby-hatted Sheriff Rinehart locked Vega back in his cell and sent word to the district judge, who was then in Taos. Melvin Mills offered his services as defense attorney, and a date for a trial was set.

Tension in Cimarron mounted as the time for the hearing approached. The natives were concerned that Cruz Vega would not get a fair deal. There was considerable underground talk of breaking him out of jail and setting him free.

McMains got word of this and sent for Clay Allison, who rode in at once. Twenty-five heavily armed men lined up behind him, all ready to prevent any such occurrence. The natives, also equipped now for battle, gathered at the other end of the street. Allison, hoping to avoid wholesale bloodshed, approached them alone.

"There's no need for trouble," he said, halting before them. "Cruz Vega will get a fair trial. If he is innocent, he'll go free."

The leader of the natives, a stocky gunman of some repute by the name of Pancho Griego, pushed forward. Allison knew him slightly and was aware he was a partner of Florencio Donohue, who employed Vega.

Griego said: "If he doesn't, my friend, I shall come looking for you."

"I'll be around," Allison replied. "But why me?"

"You are the *jefe* of the *gringos*. If Cruz does not go free, it will be your doing."

"I'm not on the jury," Clay pointed out.

"It makes no difference," Griego said. "Anyway, it would be a pleasure to make you another notch on my gun."

Allison, instantly angered, clung to his temper. It looked to him as if Griego wanted only an excuse to start trouble, that he was not so much a spokesman in the interests of Cruz Vega, as a gunman, searching for greater laurels. But it was not the time for a confrontation. The slightest thing could touch off a bloody explosion. And Griego was well backed. It appeared he had sent for all the natives in the entire county of Colfax, got them armed, and had them on hand for the trial.

Clay shrugged. "Like I said, you know where to find me." He turned back to the others in his party. Behind him he heard Griego laugh.

"Allison is fast with his tongue, not with his gun," he said.

Again anger flashed through the tall Tennessean. He was tempted to halt, to have it out with the gunman then and there. But he overcame the impulse and rode slowly on to Lambert's, rejoining the others. McMains, who had witnessed the encounter and noted the preponderance of natives in the town, hurriedly sent out messengers to summon all who were not then present to make an appearance. A showdown was not far off, he was certain.

At Lambert's Allison heard that the widow Tolby, now almost destitute, was staying with local friends. He passed the hat, made up a substantial collection for her, and then took it to her personally. Mrs Tolby, at first frightened at the prospect of coming face to face with a man she had been told was a desperate gunfighter, refused to see him. But she finally consented. He turned the money over to her and expressed his regret for her situation, after which she thanked him gratefully.

"This will take the children and me back to Indiana," she said. "Bless you and all the kind men who have made it possible."

"The parson was my friend," Clay replied. "And he was a friend of a lot of other people. We won't rest until we bring in his murderer."

Judge Henry Waldo arrived soon after that, and the Vega hearing began. Mills presented the facts as he and Isaac Rinehart had uncovered them. Vega was then put on the stand to tell his side of the story. When it was finished, Waldo considered for a few minutes. He gave his opinion to a packed courtroom.

"Gentlemen," he said, "you cannot hold a man for murder on such flimsy evidence. Actually, I find no evidence of note at all. You have one solitary fact to go on . . . that Cruz Vega happened to be on the same road at the identical time the Reverend Tolby was murdered. That, in itself, is not evidence. There is nothing to implicate the prisoner. I hereby order his release."

The decision was received in Cimarron with mixed reactions. Many thought, as did Oscar McMains, that Vega was a guilty man and that he was not telling all he knew of the affair. There were an equal number who believed him innocent, and that Judge Waldo had done the only just and logical thing.

McMains, infuriated, told his followers bluntly that he was not satisfied with the verdict, that he was not ready to let the matter die. This got back to the natives, and, fearing reprisals on the part of the *gringos*, they banded together more tightly. They began to move about in silent, watchful groups, careful never to be caught alone.

Aware he had blundered and hopeful he could dispel their fears and prove his sincerity, McMains offered Cruz Vega a job at his farm. There was much work to be done, and Vega was the man who could do it. McMains, taking no chances this time, confided in no one, not even his closest friends and allies. He did not say the move was for a definite purpose, that he was convinced Vega was hiding something, or that he fully intended to delve more deeply into the case to prove he

**183**

was correct. Putting Vega to work on his own premises was simply an effective means for keeping him nearby and readily available, when and if new evidence was uncovered.

One night a man rode into Clay Allison's yard and hallooed him to the door.

"McMains wants you to come to his place," he shouted. "He's got Vega again."

Clay saddled and went there at once. McMains and well over a hundred vigilantes awaited him. Cruz Vega, a rope about his neck, crouched beneath a tree.

"I wanted you in on this, Clay," McMains said. "It happened so fast I called the men together myself to save time."

Allison glanced about at the masked riders. "That's getting to be a habit with you," he said, moving toward them. He walked with a noticeable limp, a result of the gunshot wound received that night at the Lear ranch. "What's all this about?"

"You'll see," McMains replied. He turned to the two men holding the rope. "Hoist him up."

Vega was pulled to his feet. His eyes were wide with fright and a torrent of Spanish spilled from his lips.

"Do you confess you killed Parson Tolby?"

"No! I am innocent!" Vega screamed.

McMains motioned with his hand. Vega was drawn higher until he barely touched the earth with his toes.

"Who killed Tolby?"

"I do not know. I am innocent."

"Confess," shouted McMains, "or we'll hang you!"

"I am innocent," Vega moaned. He began to struggle, to gasp for breath.

"Confess that Donohue and Griego and Longwell and some others hired you, paid you to do it. Confess that it's true."

Longwell! Allison wondered if his ears were deceiving him. Could he be mixed up in this affair? He recalled then the trend of the doctor's conversation that night in his office. It did seem that Longwell leaned somewhat to the syndicate's way of thinking. At the first opportunity he would seek out the doctor and talk to him about it.

McMains lifted his hand again. Vega was pulled clear, swung free. He began to kick, to claw at the rope, and nod his head frantically. McMains waved to the hangmen. They released their grasp, and Vega fell, sprawling, to the earth.

"Do you confess to the murder, Cruz Vega?" McMains demanded, dropping to his knees beside the groaning native. "Do you admit what I said was true?"

The man stirred wearily. "I confess, I confess," he muttered. "Please, no more, señor, I confess."

"Was Cardenas in on it?" a voice from the vigilantes asked.

Vega nodded weakly, implicating a close friend of his who also worked for Donohue.

McMains glanced triumphantly about, then brought his attention to a halt on Allison. "Is everybody satisfied now that we have the murderer?"

"I'm satisfied," Clay said. "Take him in and turn him over to Rinehart. This time there's enough evidence to convict him, I'd say. Some of you take charge of him."

Half a dozen of the vigilantes moved forward, pulling Vega to his feet. Clay, with two men who lived in the same direction as his own ranch, mounted up and rode off.

"This should end the Tolby matter," he said as they traveled slowly through the rolling hills.

"Maybe Vega won't admit he confessed," one of the ranchers pointed out. "McMains had to get mighty rough with him to make him talk up, back there."

"A hundred men heard him say it," Clay replied. "That ought to be enough to convince Rinehart and the judge."

They reached his place, and he turned off. He was happy the killer had been caught, that it was over with, and now would become a matter for the courts. He awoke Dora to tell her and went to sleep.

At daylight he was up, ready to begin the business of the day. Before he could get well started at it, a rider rushed into the yard.

"Clay! Pancho Griego's out to get you. He says he'll kill you on sight. I came fast as I could to warn you."

"Griego?" Allison echoed. "Why?"

"Why?" the man repeated. "Ain't you heard? They found Cruz Vega, hanging from a scaffold at the edge of town this morning. He had a bullet in his back."

## XIII

November 1, 1875. The afternoon was clear, sharp with the promise of cold days not long in coming. Although the slopes of the high hills were still golden

**186**

with aspen in fall dress, Clay had noted a thin rim of ice along the edge of the water tank that morning. Winter would soon settle over the Cimarron, closing off most outdoor activities, throwing a white cloak of snow upon the land, and sending the freezing winds sweeping down the valleys and over the plains and ridges.

Perhaps it would also bring a halt to the trouble that swirled through the country. Now that McMains had unearthed the murderer of the Reverend Tolby and exacted his vengeance, maybe he would be willing to let matters rest. Pancho Griego posed the last threat. He seemed to feel that Allison was totally responsible for Cruz Vega's death and demanded satisfaction. Griego could be right. He had been the leader of the vigilantes, although McMains continually usurped that authority whenever he felt it necessary to do so. But Griego was not aware of that.

Clay had little sympathy for the gunman. By his boasting and his self-appointed position as leader of the natives, he had jockeyed himself into a situation where it was necessary he do something, or lose face. Otherwise, with the death of Vega, the whole thing might come to an end. It was Griego's fault that there was one more chapter to come. But if a shoot-out was what it would take to close the book, then he was ready and willing to meet Griego.

He rode into Cimarron, heading first for one of the stores where he had a matter of business to transact. This completed, he returned to the street. McMains was standing beside Clay's black gelding.

"You know Griego is looking for you?" he asked.

Allison nodded. "That's one reason why I'm in town." He paused, directing his hard, pale-eyed stare at McMains. "How is it that Cruz Vega never reached the jail last night?"

McMains shrugged. "It was just one of those things. It makes no difference, anyway. He was guilty."

"That could be true, but that's not the way we agreed to handle it."

"Well, some of the boys figured it was better to take care of it themselves. They didn't want to give Mills the chance to worm Vega out of a murder charge again."

"Were you there when it happened?" Allison asked in a quiet voice.

For a long time McMains did not reply. He looked off down Cimarron's empty street. "What does that matter?" he replied then, his voice rising. "Justice has been done. That's what counts."

"Justice!" Allison echoed. "Lynched and shot in the back! What kind of justice is that? I'm no lily-white . . . I've done my share of stringing up rustlers and back-shooters and the like . . . but the way this was done . . . masked men, a bullet between the shoulders, and no real proof of guilt except a confession we got by half strangling the man to death . . ."

"He was guilty!" McMains broke in. "Justice has been done . . . vengeance has been taken. You won't deny that."

"Maybe. At least, I hope he was guilty. And I hope we have come to an end to all this trouble when I'm done with Griego. It's time a little peace came to the Cimarron."

188

"Peace!" McMains echoed, his face turning scarlet with anger. "Peace! We'll never have peace so long as the syndicate has a death grip on the throat of the people. There'll never be peace until we drive out the syndicate and all the men connected with it."

McMains's voice had risen to a high pitch, shrill and cracking. Allison stared at him, realizing in that moment that he was dealing with a fanatic, a man turned wild by an inner, consuming hatred. After a moment he wheeled away, stepping to the saddle of the black. How did he ever get involved with a man like Oscar McMains? He pulled away from the hitch rail and started for the livery stable, saying no more to the yellow-toothed little printer.

He saw few people as he walked the gelding slowly down the center of the street — a native or two watched with sullen hostility as well as three or four men he knew by name but who did not speak. He suddenly felt he was a stranger in his own land, a man who had counted numberless friends among both natives and Anglos, but who now stood singularly alone. He reached the livery barn, turning the black over to the silent hosteler.

"Feed him and look after him, if I'm not back in a couple of hours," he said, and returned to the street.

He angled toward Lambert's bar. A stocky, thick-shouldered man eased into the open, took up a position halfway along the intervening distance, blocking his path. It was Pancho Griego.

"*Buenas tardes, Tejano,*" the Mexican said. "I've been looking for you."

189

"So I've heard," Clay replied in Spanish. "What's on your mind?"

"You have not forgotten my promise?"

"Cruz Vega?"

"Yes, Cruz Vega. You and your masked cowboys killed him last night. Now I shall kill you."

Allison smiled faintly. "Maybe. I will have something to say about that."

"Already you have said too much. I saw you speak with that loco McMains. He has led you to your death, friend Allison."

Clay shook his head. "It seems you are the one who does a lot of talking, Pancho. Do we settle this here and now?"

Griego spread his hands wide. "There is no hurry. There is plenty of time. I think it is polite of me if I buy you a drink first."

Allison said: "Agreed," and started forward. He watched the Mexican closely, alert for any tricks. Griego was a killer, and he was not particular how he accomplished his killings. He was said to have gunned down several men, and there was the incident in Cimarron where Griego had slain three soldiers during an argument over a faro game.

He came up abreast of Griego, and they moved on, entering Lambert's together. The saloon had only half a dozen patrons at that hour. They drew away from the bar quietly, giving the two men the entire length of the counter. Lambert placed a bottle and glasses before the pair, stepping back.

Griego, with an exaggerated display of courtesy, poured the drinks. He held his glass aloft toward Clay. "To my friend, *Tejano jefe* . . . who soon shall die."

Allison ignored the toast, waiting until the Mexican had downed his drink. Then he raised his own glass.

"To Pancho Griego, who fancies himself a gunman."

Anger flared in Griego's black eyes. He murmured something under his breath, quickly refilling the tumblers. He turned completely about, hooked his elbows on the edge of the bar, and laid his glance on the other men in the saloon. There was no smile on his face, only a scornful sullenness.

"This was a good country before the *gringos* came," he said. "With Maxwell it was still good. But you *Tejanos* have spoiled it. You fight over it like dogs for a bone. You do not remember that it always has belonged to the native people, that it is theirs to begin with. Someday it will again belong to them."

He paused, downing his glass of liquor. He wheeled slowly, facing Allison. Placing his glass on the counter, he reached up, removed his broad-brimmed hat with his left hand, and began to fan himself gently.

"It is warm for November, eh, *gringo?*"

Clay nodded. He moved away from the bar a step, never taking his eyes off the Mexican. Griego continued to fan himself, the big hat concealing the greater portion of his torso.

"Why don't we sit down at a table for a time and rest?" he suggested. "It should be a time of pleasure, a time of ease, for a man about to die."

Allison only watched, waited. Griego came away from the bar in a slow stride. Suddenly he wheeled. In that same fragment of time Allison drew. He triggered his gun fast, three times. Griego jolted from the wallop of the heavy bullets, smashing into his body. He slammed back against the bar, hung suspended for a brief instant, and then fell forward. His gun, concealed under his hat, clattered noisily as it dropped from nerveless fingers.

There was a long minute of silence while smoke boiled toward the ceiling, and the acrid odor of burned powder filled the air. Then a yell went up from the bystanders. They surged forward, all seeking to clap Allison on the back, congratulate him. They shouted for Lambert to set out more whiskey, more glasses.

Outside in the street the pound of running feet signified the coming of others, drawn by the racket of gunfire. McMains, Longwell, Mills, Donohue — a dozen more. Lambert was abruptly swamped with demand for service as a victory celebration got under way and began to gather momentum. Longwell and those with him had their look at Griego's lifeless shape, turned, and went on about their business.

There was another rush of sound in the street, this time of horses racing up and sliding to a quick halt. Several of Allison's ranch hands came in. They had got word somehow of the impending meeting between their boss and Pancho Griego and, fearing the Mexican's followers might gang up on Allison, had hurried to be on hand. They arrived too late for the shoot-out, but

**192**

they were ready if the natives wished to carry the incident further.

But there was no need. No threat of vengeance or retaliation on the part of the Spanish and Mexican natives was in evidence. Their champion had been Pancho Griego, whether by desire or not, and he had been overcome, even though he had resorted to trickery. They were willing to let it end there.

The gathering swelled steadily. Someone dragged Griego's body off to one side of the room, out of the way. Sooner or later some of his followers would arrive and claim it. Shouts filled the saloon, loud cries, and laughter. A voice called upon Allison for his famed Indian-chief war dance. He complied, and the noisy celebration went on well into the late hours.

Down the street in his quarters Oscar McMains considered his next move. Cruz Vega was dead, yes, and so now was Pancho Griego. But the men behind the murder of Parson Tolby were still at large, still walking the streets of Cimarron — Longwell and Mills. And Florencio Donohue. Also there were the higher-ups, the big, powerful politicians. Only the tool, in the form of Cruz Vega, had been removed. The real culprits were still free. How was he to reach them?

Cardenas! He suddenly recalled the name of the friend Cruz Vega had mentioned. He had almost overlooked that. Cardenas could be made to talk. Cardenas could be the key. McMains went about organizing a meeting of the vigilantes, including Clay Allison.

"We'll do this according to law," Allison said flatly, "or we don't do it at all."

McMains stirred impatiently. "That's the long way around. It takes too much time. I say we handle it just like we did Vega."

Pete McQueen moved up to side with Allison. He faced the thirteen members of the vigilantes who had gathered behind Lambert's. "I vote with Clay. Let Rinehart get out a warrant. There'll be plenty of time to see that justice is done after he's been arrested."

There was a general round of approval to McQueen's statement. The bad taste of the Cruz Vega affair was still with most of them, and, like Clay Allison, they had begun to wonder about Oscar McMains.

"All right," the printer said, throwing up his hands as a sign of defeat, "I'll go to Rinehart and swear out a warrant for Cardenas's arrest. But if it looks like Mills and Waldo are going to let him off, like they did Vega, then the vigilantes had better act."

McQueen stared thoughtfully at McMains. "Are you trying to find out who's behind the murder of the parson . . . or are you interested in seeing just how many men you can get killed off around here?"

McMains flushed angrily. "That's a hell of a thing to say to a man! I'm not trying to get anybody killed. I just made up my mind I wouldn't quit until I got to the bottom of this affair."

"Lately I've been wondering," McQueen said. "I get a little tangled up in my thinking. I'm not sure whether we're doing this for the parson's sake or just to get back at the syndicate."

**194**

McMains glared at the rancher. "Any time you don't like the way I run things, you've got a right to speak up."

"I'll sure do that," McQueen said. "And I reckon there's a few more here that feel the same."

Allison stepped between the two men. "Let it go, Pete. We'll get this Cardenas matter handled, then we'll see what the next mile looks like. Oscar, you go on over to Rinehart's office and get that warrant issued."

McMains left immediately, saying no more.

McQueen watched him depart in silence. He shook his head. "I don't know about that man, Clay. I've got a hunch there's a lot of hate inside him that keeps him thinking wrong."

"Could be," Allison said.

Sheriff Rinehart arrested Cardenas and lodged him in jail near noon the next day. By the middle of the afternoon McMains had a rider on the road to Allison's ranch, summoning him and other vigilantes to town. When, near dark, Clay walked into the printer's cluttered quarters, the fiery little man thrust a newspaper at him.

"Here . . . take a look at this."

It was a copy of the *Santa Fé New Mexican*. In it appeared an editorial in which the newspaper apologized to Dr. Longwell and Attorney Melvin Mills for mentioning their names in the previous news item relative to the Vega killing. They had not been named by Vega in his so-called confession, the writer stated. It had been only a rumor which the newspaper, unfortunately, had not verified before printing the report.

McMains was livid. "It's nothing but a cover-up," he declared, pacing back and forth. "They're both guilty as sin. That bunch in Santa Fé is just trying to hush up the facts."

Allison read the article in silence and wondered. He passed the newspaper on to the other men who had arrived in the room.

McMains continued. "What's more, I hear Mills is getting a writ. He's going to get Cardenas out of jail. That's proof he's afraid the man will talk."

"Are you sure about that?" Allison asked.

"I've got a man over at Rinehart's office now. If a writ is to be issued, he'll let me know."

"We'll wait and find out," Allison said. "You can reach us at Lambert's."

The rumor was verified a short time later. Near midnight the vigilantes surrounded the jail. Quietly and efficiently they removed Cardenas and took him to the same place where Cruz Vega had been forced to confess.

"Do you know who paid Vega to kill Tolby?" McMains asked.

Cardenas shook his head sullenly. "I don't know anything about it."

"Maybe you and Vega both did the job," the printer suggested.

Cardenas stubbornly moved his head. "I don't know anything."

**196**

"I'll give you just one more chance to talk," McMains said, "otherwise you'll hang like Vega did. Put the rope around his neck."

Protesting violently, Cardenas was dragged beneath the tree. The rope was tossed over an outreaching limb.

"All right," McMains said through his mask, "speak up or you're a dead man. Who hired you and Vega to kill Parson Tolby?"

"I don't know."

"String him up!" McMains shouted.

Cardenas's feet dangled above the ground, and he began to thresh about.

"Was it Doctor Longwell and that lawyer, Mills? Was it Florencio Donohue? Hurry up . . . speak!"

Cardenas began to strangle. "Yes . . . yes! They were the ones!"

The rope slackened. Cardenas fell to the earth in a moaning heap.

"There!" McMains exclaimed triumphantly. "You all heard it. You know now . . ."

A sudden commotion off to one side of the party broke off his words. Sheriff Rinehart with four heavily armed deputies pushed their way into the center of the gathering.

"Don't any of you reach for a gun," he warned. "Not unless you want a bellyful of buckshot."

He brushed by McMains to where Cardenas lay. He reached down, took the man by the arm, and helped him to his feet.

"You all right, *amigo?*"

Cardenas recognized the lawman and began to pour out his story in a torrent of Spanish. "I did not kill anyone, sheriff. They made me confess. I did not want to die."

"You won't die," Rinehart said. "Not here, anyway." He turned, faced the silent rank of masked men. "I'm taking my prisoner back to jail. If any of you try to follow, we'll use these scatter-guns on you."

There were no attempts to halt the lawmen and their prisoner. They were allowed to depart in silence When they were beyond earshot, McMains removed his mask and turned to the vigilantes.

"You all heard him. He confessed. It was Mills and Longwell and Donohue that hired them to murder Tolby. I'm dead certain there were others. We've got to find out who they are."

"He took back that confession," someone pointed out. "He'll probably do the same thing again in front of the judge."

"There's only one thing we can do," McMains said, "and that's get him again. This time we'll make him tell everything he knows about it."

"Not tonight we won't," another voice spoke up. "If we try, somebody is going to get killed."

"And by tomorrow morning Mills will have him out on that writ and hid away where we'll never find him," McMains insisted. "We'll have lost our best bet."

"Maybe not," Allison said, coming into the conversation. "I think Cardenas does know something. We'll give Rinehart and his boys a chance to get him back inside jail and quieted down, then we'll spring him again. I know this Cardenas. He killed a man over in Taos a few years ago. He was sentenced to hang but somebody high up got him off. He's the kind who could be hired to do a job of murder."

In the cold, dark hours before dawn the vigilantes acted again. They took Cardenas from his cell and extracted a second confession from him. This time somebody wrote it down, and Cardenas placed his mark to the paper. He was then escorted back to the jail to await trial, faced with the confession he had acknowledged. Two men conducted him to the door of the stone building. They halted there while one man fumbled with the lock. In the stillness of the early hour a gunshot suddenly cracked. Cardenas spun half about, fell heavily, dead before he hit the ground. The vigilantes scattered, fading off into the darkness, no one certain who had fired the fatal bullet or whence it had come. All that was positive was that Cardenas was dead.

Cimarron was in an uproar the following morning. The *News & Press* came out with a stirring story, accusing Clay Allison of being the ruthless leader of a bloodthirsty violent gang dedicated to murder from behind masks and holding Colfax County in a state of fear and confusion. Allison, hearing of it, called on the editor, Dawson. He hauled the man up short by his shirt front and punched him soundly on the nose.

"Any more such remarks," he warned, "and I'll do much worse."

But the damage had been done. The natives at once concluded that Allison was in no way the friend they had once thought him to be and was, indeed, their worst enemy. Even the *gringo* newspaper said so. They armed themselves for protection, and more fuel was thus heaped upon the steadily burning Cimarron country conflagration.

Several of the town's citizens called upon Isaac Rinehart, demanding Allison's arrest. The sheriff was agreeable, but Clay was no ordinary man to bring in. Besides, he was never alone now. There were always some of his cowboys with him. Rinehart did the logical thing. He sent a message to Governor Samuel Axtell in Santa Fé. He gave the details of the situation in Cimarron, asking for military assistance from Fort Union.

McMains, meanwhile, spurred onward by the written confession Cardenas had signed, camped on the lawman's doorstep and demanded that warrants be sworn out for the arrest of the three men Cardenas had named — Mills, Longwell, and Donohue. Rinehart, plagued on all sides by ultimatums, closed his ears to everyone and waited for a reply from Axtell.

Rumors began to make the rounds that the natives were gathering for a showdown fight. They were enlisting the aid of nearby Indian tribes, convincing them they would share the land again if the *Tejanos* were driven out. McMains sent out for more help, his story to the settlers and squatters being that the Maxwell Land & Railway people were back of it all, that they were arming the natives and the Indians in an all-out effort to drive them out of the country. The response to that was immediate. Cimarron began to fill up with men ready to fight to the last ditch.

"Get behind Clay Allison," McMains told them. "You all know him. You know what he stands for in this country."

Those were the magic words, and McMains well knew it. Unbidden by Allison, an army took form, grew in Cimarron, awaiting only his command. Guards took up posts and ringed the settlement. Men were dispatched to keep close watch on the Indians, camped in the hills behind the town. They were told to report any concerted move on the part of the native population.

Several citizens packed and moved out, unwilling to become a part of the bloodletting that was sure to come. The majority stood fast, believing the governor in Santa Fé would accede to Rinehart's plea and supply the necessary aid from the fort. McMains continued his agitation for the arrest of the three men he believed involved in Tolby's murder. A delegation of citizens called upon him, advising him that, even if Rinehart issued the warrants for the arrests, they would not permit the lawman to execute them. They would agree to nothing, they told the printer, so long as the town was in the hands of Clay Allison and his cowboys.

McMains drove them from his office. If Isaac Rinehart did not act, the vigilantes would take matters into their own hands. He would give the lawman twenty-four hours more in which to do something.

Allison, with McQueen, was still trying to learn who had fired the bullet that killed Cardenas — a vigilante or a someone interested in closing the man's mouth before he could talk. He was getting nowhere. Advised of McMains's threat, he immediately declared no such thing would ever take place while he had any control over it.

Caught up in the swiftly moving events, he decided he would try again to hear the truth, if possible, from Longwell himself. He had come to consider the physician a friend, remembering the care and attention the doctor's wife had given him when he was wounded. He rode to the physician's home. After some delay, Mrs Longwell opened the door.

"I would like to see the doctor," Clay said. "There's been a lot of talk that I want to get the straight of. I've tried to reach him before, but he somehow is never available."

Mrs Longwell glanced beyond him to the dozen or more heavily armed cowboys, waiting in the street. There was no friendliness in her voice when she replied. "He's not here, Clay. And I don't know where he is."

Allison shook his head. "He doesn't need to fear me, Missus Longwell. Neither do you. I'm just trying to iron this thing out."

The physician's wife stepped back. "The doctor is not here. I don't know when he'll be back," she said, and slammed the door.

Allison turned and walked slowly back to his horse. An hour later he was told by one of the guards that Longwell had been seen riding fast toward Santa Fé. Should they go after him and bring him back? Clay shook his head. No, let him go. Why force him? If a friend felt as Longwell evidently did, fearing him so greatly he would flee, then let him go.

McMains seized upon Longwell's flight as an admission to guilt. "Mills is gone, too," he pointed out. "Left town yesterday, I hear. That proves he was in on it, also. We had better get Donohue before he lights out!"

The word went around swiftly. Longwell and Mills had fled. The vigilantes were looking for Florencio Donohue and would capture him before he, too, could escape. A delegation of natives stopped Allison on the street. They repeated the promise the businessmen had made earlier to McMains: they would fight until every last Mexican, Spaniard, and Indian was dead before they would allow him and his *Tejanos* to take Donohue. Allison replied that he did not want the man, that if anyone did, it was the sheriff. The natives were not placated. For a man to be locked in a cell by the lawman meant only that he was more easily available for the *Tejanos* to lay their hands upon him.

The November ninth issue of the *Santa Fé New Mexican* advised the world that Cimarron was an armed camp in the hands of a vigilante mob that would not relinquish its grip until certain men were turned over to it for drastic punishment. Rinehart sweated out the interminable hours. There had been no reply from Governor Axtell, no word from Fort Union. He knew he could not keep the opposing factions apart much longer. Tension was such that sooner or later an incident would touch off the explosion, and Cimarron would become a battleground.

And then the answer came. Soldiers would be dispatched from the fort. They would arrive soon. Hold out a bit longer. As for Clay Allison, dodgers were being printed up for immediate distribution. He was being declared a dangerous outlaw — wanted, dead or alive. The reward placed on his head by Governor Axtell was five hundred dollars. The date was February 21, 1876.

## XIV

An aroused and angry Melvin Mills arrived in Cimarron the next day. He went directly to McMains and Allison. He had not run away, fearing justice, as they had said. He had been in Trinidad, appearing before the court on a mining case. He was not afraid to face his accusers and had returned to learn what was taking place. He would stand trial that very day, if they wished. A crowd gathered about the lawyer, threatening and ready for mob action. A rope suddenly was produced.

"Hang the murderer!" a voice shouted.

"String him up!"

The demand caught fire, sweeping through the streets. Allison looked beyond the group, seeing the natives and Indians silently assembling along the fringe of the town. Melvin Mills meant nothing to them personally; he was just another *gringo*. But he represented the opposition to the *Tejanos*, and that somehow placed him on the same side of the fence as Griego, Cardenas, and Cruz

204

Vega. They were armed, and Clay recalled their earlier promise. Blood would flow soon in Cimarron unless something was done and done quickly.

He raised his hands above his head, calling for silence. The hubbub gradually died.

"Mills says he is willing to stand trial. Let him do that."

"When . . . a year from now?" a voice demanded. "I say we hang him while we got a chance. We know he's in with the bunch that's behind all these murders."

Allison waved down the immediate chorus of assents to that suggestion. "Trial will be held today, here in Cimarron."

A friend of the attorney's pushed forward. "What are you trying to do, Allison? Railroad Mills into jail? He won't have a chance."

"You think he's got a chance with this mob?" Clay demanded. "Personally, I don't give a damn what happens to Mills . . . except I don't want to see him lynched. The best place in the world for him would be inside a cell where they couldn't get to him."

Mills's friend nodded. "I guess that's right."

"Here's what we'll do. You pick twelve men, and we'll pick twelve. They can form a grand jury and dig into the matter. We'll let them decide if he's guilty or not."

Mills was consulted on the plan and was immediately agreeable. He selected the men who would represent him. Allison and McMains chose the twelve for the opposition. The inquiry got under way at once. And while questions, answers, charges, and counter-charges hurtled back and forth, Cimarron waited in tense anticipation for the results. Noon came, then afternoon passed, and there was still no word. McMains's followers, who had clamored for immediate punishment in the form of a hangman's noose, began to grow restive. The natives, having no reports on the fate of the *gringo* for whom they stood, grew suspicious, fearing that somehow they had been tricked.

Allison, dreading the approach of night, put his cowboys to patrolling the streets with orders to keep everyone indoors, away from the building where the inquiry was being conducted. Immediately there were several minor clashes as the cowboys carried out instructions, but no serious incidents arose.

And then, just at dark, an Army officer rode into the plaza. He approached Allison, giving him a stiff soldier-to-civilian salute.

"I am McLellan from Fort Union. My men have surrounded the town. I order you and every man here to surrender your firearms."

Some of the old aversion to Yankees swelled up in Clay Allison. He did not appreciate the officer's supercilious manner, and for a long minute he considered the possibilities of ignoring the order and telling the bluecoat to go to hell. It would mean wholesale bloodletting, and there had already been enough men killed and wounded in the Cimarron country the past year.

He gave the order, and his followers laid down their guns. The natives and the Indians followed suit, and the Army took over, setting up camp in the plaza. The questioning of Melvin Mills recessed for the night, and the lawyer was placed in jail with an armed guard thrown around the building for his protection.

The next day, Judge Henry Waldo came into town to take charge of and preside over the hearing. McMains immediately set up a clamor for the jurist to order the return of Longwell that he might also be made to face trial along with Mills, but Longwell refused to heed and remained in Santa Fé.

The investigation continued with neither side making any headway. Very little proof could be offered that clearly implicated the attorney in having had a hand in the murder of the Reverend Tolby and the others slain on the Cimarron, and the would-be trial rapidly degenerated into little more than a name-calling contest. McMains, seeing the handwriting of failure on the wall in the guise of an acquittal, began to agitate among his more gullible followers for vigilante action in spite of the soldiers present in the settlement.

Allison acted again. He sought out a local justice of the peace, petitioning him for a withdrawal of charges against Mills and a declaration of the lawyer's innocence. The justice granted the writ, and Allison presented it to Waldo, who immediately declared the hearing at an end and Melvin Mills a free man.

Allison and a dozen of his cowboys, unknown to McMains, escorted Mills to a waiting horse a short distance down the road to Santa Fé and put him in the saddle.

"My advice to you," he said to the attorney, "is to get out of here and stay out. Don't come back to Cimarron if you value your life. Next time I may not be around to protect you."

"Protect me!" Mils exclaimed angrily. "It's because of you I've had to go through all this. People in Colfax County wouldn't feel as they do if it weren't for you and Oscar McMains."

"Maybe," Allison replied, "but that can't be helped now. The best thing for you is to stay away from the Cimarron country."

"I'll do just as I please," Mills declared. "And don't think you've seen the last of me. I'll square up with you and McMains, Allison, if it's the last thing I ever do."

The lawyer, having accepted Clay's help nevertheless, started off down the road for the capital city. Allison watched him until he was out of sight, then turned, and rode back to town with his men. McMains would become a raving madman when he learned what had happened. Likely he would attempt to persuade some of the vigilantes to act, this time against Florencio Donohue. That man was now the only one left in Cimarron on whom the printer-pastor could vent his hatred.

When they reached the edge of the settlement, two riders approached and halted them.

"Clay, they've got a wanted poster up for you," one of them reported. "The governor has offered a five-hundred dollar reward, dead or alive."

Allison, amazed, was unable to believe it. "Did you see that dodger yourself?"

The cowboy nodded. "It's tacked up on the board in front of Rinehart's office. I read it myself."

"I sure have to see that," Allison said, and headed on into town.

With his riders backing him, he pulled up in front of the jail and dismounted. Handing the reins of the black gelding to one of the men, he walked to the bulletin board used generally by the sheriff for legal notices of sales and auctions. The poster was there plain for anyone to see. He was declared outlaw with a price on his head.

Angrily he wheeled about, stalked into Rinehart's office who was known to be a pro-ring man.

"Where's the sheriff?"

The deputy motioned vaguely toward the town. "Out somewheres."

Allison studied the man for a moment. "He wouldn't be out talking to the Army about me, would he?"

The deputy shrugged. "He might be."

Allison spun around, moving through the doorway. He came face to face with Rinehart, apparently just returning from his meeting with McLellan. Allison pointed to the poster.

"What's this all about, Isaac?"

Rinehart leaned back against the wall of the building. "You know as much about it as I do, Clay. I got it in from Santa Fé this morning."

"Then went straight to the Army and asked them to take me in, is that it?"

Rinehart stirred. "Well, I did talk to McLellan."

"Did he agree to do your job for you?"

Again the lawman moved uncomfortably. "Matter of fact, no. He said it wasn't an Army problem."

Allison laughed. "That's the first time I ever knew a Yankee soldier to use good sense. Do you figure to do it yourself, Isaac?"

Rinehart shook his head. "Don't make things any tougher for me than they already are, Clay. I'm just trying to do a job. I'm going to let it ride until I know more about it."

"That's a good way to look at it," Clay said. In a way he felt sorry for the old lawman. The past months had been trying ones for him, with troubles besetting him at every point. He added: "Now, I don't plan to let anybody collect that reward. You might pass the word around. But any time you'd like to talk things over, you know where my place is."

"Sure," Rinehart murmured.

"And I'll be riding in, off and on, the same as usual."

"I know that, too," the lawman said and, turning, went into his office.

## XV

Oscar McMains never gave up the battle. He continued to hammer away at the hated syndicate, at the political ring in Santa Fé, and at all those he felt were in some way connected with the murder of Reverend Tolby. But he did it without the aid of Clay Allison and those who followed the handsome rancher.

Clay had come thoroughly to know and understand McMains in those days preceding the Mills hearing and now recognized the printer for what he was. Consequently, once Melvin Mills was safely out of

Cimarron, Allison refused flatly to have anything more to do with McMains, advising his friends to follow a like course. McMains was a fanatic, a troublemaker who would do anything — cold-blooded murder not excluded — to gain an advantage or prove a point. Clay Allison was not making the mistake of believing him a second time, and he warned McMains not to connect his name in any way with his activities. McMains deplored the desertion. He needed Allison and the respect the man commanded. But Clay had enough of the McMains brand of intrigue. He was through.

On his own and at the head of a select band of honest men, Clay rode the Cimarron, continuing to do what he could to protect those unable to stand against the syndicate's hired dispossessors that winter. There was much violence and gun play, enough to satisfy any man, but, when matters began to taper off with the coming of warmer weather, even he was glad to put his mind to ranching chores. With spring came new and different developments.

Rinehart received a new wanted poster on Clay. The reward had not been changed, but a new charge had been added. He was wanted for questioning as to the disappearance of Chunk Tolbert's friend, Cooper. It was a startling turn, one he found difficult to believe. He knew nothing of Cooper other than that he had seen him well on his way to Colorado that day of the Tolbert shooting. What could he tell them about the man?

He was standing on the porch that fronted the Lacy ranch house when one of his cowboys raced up, drawing to a halt in the yard.

"Clay . . . get out of here fast! Soldiers are coming for you!"

Allison walked into the open. "Soldiers?" he repeated. "What do you mean?"

"They've been to your place and found out you were over here. There must be a couple hundred of them."

Allison laughed. "They're sure coming well prepared. The sheriff with them?"

The cowboy nodded. "He was the one who did the talking to your wife. I've passed the word. The boys will be showing up pretty quick."

Allison considered for a few moments. "No need," he said after a bit. "I'll first see what Rinehart's got on his mind."

"We already know what he's got on his mind. They figure to arrest you for that Cooper deal at the Clifton House. They think you killed him."

Clay said: "Well, I sure didn't. And I can't tell them who did, if he's dead."

"I can't see as it makes any difference," the cowboy said. "You say the word, and we'll take over."

"Sit tight. We'll hear what Rinehart has to say."

The soldiers came into view shortly thereafter. The sheriff, a young captain at his shoulder, approached Allison somewhat warily.

"Clay, I'm going to have to arrest you. Orders from the governor. You know what it's all about, I reckon."

Allison said: "All about nothing far as I can tell. I don't know anything about this Cooper."

The lawman nodded. "If you say that, I believe it. But you'll have to go to court." He paused, glancing about as several riders wheeled into the yard. Allison's followers were gathering swiftly, primed to fight. The lawman swung to the Army officer.

"Captain, this man has to be taken to Taos for arraignment. I'll need you and your men to accompany us."

The young officer shook his head. "My orders call for aiding you in the arrest, no more than that. If you need to take him to Taos, you'll have to do it yourself. That is, unless you want to wait until I can get in touch with headquarters."

Allison broke in. "Why Taos, Sheriff?"

"Orders from Santa Fé," Rinehart answered. Again he swept the growing crowd of armed cowboys with his eyes. "Expect that's the reason, Clay. These men of yours will make trouble if the hearing is held in Cimarron . . . and God knows we've had enough of that."

Allison smiled. "All right, Isaac. You don't need to fret . . . and you won't need any soldiers. I'll go with you to Taos, but it will be on my terms. I keep my gun, and it'll be just the two of us. No deputies."

An injured look crossed Rinehart's seamed face. "You know me better than that, Clay. Money doesn't mean that much to me."

"Maybe not to you," Clay replied. "About somebody else I wouldn't be so sure. And I like to keep the odds even."

Rinehart thought for a time. "You'll give me your word that you'll go peaceable, and that I won't have any trouble from your boys?"

"You've got my word," Allison said. He faced the riders, awaiting his instructions. "No need for you to come along. Just stick around home. If I need you, I'll send word."

Rinehart was satisfied. He knew Allison's word was good, and he need worry no more about it. They returned to Cimarron, where Clay learned that McMains also had been arrested. He, too, was to face trial in a distant town — Mora.

They made their preparations for the sixty-odd mile journey and set out near the middle of the afternoon. It was a long ride, and Clay Allison was alternately light-hearted and thoughtful during its course.

"What's behind this, Isaac?" he wondered. "Why would they dig back and bring up this Cooper? Who is so interested in him?"

Rinehart did not know. "My instructions came straight from the governor," he said. "No details, no explanations, no nothing. Just take you to Taos for an arraignment."

They arrived in the mountain settlement late the next morning. Clay delighted acquaintances along the street by exchanging his wide-brimmed hat for Rinehart's derby and wearing it into court. He appeared before the judge, heard the charges, and was then bound over for the regular fall term. Bond was set at five hundred dollars.

"You will collect the appearance bail," the judge charged Rinehart, "and be responsible for the prisoner."

But Isaac Rinehart didn't feel it was necessary. He said nothing about the money to Clay on the ride back to Cimarron, and the rancher made no offer to pay. Allison's word that he would appear in Taos for the hearing at the specified time was enough for the lawman.

Back on his ranch and following the daily routine of living, Clay began to wonder about the matter. Things had moved so swiftly after the new charge had been placed against him that he had not had time really to think it through. He could not understand how such an accusation could be lodged against him, and the idea of being considered an outlaw by the state government rankled him more deeply than it had at first. He was no desperado. He was a rancher, a cattleman, living and doing what he considered his right and duty. That the governor should brand him as an outlaw seemed far from just.

"I'm going to Santa Fé and talk to Axtell," he told John one morning, a few days later. "I figure to get this thing straightened out."

"You can't just ride into Santa Fé with a price on your head," John objected. "There's bound to be somebody who'll try to collect it."

"I'll take that chance," Clay replied, and made ready to leave.

When he reached Cimarron and turned into Lambert's for a drink, he learned something of interest. Governor Axtell was not in Santa Fé at the moment. He was, in fact, on the road between the capital and

Raton, headed for Denver, where he was scheduled to attend a meeting.

"I understand he plans to spend the night at the Clifton House," Henri Lambert said.

Allison departed at once. He rode hard and, late that afternoon, overtook the coach in which the governor was traveling. Since there was nothing definite to the information that the territorial chief executive would spend the night at Stockton's place, Allison took no chances. He boarded the coach in highwayman fashion and sat down on the seat opposite Axtell.

The governor was first startled, then angry, after Clay introduced himself. He settled back and glared at the rancher. It was early June, 1876.

"What do you want from me? A pardon?"

Clay shook his head. "Only some answers and an explanation. No more than that."

Axtell looked at him sharply. He was puzzled. "An explanation of what?"

"Why did you declare me an outlaw and put a price on my head? I'm no outlaw."

"You caused quite a bit of trouble in Cimarron, from the reports I received. You and your wild bunch of cowboy vigilantes. And still are."

"We acted only in what appeared to be the best interests of everybody concerned. There's two sides to that story, Governor."

"Granted," Axtell said. "And you'll have a chance to tell yours in the courtroom at Taos."

"But this new charge you brought up says I'm wanted for questioning over a man named Cooper. Why

Cooper? I admit I had a run-in with his friend, Tolbert. But why bring up Cooper?"

Axtell shook his head. "Mills thought it was the best . . ."

"Mills?" Allison echoed. "Melvin Mills? Is he the one behind this? Is this his idea?"

Axtell flushed. "Mills is handling it, yes."

That explained many things. Mills was carrying out his promise, his threat. He couldn't find anything to hang onto Allison in Cimarron, so he was reaching back into the past and dragging out the Tolbert-Cooper incident.

"This is a spite deal, Governor," Clay said, keeping the anger from his voice. "Mills has had it in for me because of the trouble in Cimarron. And the funny part of it is that I'm the man who saved his neck. I got him out and on his way to Santa Fé, likely before something bad happened to him. Looks like the joke is on me."

"You're only up for questioning," Axtell said.

"No matter what I'm up for, I see I can't expect a fair trial if Mills is behind it."

"Whose idea was it to hold it there?"

Allison looked at Axtell blankly while the coach rocked and swayed over the road. "Yours . . . at least that's what the sheriff said."

"No, it wasn't mine," the governor said instantly, and then caught himself. "Well, no matter. I understand you never paid the bail money."

"No, it wasn't necessary. I said I would be there, and I shall. The judge didn't need to try and make me guarantee an appearance by putting up cash. Now,

217

maybe he should have enforced payment. Things have changed since I know who is behind all this."

"It seems so," Axtell murmured. "What if I gave you my word you'll receive a fair hearing. Would that make a difference in your thinking?"

Allison studied the executive's face for a moment. "Your word and your hand on it would."

Axtell extended his hand. Allison accepted it. "Good enough for me, Governor," he said. "I'll be there."

## XVI

Despite the seven-thousand-foot altitude of Taos, the courtroom was stifling that summer day when Clay Allison's trial began. Judge Henry L. Waldo was on the bench and W. S. Ritch, a stranger to Clay, was the prosecuting attorney. He looked in vain for Melvin Mills but never saw him. For the defense, a young lawyer new to the Cimarron country, Charles Springer, had been engaged.

Outside the crowded building a ring of Fort Union soldiers had been thrown. Rumors had reached Axtell that Allison's cowboys were quietly assembling in the small mountain settlement, ready to take a hand if matters did not go to suit them. It was rumor only. True to his word Allison had instructed his followers and friends to stay clear of the proceedings. Someone seeking to prejudice both Axtell and the court had circulated the false information.

Ritch made a highly inflammatory speech, calling to Allison's mind some of the vicious tirades he had heard from the lips of Oscar McMains. It was apparent to all that he had a very flimsy case and sought to conceal that fact by dragging up every unsavory incident and rumored activity connected with Clay Allison.

"He has been the scourge of the Cimarron," Ritch declared. "He has plundered and murdered at will. No one knows how many good and honest men have died at his hands or at his orders. Usually they were shot in the back. He has a history of violence, a background of trouble. From the day his Indian mother gave him birth, he has been a constant problem. And in the War Between The States he stood for neither side but led a rapacious band of guerrillas in murderous raids and forays upon helpless people."

Allison sat in moody silence, listening to the lawyer speak, hearing Springer raise his interrupting objections, seeing Waldo pound his desk for order when the audience grew noisy or demonstrative at some remark or assertion. Suddenly he was sick of the Cimarron. He did not think such a moment could ever come, but it had. The old urge to move on, to see new country, other towns and places, was on him again. That he had remained on the Cimarron for so many years was unusual for him — a tribute to Dora, and the fact that the valleys and hills of New Mexico had always been close to his heart. He had loved the Cimarron, just as Dora loved it, and it would be hard to leave. But now there was a bad taste in his mouth.

"Cooper was a good man," Ritch insisted. "Even a harmless one. There was no reason for Clay Allison to do away with his life, to murder him . . ."

Springer was on his feet again. "Objection, Your Honor! That this Cooper is dead has never been proved. I challenge the prosecuting attorney to produce one shred of evidence, indicating that he is deceased. I challenge the prosecuting attorney to produce a body, or anyone who ever saw the dead body of this Cooper."

"Sustained," Waldo muttered. "The prosecuting attorney will kindly stick to facts."

"Griego, Tolbert, Vega, Cardenas are only a few of the men we know positively were murdered by Clay Allison. Many more could be added to the list if the defendant or some of his wild bunch could be made to talk. The number, I fear, would astound you. And add to it those luckless men he encountered in previous years when he rode the trails for cattle companies. How many innocent men were lynched by him and his lawless followers on the excuse that they were rustlers?"

*He would quit the Cimarron, move somewhere new, start again. Maybe this time in another business. There was money to be made as a cattle dealer, buying and selling. Maybe he would take a fling at that. And there was gold mining. Some he knew had done right well digging out the precious metal.*

"He walked the streets and rode the highways of the Cimarron country, a veritable arsenal in absolute defiance of all concepts of law and order," Ritch intoned. "He laughed in the face and at the rights of duly elected peace officers, went to great lengths in making their lives miserable. He is the shining example of lawlessness for all the world to look upon and, as such, the territory and all men charged by it to uphold the law must see that he does not go unpunished."

Springer got to his feet. He bowed politely to the court and then calmly and methodically ripped Ritch's case to ribbons. He brushed aside the statements that referred to Allison's past, constantly reminding the court that the matter to be considered had to do with one Cooper, allegedly missing and assumed dead.

"The facts that Clay Allison's mother was not of Indian descent . . . that the guerrilla who operated at the close of the war was not Clay Allison but a man with a similar family name . . . that the persons known to have been killed by Clay Allison were not shot in the back but participants in a fair and honorable fight . . . as several witnesses will testify to, if called . . . are beside the point. But they serve to illustrate the inaccuracies the prosecuting attorney is guilty of. No one, nothing, is to be considered here but the matter of one Cooper. And to that end the prosecuting attorney can supply this court with no facts. He does not even know whether Cooper is alive or dead!"

Allison listened to the outbreak of applause. He heard Waldo gavel the room back to silence.

*Mining for gold or anything else really had no appeal for him. No use starting off on something he didn't like. And he should stick to a business he knew. He wasn't getting any younger. He was thirty-six, almost thirty-seven. A bit late to be learning a new way to make a living. He would talk it over with Dora. That was the important thing. He wanted Dora to be happy with whatever he did.*

221

Springer was still speaking. "He is a respected man, well thought of by the many who know him, either personally or by name only. He is honest. His word is good enough for any man . . . even to the law for whom the prosecuting attorney shed so many tears and felt such great sympathy. The sheriff deemed it unnecessary to insist on the cash bail the court imposed as a guarantee of appearance at this hearing by my client.

"The sheriff asked only his promise to be on hand. And he is here, gentlemen, as you all may see. No, I submit that we are dealing here with an honorable man, not a savage desperado, as my opponent would have you believe. And I call again to your attention no proof of crime has been presented, or will be presented. As intelligent men, I ask you, can you convict an honorable man on such evidence . . . or lack of evidence?"

Axtell had been true to his promise for, in the end, Clay Allison was a free man. The trial had been fair, and Charles Springer had handled the case capably. Ritch, who actually had no case at all, was satisfied that justice had been done. Clay, pleading guilty to assault, was fined one hundred dollars plus court costs. All charges against him were dropped and the reward poster rescinded. He returned to Cimarron more influential and well thought of than ever before.

But the restlessness did not leave with his resumption of the normal way of life, as he had thought it might. Somehow he had the feeling of a man who had just won a major battle but lost a war. He saw, or believed he saw, less friendliness in the eyes of men, particularly the natives. In its place there was only respect and not a little fear. If the court had declared him an honorable citizen, there were a few around Cimarron who did not concur.

McMains, in his trial at Mora, was found guilty and fined heavily. Only a technicality saved him from the hangman's noose. He reportedly stated that such a situation would never have come about if Clay Allison had been at his side — and broadly implied that such would have been the case had it been possible for Clay to do so.

"McMains!" Allison exclaimed when he heard. "I wish I had never met the man! He's worse than a locoed steer . . . crazy as a coot on this syndicate thing. For a little man he can stir up more trouble than a whole army!"

The local newspaper appeared with an article linking Clay once more to McMains. Allison immediately called on the editor, a newcomer who had succeeded Dawson and with whom he was unacquainted.

"Don't you mention my name with Oscar McMains again in any way," he told the man. "I have nothing more to do with him and never intend to. Let the matter drop."

"I run the newspaper," the editor said bravely. "I'll print what I see fit, and when I see fit."

"Not about me," Allison said. "I got in with McMains only because I wanted to see the killer of a friend brought to justice. Everything else that happened afterwards was a result. I'm through with it now. If you're so anxious to print something about me, print what I just said . . . it's the truth."

The editor saw it otherwise. He came out with several editorials that raked open old sores and scratched barely healed wounds. Allison, standing one night with a friend of his, Joe Curtis, in Lambert's saloon, read the latest tirade. He laid aside the paper and finished off his drink.

"Come on, Joe. We've got a little job to do."

Curtis looked up at him, grinning. "The newspaper?"

Allison nodded. "I warned that editor. Now I mean to teach him a lesson or two about getting things right."

They procured a buckboard from the livery stable and late that night drove up to the front of the Cimarron *News & Press*. The building was dark. They entered with no difficulty, ripped what parts they could off the printing press and loaded them along with several cases of type and other equipment onto the light wagon. They drove them to the Cimarron River and dumped the entire load into the deep water.

"By the time he gets all that fished out, maybe he will have had time to get his facts straight," Allison said as they rode back to town. "Can't keep a man from talking about me, but I sure can insist on it being the truth."

But there was nothing left for him on the Cimarron. He had known that with each succeeding day, and that night, as he made his way home, he came to a conclusion: it was time to move. He needed a change, a new life. He talked it over with Dora again, and the next morning he called John and Monroe to him.

"We're leaving," he said. "I'm turning the ranch over to you to run. Dora wants to visit relatives and friends in Sedalia for a spell. When that's done with, I don't know where we'll head for. I'll let you know."

The visit to Missouri lasted three months. Clay and Dora returned to the ranch in the Cimarron country but paused there only briefly. Clay had his mind made up about the future.

"I've decided to move to Colorado. I'm going into the buying-and-selling end of the cattle business."

It was like the old days in Texas again — the easy, carefree life but without the hard labor of driving herds over endless trails. Clay rode back and forth across northern New Mexico and southern Colorado, as far east as Dodge City and the other market towns in its vicinity. His own men hunted up sellers. And business was unexpectedly good. The demand for beef held firm, and Clay Allison prospered as he never had before.

He rode the finest horses, dressed in the best clothing money could buy, generally in co-ordinated outfits that distinguished him from all other men. His reputation had preceded him from the Cimarron as a man of both strength and honor — and as a hell-raiser *par excellence* when the occasion arose. Peace officers and saloonkeepers soon fell into the same state of mind as those of other towns when they saw him ride in, bent on having a good time or celebrating some particular event. By 1877 he was a firmly established citizen of the area, known to almost everyone and relied upon by most to champion any worthwhile cause. And there were many causes.

In the town of Trinidad there was a young woman by the name of Geraldine Shaw. She was an attractive girl who did sewing for some of the local women, generally at the home of her widowed father with whom she lived. Brigido Cordova was one of Trinidad's peace officers. He had noticed Geraldine on the street several times and became interested in her. At their first meeting, she turned him away in no uncertain terms, but Cordova was a persistent man who, because of the authority his job gave him, usually had his own way with the women he took a fancy to.

He pressed his suit, and Geraldine Shaw, fearing she was not strong enough to hold out against him, confided to her father. Shaw served warning on Cordova that, lawman or not, neither he nor his attentions were welcome, and that he was to stay away from Geraldine.

Cordova, brooding over what he deemed an insult, decided to pay a call on the Shaws and have it out with them. Geraldine saw him coming and warned her father, who immediately locked the door. Cordova, enraged, took up a position on the front porch and began to hammer and kick at the panel.

"You think you are better than me," he shouted. "I'll show you. You can't treat me this way. I'll break down this door."

The flimsy panel began to yield under his assault. Shaw, doing what any father protecting his child will do, seized his rifle and shot through the door. Cordova was killed instantly.

Word of the deputy's death spread rapidly. His friends began to gather in front of the Shaw place. Someone produced a rope, and the cry to lynch the old man went up. Matters suddenly were out of control, with peace officers and responsible citizens unable to cope with them.

A merchant in the crowd suggested: "Someone go get Clay Allison. He can handle this."

Two men set off for the cattle broker, who was staying with cowboys at the edge of town. The information spread through the gathering of Cordova's friends who were thirsting for Shaw's life — Clay Allison had been sent for and would arrive in a very few minutes. The crowd began to melt away, and, when Allison and his riders appeared shortly after that, there no longer was any lynch mob in evidence. The mere power of his name had been sufficient to scatter the Cordova avengers.

In the Colorado town of El Moro, Allison encountered a man known only as Buckskin Charlie. They met one day in Harrington's Saloon and fell to discussing the merits of hunting. Eventually they got into an argument over the best method to be used in stalking deer.

"On a horse," Clay insisted. "Deer are accustomed to horses and cattle. A man can slip up on a deer easy that way."

Buckskin Charlie could not see it. "The only thing is for a man to get down on his hands and knees, like the Indians do. It's the sure way, and, if you weren't wearing that knife and gun, I'd make you admit it."

Allison got to his feet, removing his weapons. "All right, start making me admit it."

227

Buckskin Charlie lunged, and the fight was on. They wrestled about the saloon for a bit, then stood toe to toe and slugged it out. The fight raged back and forth for a lengthy half hour, and finally Buckskin Charlie was on the floor, completely out. At first bystanders thought him to be dead, but a closer examination showed he was only severely beaten. He was carried to the hospital for treatment.

Later that day Clay, bathed and refreshed, was sitting in the lobby of the New State Hotel, close by Harrington's. It was his usual place of abode when in El Moro, and he often sat near the front window and watched the street while waiting for a buyer or a seller he was to meet.

Directly opposite a physician by the name of Menger maintained an office. While Allison did not know the medical man personally, he disliked the dusty, well-worn stovepipe hat he affected. To Clay it seemed out of place in the West, as he once told the room clerk, and some day he planned to tell the physician so.

That time came shortly before the supper hour. Allison, keyed up by both the brawl and generous portions of Harrington's liquor, saw Menger come from his office and start toward the hotel. Clay walked back to the desk, borrowed the double-barreled shotgun kept behind the counter for protection against holdups, then stationed himself in the hotel's doorway.

As Menger walked by, Allison took careful aim, leveled the weapon, and blasted the stovepipe hat to shreds. He calmly returned the gun to the clerk and, taking the dumfounded doctor by the arm, escorted

**228**

him to El Moro's principal store where he personally bought for him the finest Stetson in the house.

A cattle buyer named LeFevre was another man to feel the lash of Allison's temper. Caught in the act of manipulating a questionable deal, he took offense when Allison called his hand and termed him a disgrace to their calling.

"Without that gun you've got on, you wouldn't have the guts to talk to me that way," LeFevre said. He was a much larger man than Clay, taller and heavier.

Allison removed his gun belt and knife. LeFevre, like Buckskin Charlie, had his try. And also like Buckskin Charlie he took the beating of his life.

Clay Allison's love for good horseflesh never waned. He rode a fine black most of the time he lived in Las Animas, a town a few miles across the New Mexico border in Colorado, and was proud of the tricks the animal had learned. He never bothered to tie him to a hitching rail, simply allowing him to stand. When he was ready to ride, he whistled and the black came to him immediately. He sought to teach the animal to drink beer in order to share in celebrations, which were quite numerous, but the horse usually passed up the offering.

One day Allison had just completed a most profitable deal and decided the occasion required commemorating. He was alone, his cowboys having ridden on once the deal had been consummated. He entered Harrington's Saloon and called for a bucket of beer for his horse. The bartender complied, and Clay returned to the street where the black waited patiently. Allison set the beer down before him.

"Drink up, partner," he said. "It's you and me, old horse. The boys have gone, and John's not around. We'll have to do our celebrating together."

The horse nuzzled the bucket, tasted the beer, and promptly tipped it over. Allison laughed and, kicking the pail to one side, walked back into Harrington's. As he entered, he drew his gun, pointing it toward the ceiling.

"It's my day to howl!" he shouted. "And I'm sure going to have me a time doing it!" He emphasized the last remark by emptying the pistol.

Upstairs, in the room directly overhead, five men were engaged in a quiet game of draw poker: Jake Gross, young Miguel Otero, A. M. Blackwell, F. B. Nichols, and Pete Simpson. When bullets suddenly began to splinter through the floor beneath their feet and thud into the table on which they played and the chairs in which they sat, they scattered like startled quail, each man seeking a safe place to stand.

"It's Allison, sure as hell!" Gross yelled. "He may keep this up for hours."

"I'm not worried about how long he keeps it up," Simpson shot back. "I want some place to go right now."

A huge, nickel-trimmed Charter Oak cookstove stood in one corner of the room. The five men saw it at the identical moment and had the same thought. They rushed across to it, leaped aboard, thus placing its heavy iron body between themselves and the floor. It was somewhat crowded for five big men, but it served its purpose.

**230**

## XVII

In December, 1876 Clay had met his brother John in Las Animas. He had sold the ranch, land, buildings, and livestock to John for seven hundred dollars. There were papers to be signed, and certain other business matters to be transacted. They hurriedly got it all out of the way and headed for the nearest saloon for a drink.

"It's been a long time since we've been on a spree together," Clay said. "What do you say we have us a real time while you're here?"

"Suits me," John replied. "About all I've been doing since you left the Cimarron is work."

They rode into the main street of the settlement and pulled up before Clay's favorite saloon. Across the street Sheriff John Spear and his deputy, Charlie Faber, lounged against the front wall of the jail.

"Come on," Clay said. "I'd like for you to meet a friend of mine." He led John to where the two lawmen stood. "My brother, John, Sheriff," he said. "John, this is Sheriff Spear and his deputy, Charlie Faber."

The men shook hands all around. Faber looked John over speculatively. He spat. "Not another Allison, for hell's sake! Things are getting worse around here."

Clay looked at the man closely, not certain if the remark was meant to be humorous. Apparently it was not. Faintly angered he said: "I've given you no trouble, Charlie. You have no call to make a remark like that."

"Maybe," Faber replied. "And it could be that's so only because we're keeping mighty close tabs on you. They say you're a real big man back where you come from. Well, we're not a bunch of greenhorns up here. I've had to cut your kind down to size before."

"My kind?" Allison repeated, his voice suddenly quiet.

"Yes, your kind. Big talker. Fast gun with your mouth. I reckon you ought to know I got a few notches on my gun, too."

"Forget it, Charlie," Spear broke in, realizing that matters were getting out of hand. "There's no point in starting trouble."

"I'm not starting trouble," Faber replied. "I'm just warning this so-called badman he'd better not get out of line around here. I'm ready to find out just how good he is with that gun any time he calls the play."

Clay stiffened.

John saw the sure and unmistakable signs of violence settle in his brother's eyes. He took him by the arm. "Come on, Clay," he urged gently. "Let's get that drink."

Allison hung back for a moment, never removing his gaze from the deputy. "I'm not sure if I want to turn my back on this trigger-happy tin star or not," he murmured.

Spear stepped in between the two. "Never mind, Allison. Charlie's just shooting off his mouth. But watch yourself while you're in town. Don't start no ruckus."

Allison relented. He nodded and followed John back into the street. Shoulder to shoulder they walked into the saloon.

"What's chewing on that deputy?" John wondered after they had taken a place at the bar.

Clay, his anger cooled now, shook his head. "A friend told me the other day Faber had been doing some wide bragging. He said he was going to get me in a gun fight some day and take my scalp. It seems he wants to build himself a reputation as a tough gun marshal. I figured it was just whiskey talk. Now I'm not so sure."

"I'd say he was just hunting a chance to start something."

"He'll find it if he crosses me once more like he did out there," Clay said quietly.

With their bottle and glasses they moved away from the bar, settling down at one of the corner tables. They quickly forgot about Charlie Faber and began to enjoy themselves, talking about old times on the Cimarron, the early days by the Brazos, even the bitter, lean life they had known in Tennessee. John wanted someday to return to the old homestead, as did Monroe. Farming was what they liked and thoroughly understood. Not that ranching and cattle raising had not been good to them, but both yearned to get back to the soil.

"Not me," Clay said. "I'm never going back to that country to live. Nothing there for me."

The day wore on, turning finally to night. The saloon began gradually to fill as evening customers entered. Clay called them all over, introduced them to his brother, having a drink on each occasion.

The piano player showed up and fell to his job. The half dozen girls who worked the floor came on duty, and dancing began. Clay stood drinks for all.

"Come on, John," he shouted in high spirits. "Let's show them how we used to do it at Lambert's."

**233**

The merriment increased and with it the noise. More patrons came in, attracted by the laughter and the loud shouting and singing, and began to participate.

"The big chief goes on the warpath!" Clay yelled, and began to remove his clothing. "Let's give them the war dance, John!"

John began to disrobe. In very few minutes the pair was giving their version of an Indian dance, clad only in boots, drawers, and gun belt. Others took up the idea and confusion soared.

The doors of the saloon pushed back. Deputy Faber took up a stand just inside. The laughter died away; the piano ceased. Faber glanced about the room, bringing his surly attention to a halt on Clay. He looked him up and down slowly.

"Get rid of that gun," he ordered. "No weapons allowed in here."

Allison stared at the lawman. He let his eyes sweep the rest of the men in the saloon. Every man there had a gun on his hip. He turned back to Faber.

"Go to hell, Deputy. You make everybody else take off his gun, then I'll shed mine."

Faber glared at him for a moment, wheeled, and went back into the street. The piano struck up again, and the celebration resumed its noisy course. Clay called for a fresh round of drinks for everyone in the house. It was as the nights at Lambert's, the good times he had seen in Cimarron.

Then he was aware the saloon had abruptly fallen to silence once more. He turned to see the cause. Faber was back, a shotgun in his hands. A dozen or more friends were with him.

"I'm telling you for the last time, Allison," the deputy said, "drop your gun belt."

Clay turned slowly around to face the man. John eased up to his side. "And I'm telling you that when the rest of them in here do that, I'll do the . . ."

Faber brought the shotgun up fast, fired hurriedly. John Allison reeled backward, clutching at his side. Clay's pistol was out almost before the shotgun's blast was over. He emptied his weapon into the deputy, saw him stagger, and go down. He reloaded while smoke coiled about him, waiting for the men who backed Faber to make their move. They chose to pass it up, melting back into the darkness of the night.

Clay wheeled to his brother. Tears streamed down his face. It was the first time John had ever been hurt.

"It's not too bad," one of the girls said, examining the wound. "The doc can fix him up real easy."

Clay began to laugh, showing his relief. He crossed the room, seized Faber by the hair, dragging him to where his brother lay.

"Look here, John. Here's the son of a bitch that shot you. I got him for you. He's stone dead!"

The saloon doors banged open again. It was the sheriff this time, along with several merchants and the town's banker. Clay, gun still in hand, crouched beside his brother and faced them.

"What's going on here?" the lawman demanded. "That Faber there? Is he dead?"

"He's dead," Allison replied. "I killed him."

"Charlie started it," a man in the crowd spoke up. "He fired first, tried to shoot Clay there with that shotgun. Hit John instead."

The sheriff glanced about the saloon. "Is that the way of it?"

A dozen confirming replies broke out. The lawman nodded to Clay. "Put away that gun, Allison. You'll have no cause to use it." He knelt down beside John. "Is your brother bad hit?"

Clay said: "I don't think so. I'd appreciate it if somebody would get a doctor."

Several men moved for the doorway immediately. The sheriff glanced at Faber, then unpinned the badge from his vest. "I figured this was going to happen some day. Charlie's been honing for trouble. He was always wanting to take on somebody with a reputation."

"I heard him tell the other day how he was going to have it out with Mister Allison," the bartender volunteered.

"Well, looks like he did, only it didn't work out like he wanted," Spear said dryly. He swung back to Clay. "I'll have to hold an inquest, Allison. I reckon you're in the clear, but we still have to go through the motions. I expect you to stay around until it's over."

Clay said: "I'll be here, Sheriff. I want to look after my kid brother, there."

John recovered and returned to the Cimarron country after a preliminary hearing, held in Pueblo, dismissed any charge against either of them for lack of evidence. Clay rode on to Trinidad where he received a message from a drifting cowboy who sought him out.

"Mister White said to tell you Wyatt Earp shot down George Hoyt," the cowboy told Clay. "Earp killed him without no good reason. He wanted you to know that."

Allison brought the drifter a drink and sent him on his way. He thought about the news he had heard. He was no stranger to Dodge City where Earp was marshal. He had gone there often. Hoyt had been a friend as was White who, with a partner, along with several other enterprises operated a store where Clay generally purchased his clothing.

Clay knew and respected Wyatt Earp, but it was hard to understand why the lawman would find it necessary to kill Hoyt, ordinarily a mild and harmless sort of man. White must have figured there was something wrong, too, or else he would not have taken such pains to send word to Trinidad. He would simply have waited until Allison made one of his periodic visits to Dodge City and then informed him. Clay decided this was something that needed looking into and immediately headed out.

He had little use for trigger-quick lawmen who shot fast and without thought. In his estimation they were as low as the gunslingers they hunted. He remembered the time when one such lawman had killed another friend of his, Joe Smith, for no reason other than to prove his merit as a tough marshal. He and Smith had both been working for the Turkey Track spread over in the Panhandle. He spent the entire night hunting for the lawman who had taken cover when he learned Allison was searching for him. Bat Masterson had been in town at the time and McNulty, who owned the

Turkey Track, did his best to dissuade Allison, fearing the two would come together. Bat had stayed out of Allison's way. He wanted no trouble with a man of Clay's caliber and the gang of drunken cowboys who trailed along behind him to see the fun. Likely he was not afraid of Allison. It had simply been good sense to keep clear of the Tennessean's path at the time. Clay viewed gun marshals and gunslingers in the same light. Daybreak and McNulty finally combined to bring the search to an end, and he had ridden back to the Panhandle with the rest of the crew, his hatred for killer lawmen even more intense.

Now as Allison entered Dodge City's Main Street, he slanted for White's place. Stabling his horse at the rear, he gained the building by its back door. White was not in. It was late summer, dry and hot.

Clay, mopping the sweat from his forehead, said to the clerk: "When White comes in, tell him I've gone over to the Long Branch for a couple of drinks. I'll meet him there."

The saloon had its usual number of patrons for that hour of the day, and Allison settled himself at a table in the back after picking up a bottle and glass at the counter. He saw a few men he knew, spoke to them, talked for a time with one who had some beef to sell, and arranged to get in touch with him at a later date on the matter.

Three hours passed. White had not shown up when Allison arose, leaving the saloon. He stepped into the street and paused there to consider what he should do next — wait for White or look up Wyatt Earp.

At that moment the familiar figure of Bat Masterson moved toward him from an opposite corner. Masterson pulled to a halt before him, extending his hand.

"Hello, Clay. What brings you to Dodge?"

Allison shook his head. "I'm looking for Earp. I want to get the straight of his shooting down George Hoyt."

Masterson nodded. "I see, but why? Is there something you don't like about it?"

"I don't know . . . that's why I'm here. George wasn't the kind of man that needed killing."

Masterson shrugged. "George got drunk. He took a few shots at Wyatt, and Wyatt winged him. He died a few days later."

"George Hoyt tried to kill Earp? That's a little hard to believe, Bat."

"Well, believe it or not, that's the way it happened. It appears to most of us that somebody got George all fired up with liquor, then hired him to make a try. Wyatt's got a few enemies here in town. High-ups who don't like the way he's clamped down because it's costing them business."

"Did George say that before he died?"

"Not to me. I heard he'd said it. He wouldn't give any names."

"That could be the way of it," Allison said. "Still, I reckon I'd like to talk to Earp."

Masterson thought for a long moment. Then: "It might not be a very smart idea, Clay. You've had quite a few drinks, and you haven't shucked your gun. Why not let it go until latter?"

Allison said: "No, I'll see him now."

Masterson half turned, then stepped back. Earp had just come around the corner and was entering the street. Clay moved out slowly to intercept the assistant marshal.

"Wyatt," he said when they met, "I got word you shot down George Hoyt. I'd like to hear your reasons why."

The lawman studied Allison's face for a time. Around them the street cleared quietly. "I had one good reason, Clay. He tried to gun me. I got him instead. How did you hear about it?"

"Friend of ours sent me word."

A strange expression crossed the lawman's face. His eyes hardened, and Allison felt the sudden, irresistible pressure of a gun barrel in his side.

"Get on your horse, Allison, and ride out," Earp said coldly. "Get out of Dodge . . . fast."

Anger rushed through Clay. He had not expected Earp to resort to his gun. "What's the deal, Wyatt? Why the iron? Did you think I was going to throw down on you?"

Earp shook his head. "I didn't think anything. Just leave town. Now."

Clay lifted his glance, looking beyond the lawman. Masterson now stood on one side of the street, a rifle in his hands. Farther along, on the opposite corner, Town Marshal Charlie Bassett had taken up a position, a weapon also ready.

Allison brought his attention back to Earp. "All right, have it your way." He turned to head for White's store to get his horse.

He was having a difficult time understanding Wyatt Earp's actions and those of Bat Masterson and Marshal Bassett. It came to him a moment later. Could it be that he had purposely been drawn into a plan for ridding Dodge City of Earp? Had he been informed of George Hoyt's death — or intentionally misinformed — by one of those who was opposed to Earp in the hope that he would come to Dodge and gun down the lawman? That would account for Earp's drawing on him when there was no reason to do so. It also would explain the presence of Masterson and Bassett, armed and in strategic positions to catch him in a wicked crossfire if a shoot-out evolved.

He halted and started to turn around and explain to Earp that he had no intention of playing the role of executioner for the moneyed interests of Dodge — and maybe losing his own life in the process. At that moment, someone he did not know was beside Earp, handing him a double-barreled shotgun. The lawman raised the weapon suggestively when he saw Clay stop.

"Keep going," he said.

"There's something about this deal I don't quite understand," Allison said. "I think we ought to talk it over . . ."

"Keep on going," Earp repeated. "And don't stop again like that unless you want me to cut you in two."

Allison shrugged and continued on. He entered White's, but the merchant was still away. He obtained his horse, mounted up, and rode back into the street. Earp still stood where he had left him. Now there were others behind him, backing him up. Clay walked his horse slowly toward the lawman.

"Wyatt, looks to me like this is some kind of a sucker play, meant to get us both killed . . ."

Earp, never a man to parley when he was certain trouble was nearby, lifted his shotgun. "Turn around, Allison, and ride out. Otherwise I'm going to get you."

There was no point in trying to talk to the lawman. Allison could see that. Earp was convinced he was in town for no good purpose. And there were many who apparently felt the same, judging by those who stood behind him: Masterson, Bassett, Luke Short, two or three more.

But Earp must have had some doubt in his mind about the affair. He was the sort of man who kept the peace by the power of his gun. If he were certain Clay was out to kill him, he would have wasted no time in conversation. Allison had a strong hunch the lawman saw the possibilities of a put-up job designed to draw them into a fatal gun fight and was having none of it. But he also was taking no chances.

Allison wheeled his horse around, doubling back along the street. There would come another day. He would get with Wyatt and talk things out. Maybe they could figure out just exactly who it was that would like to see them both dead.

## XVIII

Soon after the Earp affair, the urge to move again possessed Clay Allison. With Dora he traveled to Hays,

242

Kansas, where he felt there were greater opportunities for his cattle-brokerage business. Trading had suffered a steady decline in New Mexico and Colorado, and he saw considerable advantage in being near to Dodge City, Abilene, and other such markets.

In reality, Allison was growing tired of being a beef drummer on horseback. The shine had worn off his new vocation. He disliked very much being away from Dora so often, and, when business proved to be little better in the Kansas area than it had been in Las Animas, his thoughts swung back to his first love — cattle raising. Perhaps it was the advent of prohibition in his newly adopted state in December, 1880, that helped crystallize the matter in his mind, for shortly after that he pulled stakes to settle along the Washita, in Texas, and there began building up of a new ranch.

The old magic touch was still his, and the venture prospered. The three thousand dollars he had invested in a starter herd multiplied several times over very quickly. He became an important figure in the small town of Mobeetie, near Fort Elliott, and throughout the surrounding area. His reputation as a dangerous man had gone before him, and he engaged in several bitter clashes, usually with passing gunmen or soldiers from the fort.

The town soon organized, electing a man named Henry Fleming as their sheriff. Rustling was becoming a big-time operation in Hemphill County, and the need for law of some status was felt. Fleming, however, found his time occupied by drunks and gamblers who continually plagued the town. Also nearby cattle trails kept a steady supply of drovers feeding into Mobeetie, many of whom were old acquaintances of Allison's who always insisted on a full-scale celebration.

It was in Mobeetie that he again performed his famed big-chief act for the final time, so far as the record goes. Just what the occasion was is not clear, but he stripped in the usual way and rode up and down the streets of the settlement, yelling and shooting off his pistol. Sheriff Fleming later joined him in a saloon, apparently willingly, as there was no subsequent arrest, and Fleming's dislike for such antics was well known.

Marauding Indians and greedy rustlers began to cut deeper into the profits of ranchers, and new aids were sought to supplement the efforts of Sheriff Fleming. A request was made to Texas Ranger headquarters, and George Arrington, a tough little captain with a particular hate for Indians, was sent down to take over.

Allison and Arrington came to immediate cross purposes when the ranger attempted to arrest a man with whom Clay was transacting a business deal. Allison refused to allow Arrington to take in the man until he had competed the matter, which was the purchase of some stock from Allison's herd. The ranger was forced to sit by and wait until the next day, when the deal was finished.

Arrington's attempt to halt the wholesale rustling made little progress, and eventually, with Charles Goodnight and other interested ranchers, Clay joined in the formation of the Panhandle Cattleman's Association. It was something like the days on the Cimarron when men banded together as vigilantes to control outlaws and cattle rustlers and fight for their rights.

Goodnight was elected president, and he immediately appointed a relative of his and a man named Pete Eaton as detectives to run down the thieves. They worked at it steadily, but, like Fleming and George Arrington, seemed to get nowhere, turning up only minor criminals while the larger ones continued to grow fat on local herds.

Allison, typically, took matters into his own hands. He was always a believer in personal action, anyway, and with his cowboys he began an around-the-clock watch over his cattle. His orders to his men were to shoot first and ask questions last, if they came upon anyone driving beef or branding stock that were not theirs. He took to riding the range continually, night and day, and soon he had the answer he sought.

Two brothers, both stanch members of the association and well thought of in the Panhandle, were seen by Allison and several of his men branding calves that were not their property. Thinking it over, Clay decided to leave the matter to the association. He contacted Goodnight and reported his findings. The head of the association found it difficult to believe, but he called a special meeting.

The brothers came and took places in the audience. Goodnight, reluctant to bring out the bald accusation, stalled and hedged. Allison, disgusted with the way the meeting was being handled, finally rose to his feet.

"Mister President, do you want to know who the big rustlers are in this county?"

245

Goodnight, relieved of the responsibility of making the charge against the brothers, said: "Naturally, Mister Allison. If you have any information as to who . . ."

"You know damned well I've got it!" Allison shouted. He wheeled, faced the brothers, and pointed a finger at them. "There they are. I caught them red-handed myself. They can't deny the truth."

Before anyone could move, the brothers were on their feet. They snatched their guns off the table where they had earlier checked them, threw down on the startled members of the association, and backed out the door. Slamming it shut, they raced for their horses and escaped into the night.

Allison was furious, both at himself for being taken unaware and not having his pistol handy and at the association for being such a meaningless and ineffectual group. He should have acted on his own when he first saw the rustlers. Then there would have been an end to it. Now they were free to continue operations — if not in the Panhandle, then elsewhere.

He kept pretty well to himself after that, and some time later, after John and Monroe joined him in the Hemphill County venture, he decided possibilities might be better in New Mexico's Lincoln County. In 1883 they sold out and, with Dora and their first child, a daughter, Patsy, headed down into the Seven Rivers country in the southeastern section of the territory. John and Monroe did not elect to accompany Clay at this time. They wanted a look at the West, at the South, and had a need to see again their old home in Tennessee.

Seven Rivers, Clay felt, was the answer to any cattleman's dream. A man could still ranch and raise beef in the customary fashion without windmills and barbed-wire fences to mar his view, as was getting to be the way back in the Panhandle. He needed no introduction to those who were there ahead of him, making up the village of Seven Rivers and operating the scattering of spreads. Almost to a man they welcomed his arrival, believing his reputation would bring about a greater respect for law and order. The name of Clay Allison linked with any group or organization immediately commanded consideration, and the cattlemen of the Seven Rivers country felt rustlers and desperadoes, in general, would give the area a wide berth when they learned of it.

Allison, however, was wary of organized groups after his experience in the Panhandle, and he was at best a member in name only of John Chisum's Lincoln County Stock Association. He believed in the power of his own gun, and in those his cowboys carried, figuring he could be far more effective than any association. It was best that a man look after his own, anyway. That he walked tall insofar as rustlers and raiders were concerned was borne out by the small amount of trouble and interference he met on the various trail drives he made with his herds into New Mexico and points farther on.

New Mexicans, Kansans, and the people of southern Colorado alike remembered him well, and the reflection of their knowledge spread eventually into more distant areas, particularly Wyoming, where an incident in Cheyenne gave it impetus. Clay had been suffering considerably from a bad tooth, and Dora urged him to have it pulled when he reached a town where a dentist was available. In Cheyenne to sell a portion of his herd, Clay decided to have the matter attended. He sought out a dentist who, figuring he had an easy mark with far too much money, concluded he would make a good thing out of it. He informed Clay besides the bad tooth that must be pulled, there were others that needed filling. Allison, agreeable, allowed him to begin, but, after an hour during which the man hurt him painfully and accidentally broke another tooth, he got out of the chair and departed in disgust.

He went to another dentist, this one an honest practitioner, who told him what had taken place. He had no teeth that needed filling. His sole problem was the decayed molar, and the first dentist had played him for a sucker. He repaired the work that had been done, and Allison felt much better. But not toward the quack. He went immediately to the man's office. He yanked him from the chair where he sat relaxing, throwing him to the floor. With a large pair of forceps he wrenched one of the dentist's front teeth and would have removed another had not bystanders, drawn by the dentist's screams, come to his rescue.

Drought, however, was something Clay could not overcome by sheer muscular strength or his fast gun. He was up against an enemy that could not be whipped, and, being the good cattleman he was, he recognized the futility of fighting indefinitely. It had begun in the Seven Rivers country in 1886 and had steadily grown worse. Besides, Patsy was becoming of school age, and there was no fit place for her to attend in Seven Rivers. When the interests of Dora and their daughter were at issue, they received prior and top attention.

Clay decided Pecos, in Texas, was the right place to which they should move. Ranching was still a good business in that section of the country, and the town was an up-and-coming settlement. Patsy could attend a proper school, and Dora could live in much more ease and comfort. She was expecting their second child soon.

John and Monroe, who had joined Clay in New Mexico after returning from their tour of the West and the South, concluded the move was not for them. They wanted to return to farming in Tennessee. When the Seven Rivers ranch was sold, they took their share and started east. Clay, with Dora and their daughter, drove south into Texas — to a new and final chapter in his life.

## XIX

This was the way he had always wanted it. This was as it should be. The ranch along the Pecos River was a going concern, and he had a good man, John McCullough, he could trust and depend on to ramrod the outfit while he was away. McCullough was a distant relative of Dora's. Clay bought a nice house in town for his family, and they were settled and comfortable. He liked this idea of commuting back and forth from home to ranch. It made for an easy life and permitted him to spend much more time with Dora and Patsy.

One afternoon as he jogged slowly toward Pecos, he wondered how John and Monroe were doing in Tennessee, if they were actually back to farming. They had always preferred working the soil to ranching and had raised cattle only because he had wanted it that way. Now, for the first time, they were on their own, doing what they wanted to do. Maybe, after the baby came, he would take the family to Tennessee for a visit. He had no great love for Wayne County, but it would be nice for Dora and the children to see the old place where he had been born.

A rider, coming up fast from town, caught his attention. After a time he recognized the man as John McCullough and sensed at once that something was wrong. He drew to a halt as the foreman approached.

"What's the trouble?" he called.

"I hoped I'd catch you before you reached town," McCullough said. "I just rode in from looking over that stock of ours at Seven Rivers. I bumped into a hardcase in a saloon in Pecos. He says he's looking for you."

Allison frowned. He had changed little from the days on the Cimarron. He was still tall and lean, his eyes cold blue and piercing. His skin, perhaps, had darkened considerably, but any man knowing him twenty years back would recognize him instantly.

"Why is he looking for me? Did he say?"

"No. I figure he's just another gunslinger hoping to add to his list," McCullough said. "Somebody called him John."

It never ended. Allison shook his head. "He's a stranger to me."

"Well, he's laying for you. He told me to tell you so. When you get to town, be on the watch for him. I wanted to warn you so's you could be ready."

"Obliged," Clay said. "I'll look him up. What saloon was he in?"

"The Cantina."

"I see. How were things at Seven Rivers?"

"Dry as popcorn. We ought to move that herd over here, but I don't think we can, not until we get some rain between here and there."

Allison said: "We'll talk about it later. See you at the ranch."

He continued on to Pecos and rode straight to The Cantina. Word of the gunman's challenge to Allison had spread, and at Clay's appearance the street cleared immediately. He dismounted and entered the low-roofed building. Inside the doorway he paused, glancing about. There were half a dozen customers at the counter.

"Which one of you is John?" he asked.

There was a long moment of quiet and then one of the cowboys turned around slowly. "That's me."

"I'm Clay Allison. I understand you're looking for me. What's on your mind?"

John stirred uneasily. He looked about the small room, as if suddenly seeking a friend. He stood alone.

"What about it?" Allison pressed.

John looked down at the floor. "I reckon that was just whiskey talk, Mister Allison."

"Mighty strong for whiskey. Are you sure that's all it amounts to?"

"I'm real sure," John mumbled.

"Well, I'd like for you to know you're welcome to try your hand with me. It's been a rule of mine to always accommodate a man who gets the notion he'd like to take my scalp."

"I guess I was a little drunk," John said. "I always do talk too much when that happens."

Allison moved into the saloon. "If whiskey makes you brave and talk big, maybe you ought to have a drink right now. Bartender, give us a bottle."

John laid his elbows on the counter. Allison poured out two drinks, took one himself, and waited while John picked up the other.

"Drink it," he ordered.

John complied.

"Are you getting the urge to talk big again?"

John wagged his head. "Leave me be, Mister Allison. I don't want to fight you."

Clay stepped back. "All right, John. We'll let it pass, but, if I ever hear of you opening your mouth about me again, you'll not get off this easy. Is that understood?"

"I understand," John murmured, and turned away.

Allison had another drink and went back into the street. He started for his home, the old McNally place on the corner of Fifth and Cypress, when a shout from the front of the town's largest store halted him.

"Clay, the fireworks you had me order for Independence Day got in."

Allison nodded. "Fine, hang onto them, Ben. I'll send some of the boys by and load them up in the next day or so."

He headed again for his home where Dora and Patsy would be awaiting him. The street was alive again, now that the threat of gun play had passed. As he rode along slowly, he spoke to many who had become his friends since he had moved into the Pecos country. He guessed he would stay put this time. It was a good place for Patsy and the coming baby to grow up in. And a man couldn't ask for better ranching conditions.

He reached the corner and threw his glance toward the McNally house — his home now. A horse stood at the hitching post fronting it. He recognized the cowboy who lounged against the fence as Joe Harkey, one of his own riders. Harkey moved out into the street to meet him as he approached.

"Mister Allison, I've been waiting to see you," the cowboy drawled.

Clay dismounted. "Is that so, Joe? What's wrong?"

Harkey said: "Well, knowing how you feel about the boys that work for you, I figured you'd want to know about this."

Allison said: "About what?"

"That new kid from Illinois. Hank, his name is. He's gone and got himself in bad trouble."

Hank — Henry Davis. He was a youngster who had come to work for him a few weeks back. He was a greenhorn, but willing and learning fast.

"What sort of trouble is he in?"

"Over at Toyah last night one of them toughs started picking on him. He sure did give him a bad time, but Hank stood right up to him. Then this hardcase got

**253**

mad, called Hank a lot of names, and prodded him into a gun fight."

"Gun fight!" Clay echoed. "Why, that boy hardly knows which end of a gun to point."

"That's why I'm here, Mister Allison. I figured you ought to know the kid's sure going to get hisself killed unless somebody stops it."

"Why didn't you other men head it off before it got this far?"

"One reason," Harkey said. "Hank would listen to none of us cutting ourselves in. He says he wants to stand on his own feet. He's kind of proud that way."

Allison said: "I see. Who's the other man?"

"Hugh Skeller."

"Skeller!"

Clay repeated the name in surprise. Skeller was a gunman of considerable reputation. A meeting between the youngster from Illinois and him would be no contest at all. It would be nothing short of murder. Skeller apparently was looking for an easy notch to cut in his gun.

"When is this shoot-out supposed to take place? And where?"

"Daylight tomorrow morning. On the road halfway between here and Toyah."

Allison said: "You ride on back to camp. Tell Hank that McCullough wants him at the ranch. Then you see that he gets there. I don't much care how you do it, just so's it's done. I'll meet Skeller in the morning."

Harkey grinned. "Fine, Mister Allison. I sure am relieved. That boy was as good as dead."

"There's no need to tell him I'll be taking his place with Skeller. Just let him think he has to pass up the meeting because McCullough wants him."

"I savvy. Anything I should tell John about why you sent the kid to him?"

"If you get a chance, you can explain it, but you don't have to worry. McCullough will know I had a reason."

Harkey swung to the saddle. Seated, he looked down at Allison. "I reckon you don't need no help of any kind, but, if you're wanting company, I'd be right proud to ride with you in the morning."

"No need. It won't take long," Clay said. "And Joe, you might pass the word on to the boys. Those fireworks I ordered got in. Everybody can get set for a real celebration, come the fourth."

"Fine, fine," Harkey said, his smile broadening. He touched the brim of his hat and pulled away. "*Adios.* See you tomorrow."

Long before daylight the next morning Clay was on the road that led to Toyah, a small town a few miles to the southwest of Pecos where the cowboys often spent their leisure time. When he reached what he considered to be the halfway point, he halted, drawing off to one side. Almost immediately he saw two riders emerge from the brush a hundred yards farther along, riding slowly toward him. It was still semi-dark, but he could recognize Skeller with no trouble. The second man was a stranger.

He stepped down from the saddle, tied the horse, and walked to a clump of doveweed where he could await their arrival unseen. He permitted them to get within twenty feet or so and stepped suddenly into view.

Both men came to an abrupt stop. Skeller's hand dropped to the gun at his hip, then fell slowly away as he recognized Clay. There was a long, dragging moment of silence. Then he spoke.

"What are you doing here, Allison?"

"Hank couldn't make it. He had to go back to the ranch. I'm keeping the date for him."

"I've got no quarrel with you," Skeller said immediately.

"Maybe not, but I've got one with you. You must be slipping, Skeller, ramrodding a greenhorn kid like Hank into fighting you. You must need a notch in your gun real bad. Suppose you make a try for my scalp instead."

Skeller was thoughtful. After a moment he shrugged. "Like I told you, I got no cause to draw against you."

"You damn' well will have, if I ever hear of you rawhiding one of my boys again, Skeller," Allison said, suddenly angry. "Now turn around and ride out of here . . . you and your partner both. I'm not going to put up with any trouble from either of you."

"A man's got a right . . ."

"You don't have any rights around here, unless you want to fight me for them," Clay snarled. "Now, I've got some stock to look over a few miles north of here. When that's done, I'm circling by Toyah. You better not be there, either one of you."

The rider with Skeller immediately turned his horse about and started back along the road for the settlement. The gunman stared at Allison for a brief time and then wheeled around, saying no more. Clay watched them go in silence.

When he pulled up before the saloon in Toyah two hours later, the first words he heard were that Skeller and his partner had ridden northward toward the New Mexico border.

## XX

That July second was a hot one. The drought that had settled over the Seven Rivers country was making itself felt along the Pecos now, and the problem of dryness, of burned-out grass, of low creeks and rivers, and shrinking wells was becoming acute. The heat seemed to intensify with each passing day, and there was no relief in sight.

Allison, in Pecos near the middle of the afternoon, halted at the general store where freighters, Tom McDonald and Will Laramore, were loading their wagons for the run north.

"Have you two got a minute?" Clay asked. "How about having a beer with me? There's something I want to talk to you about."

McDonald said: "Sure . . . and it's a right good idea. We're finished, and a beer would go nice."

The three men walked over to The Cantina, entered, and sat down at one of the tables. Clay ordered the drinks and then turned to the partners. They were unusually quiet, as if expecting his question.

"You're both friends of Pete Cummings and Jubal Tracy," Allison said. "I'd like to know if they've been talking to you about me."

The bartender brought the drinks, placing them on the table. McDonald waited until he had returned to his station.

"Well, you know Pete and Jubal. They don't mean half of what they say . . ."

"They meant it, sure enough," Allison said, his pale eyes suddenly hard. "They've been spreading it everywhere they go. And I sure as hell don't appreciate it!"

"Anybody that hears them knows it's not the truth," Laramore said. "We all know you'd never cheat a man, Clay, out of what was due him."

"I never have and I never will," Allison said. "And I don't like folks getting the idea that I would." He downed the glass of beer, motioning to the bartender. "Bring me a bottle of whiskey. This damned beer is flat."

The teamsters exchanged glances and again remained silent while the barkeep brought a bottle and glasses, placing them before Allison. Clay, ignoring the small shot glass, poured himself a generous drink into the beer mug.

"I can't figure Pete and Jubal out. I always treated them right, same as I do all the boys who work for me. I've gone out of my way to see that they're taken care of and looked after."

258

"Like I said, they're just shooting off their mouths," McDonald murmured. "I expect they've already forgotten about it."

"No, I heard about it again this morning. There's only one thing for me to do, I reckon. Go and shut them up."

"Shut them up?" Laramore repeated, his voice rising in question.

Allison took another swallow from his glass. "That's what I said . . . shut them up. Nobody's going to run loose talking about me the way they are."

"Maybe it won't be necessary," McDonald said cautiously. "How about me and Will going to them and telling them to close their traps? We can get it stopped."

Allison shook his head. "It's too late for that. I'll do it myself now."

"Do you know where they are?"

"Sure. At the north cow camp," Allison said. "The lousy bastards! They talk about me but keep on working my cattle and earning my money just the same. It's a hell of a note."

McDonald said: "Clay, I've got an idea. We're heading out that way in a few minutes. Why not ride along with us?"

Allison took another deep swallow, considering the teamster's offer. "All right. Any time you say, I'm ready."

It was near dark when they left the saloon. Allison, well through the bottle of whiskey, tied his horse on behind one of the wagons and climbed onto the seat beside McDonald. He had grown angrier with each passing minute, and the teamster knew a killing lay ahead at the cow camp where the cowboys quartered unless he could come up with some idea to prevent it.

The rancher, moody and sullen over the wrong done him by the two men, rode in silence. He finished the bottle, hurling it off into the brush. Maybe his temper would cool now, McDonald figured. The whiskey had served only to aggravate his feeling toward Tracy and Cummings.

"Hold up!" Allison suddenly ordered.

McDonald brought the heavy freight wagon to a stop. "What's the trouble?"

"I'm going back to town for another bottle," Allison said, and leaped from the seat. "You and Laramore go on. I'll catch up when you pull in for the night."

McDonald had an urge to halt Allison, to try and talk him out of going back, but he quickly dismissed the thought. Clay was no man to argue with when he was drinking heavily. He watched in helpless silence as the rancher swung to his saddle, wheeling back toward Pecos. Will Laramore came up, wondering at the halt. McDonald told him.

"There's not much you could do about stopping him," the freighter said.

"There's nothing anybody can do when Clay's in that kind of a humor," McDonald said. "Maybe we'll get lucky. Maybe he'll stay in town, once he reaches there."

Laramore wagged his head. "Not him. When he's got it in mind to square up with somebody and starts hitting the bottle over it, he won't quit until it's done. Do you think we ought to warn Jubal and Pete?"

"How? We'd never get there ahead of Clay with these rigs. He'll be back before we get much farther."

"I saw a rider up ahead. I don't know who it is, but maybe we could get him to carry a message on to the camp. He could tell Jubal and Pete to lay low."

"It would be better to tell them to get clear out of the country," McDonald amended. "I'll unhitch one of the lead horses. Maybe you can catch up with whoever that is."

"I'll catch him," Laramore said. "I'd better, or we got two less friends."

Three hours later Allison overtook them. They had halted at the side of the road for the night. He had exchanged his saddle for a horse and buggy — and he was in no better mood than he had been when he turned back.

"You might as well sit down and rest a bit," McDonald suggested as he rolled up. "There's a pot of coffee here, waiting."

Clay climbed down from his light rig. He had exchanged his pistol also, the teamsters noted. He now wore a big, cedar-handled Colt that showed much wear and usage. The holster was dark and soft, and it was tied low on his thigh.

"No, thanks," Allison said, his voice perfectly even and controlled. "I'll just stick to this." He held up a bottle, already half empty.

"We were just talking," McDonald said, squatting beside their small fire. "We can't see any use of you riding clear out to that camp, Clay. It could be Jubal and Pete have already left the country. We'd be glad to stop and find out. And if they haven't, we'll tell them you're looking for them."

Allison stared into the fire. He appeared almost Indian, the bones of his dark, lean face highlighted by the flames. Only his pale eyes showed the anger that drove through him.

"It would be better than a killing, Clay," Laramore said softly. "Us getting their promise that they'd cut out this talk and leave the state."

"Pecos is a good town," McDonald went on. "I'd hate to see it get all riled up over a killing. There hasn't been any of that since you moved in and people feel that you just living around here has made that happen."

"Gun slicks have sure give us the go-by. If you shoot up Pete and Jubal, they're going to figure it's like the old days and soon start drifting in again."

Allison made no comment. He tipped the quart bottle to his lips, taking a long swig. Off somewhere in the night a coyote barked, and then another.

"Pecos is a mighty fine place for a man to bring up his children, too," Laramore continued. "It's safe for womenfolk. It ain't right it should change."

Clay shifted his glance to Laramore. "Do you figure that's what would happen, Will?"

"Sure as we're sitting here, Clay. It would be like opening the door to all the drifters and gun hands in the West. Not only that, Pete and Jubal are bound to have friends, maybe a relative or two, and they'd come, looking to settle up. I don't figure you'd have any trouble taking care of yourself against them, but there'd be a lot of shooting, and somebody might get hurt. Somebody innocent, I mean, like a school kid."

"You just say the word, Clay," McDonald pressed gently, "and we'll handle this for you. I'll ride on to that camp tonight and straighten out Pete and Jubal. They'll be on the trail come daylight."

Allison stared moodily into the flames. After a lapse of several minutes, he said: "All right, Tom. I've never asked any man to do what I figure is a personal job for me, but I reckon you men are right. You tell Pete and Jubal to keep out of my sight. Any word comes back to me they're still spouting off, I'll come looking for them . . . even if it takes a year to find them."

"It's a deal," McDonald said, relief running through his voice. "I'll ride out now."

"You might just as well spend the night here, Clay," Laramore said. "It'll take Tom most of the night. You can use his bed."

Allison was agreeable to that, also. He unhitched his buggy horse for the teamster to use, improvising a halter bridle. There was no saddle available, only a folded blanket. McDonald left immediately, and Clay, with Laramore, returned to the fire. They finished off the bottle between them, and Allison tossed it aside. He removed his gun, stretching out on the teamster's blankets.

"I'll make this up to Tom in the morning," he said. "I can drive for him while he catches up on his sleep. That way you won't be losing any time."

Laramore said: "Good idea," and rolled into his own bed.

McDonald was back shortly before dawn. He dropped from his horse and strode to the fire where Laramore already had breakfast going.

"All set." He grinned. "You won't be hearing or seeing that pair of cowpokes again. They were happy to get themselves off the hook."

Clay nodded. "I'm obliged to you, Tom." He refilled his cup from the blackened pot of coffee. "I did some thinking early this morning after I woke up. The time's about come for a man to realize there's other ways to settle an argument than with a gun. The country's getting too civilized for bullets. Listening to what you said about Pecos last night made me see that."

"Guns are for a man's protection nowadays," Laramore said. "Nothing else, hardly."

They finished the meal, harnessed the team, and made ready to move out. Allison tied his horse and buggy on behind McDonald's wagon.

"Climb in, Tom," he said to the teamster. "Get yourself a little sleep. I'll take the wagon."

McDonald complied willingly. It had been a long, hard ride, and he was dead tired. He curled up on the seat, bracing himself against the dashboard with his feet.

"I'll probably end up with a crick in my neck, but it don't make any difference, the way I feel now."

Allison grinned and moved back to the freight wagon. He climbed onto the seat, taking up the leather ribbons. He glanced over his shoulder. Laramore was ready. Allison lifted his arm in a forward signal and shouted the team into motion. The big wagon began to roll as the horses threw themselves into the harness.

Clay knew he had cost the teamsters a good two hours in time. Accordingly, he kept the four-up moving at a good pace. The country was level and the road dry and in fine condition through this particular section. It would be easy to make up time now. Farther on it would be a different story. The road dropped down into a narrow valley that lay between two steep hills. That strip was always rough and slow going, with rocks and deep ruts forcing a man to take it at a lesser speed.

When they reached the mouth of the cañon, Clay looked back again over his shoulder. Laramore was not far behind. McDonald was sleeping soundly on the wagon seat. He turned his attention back to the team. They were now on a slight downgrade, and the heavy vehicle was picking up speed. It began to jolt from the ruts and rocks.

Allison stood up and looked beyond the bobbing heads of the lead horses, endeavoring to see the terrain at the foot of the slope where the more level floor of the valley unrolled. There were deep gashes there, gouged to greater depth by the many wagons that had struck the valley floor over the years.

Suddenly a large rock, displaced from the slope and now lying in the roadway, caught his eye. It was directly ahead of the right front wheel. He saw it was too late to swing clear. He moved to brace himself against the sharp jolt that was certain to come. He took the precaution too late.

He felt himself pitch forward, hurtle through the clean morning air, straight for the iron-bound wheel of the wagon. He clawed at the dashboard, trying to save himself. His fingers barely grazed the splintered, weather-beaten wood.

Laramore, at the abrupt halting of the wagon ahead, pulled in sharply. He leaned over the side and saw the crumpled figure of Allison, lying close to the edge of the road. He leaped from his seat, ran forward, shouting at McDonald as he did, and knelt down beside the rancher.

McDonald, already awakened by the unexpected stop, slid from the buggy and raced to Laramore. Together they rolled Clay over onto his back. Laramore felt for his heartbeat, his own eyes on the crushed, discolored area that disfigured Allison's face and forehead.

Laramore raised his glance to his partner. "He's finished, Tom. He must have hit his head on the edge of the wheel when he was thrown from the wagon."

McDonald studied the still features of the man, lying on the cool Texas earth. "Hell of a thing," he murmured. "To live this long through what he has, then die of a fool accident like this."

Clay Allison, the legendary gunman, was dead. The date was July 3, 1887.